T0196859

1 ACROSS: HUMAN REMAINS

Creating crossword puzzles for the *Chestnut Station Chronicle* won't allow Quinn Carr to quit her diner waitress job anytime soon. But it does provide an outlet for her organizational OCD, and also lets her leave subtle hints for police chief Myron Chestnut, an avid puzzler, when his investigations need some direction. Some mysteries, though, leave even Quinn stumped—like the property deed she finds in her grandfather's old desk. The document lists Quinn's mother as the owner of some land on the outskirts of Chestnut Station, but Georgeanne refuses to discuss it.

8 LETTERS, STARTS WITH "S"

Quinn visits the site, located near a World War II Japanese internment camp that's since been turned into a museum. There she unearths a weathered Japanese doll...and a skeleton. Before she can uncover a killer, she has to identify the victim. Was it an inmate trying to escape? A guard? Or someone closer to home? As Quinn fills in the blanks, she finds an unexpected link between her family and Chief Chestnut's—one that could spell more deadly trouble...

By Becky Clark

Puzzling Ink
Punning with Scissors
Fatal Solutions

Fatal Solutions

Becky Clark

LYRICAL UNDERGROUND
Kensington Publishing Corp.
www.kensingtonbooks.com

LYRICAL UNDERGROUND BOOKS are published by

Kensington Publishing Corp.
119 West 40th Street
New York, NY 10018

All Kensington titles, imprints, and distributed lines are available at special quantity discounts for bulk purchases for sales promotion, premiums, fund-raising, educational, or institutional use.

Special book excerpts or customized printings can also be created to fit specific needs. For details, write or phone the office of the Kensington Sales Manager: Kensington Publishing Corp., 119 West 40th Street, New York, NY 10018. Attn. Sales Department. Phone: 1-800-221-2647.

Lyrical Underground and Lyrical Underground logo Reg. US Pat. & TM Off.

First Electronic Edition: November 2021
ISBN: 978-1-5161-1065-0 (ebook)

First Print Edition: November 2021
ISBN: 978-1-5161-1068-1

Printed in the United States of America

Chapter 1

"So, how did your visualization exercise go last week?" Mary-Louise Lovely asked. "You were supposed to picture your mom's spice rack unalphabetized and record your anxiety about it."

"Yes, I recall," Quinn Carr said dryly, adjusting her struggle bun. As she arranged it while walking to her car this morning, she had the jab of an inkling of an idea that maybe—just maybe—she should perhaps start doing her hair in front of the mirror again because it almost felt like she'd been struggling just the teensiest bit less the last few weeks. A visit with her therapist often disabused her of that notion, however.

Quinn sat in Mary-Louise Lovely's office in her favorite place, the corner of the love seat by the table. It was the perfect place to hold her notebook and/or binder, or notebooks and binders plural, depending on her level of anxiety and what she wanted to talk about in her session. She could also see out the large window to catch calming glances of the cobalt-blue Colorado sky, the dancing leaves of a stand of quaking aspen trees, and the occasional banded dove on the sill, offering a quizzical tilt of its head. *Are you* still *in therapy? It's already September, for heaven's sake*, Quinn pictured it, thinking. *How hard is it to get over OCD? Just quit doing that stuff.* The same thing Quinn told herself on too many occasions.

Quinn confidently handed her two-inch blue binder to Mary-Louise Lovely, who sat in the chair diagonal from her. Every week the chair seemed to be at a slightly different angle to the area rug. And every week it took almost all of Quinn's willpower not to place it in its obvious proper place.

She wondered what Mary-Louise Lovely would write in her yellow legal pad about her if she found out Quinn had dug deep to uncover the name of the cleaning company for the office building and tried several different scenarios with her schedule to see if she could arrange a part-time job on this particular crew. She could not. She decided not to mention it, but knew, deep down in her soul, that if she ever came to own a cleaning company, on the first day of training, new employees would be tested on their ability to replace furniture in the carpet indentations from whence they came.

It didn't take too many sessions before Mary-Louise Lovely invited, then waited for, Quinn to readjust the chair before she settled into it for their fifty-five minutes. "I want you to be able to concentrate," she'd said. That's when Quinn knew she was a good therapist. Or at least one she could get along with. Everything about Mary-Louise Lovely—whose full name Quinn decided long ago absolutely suited her and should always be used in its unabridged glory—calmed Quinn. Her unassuming honey-blond hair, which she wore unadorned, happily and freely brushed her shoulders whenever she moved. Her open, honest face devoid of all makeup except the tiniest bit of mascara and lip gloss. Her sensible clothes and shoes, so comfortable on her frame that it transmogrified into comfort for Quinn as well. Before Mary-Louise Lovely uttered a word of greeting, her simple presence comforted Quinn, even when taming her monster was as far from comfortable as allspice was from white peppercorns.

Quinn bounced in her chair a little as she awaited Mary-Louise Lovely's admiration of her binder.

Mary-Louise Lovely flipped through the pages. "I thought we agreed you'd use a scale of one to ten."

Quinn nodded.

"And I see here you used a scale of one to one hundred."

"To allow for nuance. My thoughts are very nuanced." Quinn leaned closer to the binder resting on Mary-Louise Lovely's knees. She flipped to the blue tab. "Here's the section for my thoughts and feelings."

"Color-coded as to time of day, I see."

Then the yellow tab, "Line graph." Red tab, "Bar graph." Green tab, "Pie chart." Quinn babbled about her process while Mary-Louise Lovely silently turned the pages.

The therapist's face showed no judgment. An impenetrable mask.

But Quinn penetrated it. She slumped against the back of the love seat, confidence dissolving like a tissue put through the spin cycle. "How is it possible to do an assignment to get rid of my OCD in a total OCD manner?" she wailed.

Mary-Louise Lovely smiled at Quinn's dramatics and handed back the binder. "If it's any consolation, the assignment wasn't going to 'get rid of your OCD,' no matter how you completed it. And I probably should have told you to record your thoughts in a quick text to yourself instead. Let's call this a case of poor instructions."

Quinn smiled despite herself. Mary-Louise Lovely had that way about her. Quinn never felt criticized or reprimanded here. One glance into her therapist's big brown eyes and ready smile immediately relaxed her. Mary-Louise Lovely would be the perfect therapist if she could only Shrinky-Dink into pocket size so Quinn could carry her around all day.

"Okay. So, we agree. It's your fault I'm chock-full of OCD. You and your lousy non-OCD instructions. How'd you ever get a license, anyway?" Quinn grinned at her.

Mary-Louise Lovely laughed softly, making her hair dance. "I want you to remember that obsessive-compulsive disorder is an anxiety disorder, but it's also a way to *deal* with anxieties, which makes it a tricky little monster."

"Hey, I heard a joke I thought you'd like," Quinn said. "A guy asks, why do you place a pine tree branch outside your front door every day? And his friend says, to keep the tigers away. So the guy says, but there aren't any tigers. His friend replies, right? Pretty effective, eh?" Quinn leaned forward with a gleam in her eye. "It's an OCD joke, get it?"

"Funny. Is that how you see your compulsions?"

"Absolutely. The tree branch is my counting steps or alphabetizing or whatever, and the tiger is my overwhelming need to organize and categorize everything." Quinn glanced at Mary-Louise Lovely. "Do I win something?"

"Do you want a gold star in your chart?"

"Do you have those?"

Mary-Louise Lovely flashed her notepad at Quinn. "Nope. Sorry."

"You're such a tease."

"I do like that joke, though. It's a really good snapshot of the OCD mindset. With any repetitive behavior, the more you do of it, the more you *need* to do it. You brought up counting your steps. You started one day counting your steps to the end of the block. Then you progressed to counting your steps all the way home from the diner—"

"I wouldn't call it progress."

"Maybe that's the wrong word. But then it turned into every time you were out walking. Some of my patients say they kind of disassociate while they're doing their rituals."

"That's how it is for me sometimes, like I'm in a trance. I look up from filling the condiments on one table at the diner, and all of a sudden I'm done with all the tables and I have no memory of doing any of them. And when I got stuck in that walking loop over at Hugh Pugh's house that day, I only realized how long I'd been doing it because I almost passed out from the heat. Imagine how poor Virginia Woof felt! A small dog like her isn't built for all that. I'm just lucky Hugh's neighbor Barbara saw me and made us come in her house and pour water down our throats."

Mary-Louise Lovely nodded. "OCD is a way to feel like you're controlling things, but it's really the other way around. People believe something bad will happen if they don't do their rituals."

Quinn stared out the window for a bit, watching the aspen leaves flutter. They were getting the telltale golden color that signified September had finally made its appearance in Colorado. Sweater weather instead of sweating weather. "I don't really think something bad will happen if I don't do things a certain way," she finally said. "But it *feeeels* like it will."

"Exactly," Mary-Louise Lovely said. "OCD is a *feeeling* disorder. We need to figure out the *feeeelings* before we can straighten out the thoughts. Unless the lake is calm, we can't see our reflection."

"Deep."

"I'm not just another pretty face." She smiled. "This week we're going to try some exposure therapy. You did the first step with the visualization exercise, but now you're going to get your hands dirty."

"Good thing I'm not a germophobe, then."

"You might wish you were after you hear what I want you to do."

"Uh-oh."

"You're actually going to randomize those spices. Maybe not even have them in the spice rack."

Quinn gasped like a Victorian princess who'd just been told to empty a chamber pot.

"Or you can have your mom do it. Because your real job is to leave them there as long as you can. But no notebook this week. Just text yourself, or me, some quick thoughts as soon as you have them. You always have your phone, so just use that. I don't want you to document this to within an inch of its life, just note whenever you feel the urge to re-alphabetize the spices, or even if you just feel the need to check on them. Note when you think about those darn spices, sitting there all willy-nilly every which way."

Quinn shuddered.

"And note if you used any of your distraction tools or if it got too overwhelming and you had to fix them. Then next time we'll talk about it and decide what to do next. We'll either do the spice rack again, or you can choose a more difficult task if this was too easy."

"Too easy? Climbing Mount Everest is too easy. Teaching my goldfish, Fang, to walk is too easy. Growing potatoes on Mars is too easy. This has already given me sweaty palms." Quinn rubbed her hands on her jeans, then held them up to prove they were already sweaty again.

Mary-Louise Lovely smiled. "You'll be fine. Have you ever jumped into a lake? It was freezing at first, but then you got used to it—habituated, we call that—and after a while, it felt like the perfect temperature. That's the idea here, too."

Quinn knew she was right, but immediately noticed her heart start pounding anyway. She was finding it hard to breathe and began "doing her finger thing," as Rico put it: touching each finger of her right hand to her thumb, then her left-hand fingers to her left thumb, over and over.

"You're feeling out of control."

"Gosh, you're *not* just another pretty face." Quinn panted. Felt a trickle of sweat along the side of her temple. Willed her fingers to stop, but they refused.

"I want you to focus on exactly what's going on right now, internally and externally."

"You're telling me I have to stop alphabetizing Mom's spices, and it makes me anxious, out of control. I want to race home to protect the pantry."

"Ask what your OCD monster wants you to do."

"He wants me to alphabetize something. If not the spices, then maybe your files for you. If I don't, he's telling me I'm pretty worthless. He doesn't want me to change."

Mary-Louise Lovely leaned forward and rested her elbows on her knees, never breaking eye contact. "Quinn, you get to decide if that's helpful or not."

"No, it's not helpful!" Quinn bugged out her eyes at Mary-Louise Lovely.

"Okay." She leaned back in her chair. "So, establish two or three things you could do instead."

"I could yell 'baba ghanoush' and go get a soda from your machine to break the cycle. I could give in and alphabetize something. I could"— Quinn groped for one more thing to do—"call my therapist and have her tell me what to do!"

Mary-Louise Lovely watched Quinn for a moment, a reassuring smile playing on her lips.

"What?" Quinn finally asked.

"Look at your hands."

Quinn looked down at her lap, her hands neatly and calmly folded in front of her. She looked up with big eyes. "When did I stop? Are you secretly a witch?"

"I've been called worse. But all I did was teach you the FADE technique. Focus on what's going on. Ask what your OCD monster wants you to do. Decide if it's helpful. Establish two or three things you could do instead. Focus, ask, decide, establish. FADE."

"You *are* a witch."

"I love that the first thing you said was that you could distract yourself. But you can't always leave a situation, so here's another distraction technique. Wherever you are, find an object to look at. Start listing specific things about it. Practice on me. What do you see?"

"You're blond, perhaps from a bottle."

Mary-Louise Lovely snorted.

"You're sitting. Ankles crossed. Yellow legal pad in your lap. Pen from that mystery writer you like, so you must have gone to her book signing." Quinn felt her breathing begin to slow.

Mary-Louise Lovely looked closely at her pen. "Very observant."

"Black pants. Expensive shoes. So cute, by the way."

"Thank you."

"Lavender top, white camisole underneath, probably—"

"Okay, that's enough. I'd forgotten just how observant you are." Mary-Louise Lovely flashed her smile. "Feel better? More in control?"

Quinn nodded.

"You moved out of your imagination and into observing the real world. If you can do this for yourself, it'll be harder for your OCD monster to take control of your imagination and work it into a frenzy."

Quinn nodded again.

"Did you notice earlier when you said your OCD monster doesn't want you to change?"

"Did I?"

"Yes, and that's very perceptive of you."

"Guess I'm not just a pretty face either." Quinn tossed her hair melodramatically over her shoulder.

"Change is hard and uncomfortable, even if it's good change. I remember when I was moving into my own apartment after grad school. I was so excited and happy, but so scared. It takes courage to change things that have been the status quo for so many years."

"Like my OCD monster."

"Like your OCD monster." Mary-Louise Lovely nodded. "Even though you'd rather he disappeared, you understand him. You're worried that whatever happens next, you won't understand. Some of my clients don't even want to begin treatment because they have an illusion of control and coping mechanisms they think are working."

Quinn thought back to that middle-of-the-night phone call she had finally made to Mary-Louise Lovely. Lost and completely broken by her OCD and depression, that business card on her parents' corkboard was a three-and-a-half-by-two-inch lifeline. Nothing had been working for her, and she'd always be grateful for that four-hour conversation in which Mary-Louise Lovely had rescued her, providing a safe haven that night and ever since. Despite the rescue, though, Quinn still felt like she was flailing in the deep end, barely keeping her head above water.

With a thoughtful expression, Mary-Louise Lovely studied Quinn, watched as the emotions played across her face. Gently she said, "At least you're trying hard to win this race with your monster."

"Yeah, but I keep tripping over my own two feet." Quinn sighed and slumped into her seat. "I can't even see the finish line."

Mary-Louise Lovely tilted her head and stared deep into Quinn's eyes. "You will. Trust me. There's a saying I like: Fall down seven times, get up eight. That's you. You persevere." At Quinn's skeptical look, she added, "You do, Quinn. You haven't given up, even when this gets hard. You do everything I ask of you. Maybe not the first time, and maybe with too many charts and graphs and too much color-coding, but eventually."

When Quinn's session was over, she relinquished her color-coded binder. Mary-Louise Lovely only had to ask three times.

Chapter 2

Later that afternoon, Quinn was polishing and organizing her grandfather Bernard Dudley's antique rolltop desk. It had been his father's and had a small brass plaque proudly proclaiming it had been manufactured in 1890. The desk landed in the Carrs' living room after Grandpa had to be moved into the Bonneville Assisted Living Center in Chestnut Station. He was in fairly good physical shape but had burned his dinner once too often in the house in Denver where he had been living alone.

Georgeanne, Quinn's mom, was still trying to get used to the idea that her father needed to go into a care facility. She liked that he was closer in proximity—ten minutes away rather than almost ninety—but it was the end of an era to her. She hadn't grown up in the house Bernard was leaving. Georgeanne grew up in Chestnut Station, and after she and Dan got married, her parents sold them the very house she—and now Quinn—had grown up in. It had been paid off for years, and Georgeanne and Dan got it for a song. Bernard and his wife, Margaret, Georgeanne's mom, dead seven years now, had wanted to try city life in Denver. It agreed with them, but now Georgeanne found herself mourning the loss of the life her parents had relished in Denver.

Georgeanne, Dan, and Quinn when she was able, went there for Sunday dinner every week until Margaret died. Then Sunday dinners became more sporadic. Sometimes Bernard came to Chestnut Station; sometimes Sunday dinner became Wednesday lunch.

Regardless, the sudden changes were hard on Georgeanne, so Quinn had volunteered to give the desk new life and deal with the assorted papers and odds and ends stashed in it so her mom wouldn't have to. It went without saying that rooting through drawers (thirty-one of them!) and organizing stacks of files and papers was Quinn's nirvana.

Quinn had lemon-oiled and buffed the outside surfaces of the solidly made and well-loved oak desk. She'd lovingly and painstakingly removed years of grime and fingerprints until the wood was hydrated and gleaming. Scratches and scuffs with stories Quinn could only imagine still remained, adding character to the antique. After she was satisfied with her work—at least for now—she went to her bedroom to collect Fang. She set his bowl in the center of the desk. "Ready for the tour I promised you?" She pointed out all the little cubbies in the desk, and he dutifully swam in each direction she pointed.

Now that the outside of the desk glowed, she began tackling the unimportant flotsam and jetsam, as well as the perhaps more significant bits and pieces of Grandpa's life that remained in the drawers. Her curiosity had made her briefly paw through each cubby as soon as the desk had been delivered, but she'd forced herself to save the official inventory for its proper time...now.

Without telling Mary-Louise Lovely, or anyone else, she'd set up a test, strictly for herself, with this desk. Would she be able to work on it only in her free time, or would it begin to consume her thoughts and commandeer her every waking moment? Would she be late to work because she had to organize "just one more cubby" or rub another coat of polish into every inch? Could she walk away, knowing the scars and imperfections remained? Would she obsessively keep trying to eliminate them, secretly, in the middle of the night, with another round of elbow grease, knowing deep down that it was impossible? Or—and this was her fervent hope—would she be able to work a bit on it, then walk away for the day, like a normal person would? If she could do that, maybe someday she could claim with conviction—a conviction she truly believed—that she was in control of her OCD, and not the other way around.

She began at the bottom drawers, where, among other things, she found a cigar box containing a grimy set of three-inch-tall World War I doughboys made of cast iron. She held each one up for Fang to admire, as she gave them a gentle scrub with a soft toothbrush and some soapy water.

There were soldiers in several different poses: standing with a gun over their right shoulder; standing with a gun held in front of their torso; marching; a medic helping a soldier with a bandage wrapped around his head and his arm in a sling; lying flat behind a gun on what looked to her to be a miniature tripod; kneeling behind a box of ammunition.

Grandpa had several soldiers of each pose. Quinn wondered if he and his friends had played with them as boys, or if this was a solitary pursuit. Had the cigar box belonged to his father? Had he begged for it as the perfect resting place for his doughboys? Commandeered it from the trash? Who had smoked all those cigars? She stuck her face in the box and took a deep sniff. Coughing, she realized that whatever aroma they'd once proclaimed had long since been replaced with the mustiness of time.

She rearranged the shelves on the built-in bookshelves in the living room, pulling out several books to make a display of the doughboys right at her eye level. She liked the contrast of the dark cast iron against the pale yellow of the shelves. *The Girl Who Kicked the Hornet's Nest*, *The Grapes of Wrath*, *Great Expectations*, *The Great Gatsby*, *Gone with the Wind*, *Goya's Art*, *Green Eggs and Ham*, and *Grimm's Fairy Tales* were all set aside for now in a stack on the desk, the books remaining on the shelf steadied by bookends. She gave the pile of books a warning side-eye as if to say, *None of you are to call to me in the middle of the night to put you back in your spot on the shelf. You'll be fine right where you are.*

Quinn dusted the empty shelf, then placed the soldiers in a pleasing tableau. Or she tried to, anyway. They were wobbly and not cooperating with her artistic vision. The frustration of getting them to stand without toppling over was made worse when she painstakingly got them to stand, only to knock them over herself when placing another. *How did Bernard play with these?* Quinn wondered. *Probably outside where he could nestle their bases in the dirt, just like real soldiers.* She smiled at the thought of her grandfather playing as a boy, then cringed at how filthy he and his friends must have gotten playing on their bellies in the dirt like that.

She made a frustrated gurgle as she knocked the soldiers over again and heard Mary-Louise Lovely's voice saying, *Fall down seven times, get up eight.* "More like seven hundred times," she muttered. She kept returning to the doughboys even when she found herself doing her finger thing. Sighing, she had no idea how long she'd zoned out. Had she been trying to arrange the doughboys in the tableau, or did she simply look like a dummy standing there in front of the shelf doing her finger thing? She knew one thing for sure, though—she'd only been concentrating on one or the other that entire time.

Some people reveled in what they claimed was multitasking, which Quinn knew wasn't even a real thing. She knew "multitasking" was simply switching attention back and forth, but not accomplishing any of it. The true path to accomplishment was steady focus and forward progress. One thing at a time, the same thing that made crossword puzzles so marvelous.

Read this clue, fill in these boxes, read another clue. Quinn felt better just thinking about it. Perhaps creating and solving crossword puzzles wasn't healthy for someone with organizational OCD, but Mary-Louise Lovely would have to pry them out of her cold, dead hands.

Quinn kept her puzzle creation a secret. Only her parents and Vera Greenberg, the publisher and editor-in-chief of the local *Chestnut Station Chronicle* knew she'd been doing it since high school. Not even Rico, her lifelong best friend, knew. But that's because he'd surely have blabbed it, and she'd have been labeled as even more of a freak at school. She wasn't ashamed of her nerdy pastime any longer but was glad it wasn't common knowledge, mainly because she had discovered recently it was a useful mechanism to plant subliminal clues in the brain of Police Chief Myron Chestnut, an avid puzzler, when he wasn't digging into crimes to her satisfaction.

It had already worked several times to steer him in a different direction in his investigations, a point of pride to her. But it wouldn't work ever again if he knew she was the mastermind behind them, because for some reason, Chief Chestnut despised her with an intensity usually reserved for internet trolls and the politically progressive.

Now, if she could only work out why he hated her so much.

She batted away the stirring of her monster, who began nudging her, suggesting she turn that brief thought into yet another all-consuming obsession. *Not now, monster.* She quickly raised a metaphorical silver crucifix, since she already had her hands full. If she took action early and defiantly enough, her monster often settled back into its murky cavern deep in her subconscious, happy to wait for a more opportune time. He knew it would come soon enough.

In addition to testing herself with Grandpa's desk, Quinn was attempting other secret small challenges, like having a messy purse as long as she could stand it and wearing her name tag in different locations on her bib apron at the diner. And now, at Mary-Louise Lovely's direction, she'd have to add in a semipublic test: not alphabetizing her mom's spices.

Quinn felt a pang of regret for not confiding in Mary-Louise Lovely today that she worried about the spice rack exercise because she'd recently found herself in her third iteration of organizing the coat closet in the last week. On Tuesday she'd arranged all the coats by size, on Wednesday by color (with subsets of light to dark shades), and on Thursday by owner.

And now she was tackling Grandpa's desk. "What am I thinking? I'm getting worse instead of better," she whispered to Fang. He swam in place, his feathery fins and tail creating slow-motion elegance in his bowl. At least until he spewed a long trail of fish poo behind him.

Each time Quinn thought she got an OCD behavior under control, a new one popped up. She'd once told Rico it felt like she carried a fully charged battery pack in the back of her head, and if she didn't aim it at something, she might explode. By now she'd hoped that with therapy and meds, it would have shrunk down to the size of a triple-A battery. Instead it had added nuclear capabilities.

She pressed her index finger on the smooth glass of Fang's bowl. When he swam over, she told him, "I'm failing at healing." Quieter, she added to herself, "Why should I keep trying if it's only going to keep getting worse instead of better?" She thought about her optimism about the desk and the reality of the coat closet, wondering if her depression had crept back in, then realizing with a start that her depression had probably never left. It was just hidden by the meds. Was that actually a better scenario? She didn't know. Mary-Louise Lovely said Quinn had seen her share of turmoil lately—an understatement—so it was to be expected that she felt a bit out of control. Quinn doubted the wisdom of refilling her prescription. If the pills were simply smothering her reality, how was that helpful? Mary-Louise Lovely always told her that she had no intention of getting rid of her OCD behaviors, just teaching her how to keep from being trampled by them. But what about the underlying depression? Quinn felt herself spiraling with these unanswered, perhaps unknowable, questions. She literally had to shake her head to erase them. A human Etch A Sketch.

She tried once more to wrangle the doughboys, but they'd have none of it. With her scrubbing toothbrush and a little baking soda paste, she cleaned the drawer they'd been stashed in, wondering how long it had been since they'd been taken out of there. She brushed the grime from the interior corners of the cigar box, then returned the doughboys to it and the box to the drawer. Was giving up on them OCD progress? It didn't feel like it. Progress would probably be to put them on the shelf and happily let them fall over however they'd like.

She made a hesitant but conscious decision to leave the books stacked on the corner of the desk, wondering how long she could stand it before returning them back to their place on the shelf. She brushed her hand across the beautifully illustrated and embossed dust jacket of *Grimm's Fairy Tales*. A test.

Quinn sighed and pulled open the next drawer, which was full of loose papers. She awkwardly wrangled the pile from the deep drawer and placed it in the center of the desk. She dragged a chair from the kitchen and settled in, leafing through the papers. As she read each one, she created a categorical pile for everything she found: medical; dental; warranties for small appliances that had probably conked out twenty years ago; copies of strongly worded but respectful letters to the editor Bernard had sent over the years to the *Denver Post*; receipts current and historical; bank statements; investment notifications.

The next paper she pulled out she couldn't quite identify, even though right across the top it said "Quit Claim Deed." Real estate? Quinn scanned the first page. "Be it known by all, that all right, title, interest, and claim to the following described real estate property is hereby granted to Georgeanne Dudley." She was surprised to find out that Georgeanne had property listed in her maiden name. She couldn't remember her ever talking about it. Quinn scanned the description, hoping it involved an exotic chateau high in the Swiss Alps, or a mossy Irish castle complete with drawbridge and moat, or a cozy seaside cottage decorated with lobster pots. Nope. None of the above. Georgeanne's property was only twenty or so miles from Chestnut Station, "bordered by County Road 34 on the west, County Road DD on the north, County Road 68 on the east, and County Road CC on the south." Quinn tried to picture these roads, but the closest image she got was a vague area east of town. Nothing exotic, mossy, or cozy about it, just rattlesnakey, dry, and covered in sagebrush.

"Quinn, wash up for dinner," Georgeanne called.

The thought of dinner made her tummy rumble, and she dropped the disappointing Quit Claim Deed packet on top of the pile again.

As Quinn filled glasses of iced tea for her parents and herself, her dad said, "Sure smells good in here."

"I made your favorite—"

"Everything you make is my favorite, Georgie." Dan actually did enjoy eating everything his wife made, even the weird stuff. Maybe especially the weird stuff. Quinn admired his sense of adventure.

"Weeknight Funfetti Casserole."

"Or as I call it," Quinn said with a laugh. "Dichotomy Dinner."

"I love Funfetti Casserole," Dan said. "It's dinner and dessert at the same time. Such a time-saver." Dan poked Quinn in the ribs. "Your mom is a genius."

"That she is, Dad. That she is. Funfetti cake mix, bacon, and cheddar cheese? C'mon…what's not to love?"

"Oh, you two." Georgeanne blushed.

"How are you coming on Bernard's desk?" Dan asked Quinn.

"I got the outside all clean and spiffy, and now I'm going through the drawers. I found some old army men that I'm going to ask him about. By the looks of them, they could have been toys he played with as a kid."

"If you find anything you think he might like to use to decorate his new place, let me know and I'll get it over to him as soon as his acclimation period is over," Georgeanne said.

Quinn nodded. "I'm making some stacks of papers for you to go through, Mom, before I bother him with them. I'm not sure what's important and what's not."

They chatted about their days. Dan regaled them, as he did most nights, with an over-the-top insurance claim one of his agents had to deal with. They had a friendly competition in his office among the agents, with Dan awarding a monthly joke trophy for the most outrageous story. Quinn had always wondered if they were actual claims or if the agents made them up to win the much-sought-after trophy awarded by their boss.

Now that school was back in session for the fall, Georgeanne once again compared and contrasted her days of semiretirement from teaching music to all the schoolkids in Chestnut Station. In those days, she traveled a weekly route educating every student from preschool to high school as the town's only music teacher. Now she gave a handful of people—kids and adults—private piano lessons in her basement music studio. This autumn, though, for the first time that Quinn could remember, Georgeanne didn't seem to regret her decision to retire. "I don't need all that real estate in the basement like I used to, so if we need to move Dad's desk down there, I can make room."

"I don't know," Dan said. "It's such a beautiful piece it would be a shame not to have it on display in the living room."

"It makes me a little sad to see it here instead of at Mom and Dad's place, but I suppose I'll get used to it. I'll decide later."

"Oh, speaking of real estate, Mom," Quinn said. "I found what looks like a property deed in your name in those papers in Grandpa's desk. I didn't know he gave you any property."

Ignoring Quinn, Georgeanne passed the baking dish to Dan. "Want some more?"

"Don't mind if I do." He served himself another piece of dinner cake.

"Where is your property exactly, anyway, Mom? I can't picture it, but it looks like it's out east of town somewhere."

"It's nothing, Quinn. There's no property out east somewhere."

Quinn laughed. "There's plenty of property out east."

Georgeanne rolled her eyes. "There's no property out east somewhere *in my name*."

"There's a paper in Grandpa's desk that begs to disagree with you."

"It's nothing. And don't be bothering your grandfather about it. His memory isn't what it used to be. He doesn't need you muddling things up in his brain." She served herself another piece of Funfetti Casserole and then pointed her fork at Quinn. "Have you refilled your meds yet?"

"I was going to but…I couldn't find the time." That excuse sounded as weak to Quinn as it obviously did to Georgeanne.

"Now that Jake has hired more help at the diner, you should have more time, not less. You should thank him."

"I'll add it to my list," Quinn said, stabbing the last bite on her plate. She saw Georgeanne and Dan exchange a parental look not meant for her to see. Quinn joked that OCD stood for Occasionally Complicated Daughter, and she knew her parents wouldn't disagree.

"But about that property. Is that my inheritance? Did you want it to be a secret, so we don't have a *King Lear* situation? Do you want me to go all Cordelia on you and publicly declare my love before I can get my share of the kingdom?"

Dan laughed, but Georgeanne snapped at her. "That's not funny. And I told you to drop it. It's nothing." She shoved away from the table and started cleaning the kitchen.

Quinn recoiled as if she'd been slapped. Georgeanne rarely snapped at anyone, especially Quinn, not in all of her thirty-one years. She looked at Dan, searching for an answer to her mother's outburst but finding none. Dan looked just as surprised as she felt.

There was no way that property deed was nothing. Quinn didn't believe Georgeanne for a minute.

Chapter 3

The next morning before Quinn headed for work at the Chestnut Diner, she detoured into the living room to check the location of the property in Georgeanne's name, but the deed wasn't on the stack of papers where she'd left it on the desk yesterday. She checked the drawers and all the cubbyholes. While she was there, she rubbed a finger on the embossed cover of *Grimm's Fairy Tales* and fought the urge to return it and the other books to their rightful home on the shelf.

Quinn wandered into the kitchen, trying to assess her mother's mood. Was last night an anomaly, or was it ongoing?

"I made you toast," Georgeanne said, handing her a plate.

"Thanks, Mom." Whew. Anomaly. Thank goodness. She still didn't want to come right out and ask about the deed, though. She tried a roundabout. "Hey, did you get a chance to look through the piles of papers on Grandpa's desk yet?"

"No, I haven't touched any of it." Georgeanne hurried out of the kitchen without finishing making Dan's oatmeal, abandoning her practically full coffee cup on the counter.

Quinn nibbled her toast, waiting for Georgeanne to come back. She stirred her dad's oatmeal, then turned off the burner under it before leaving for work.

As she walked to the diner, one thought kept looping through her brain, a syllable for every step. "What's out there that Mom doesn't want me to know?"

* * * *

When Quinn reached the diner, Jethro the bloodhound was sprawled in front of the door as usual, while Virginia Woof sat demurely out of the way. Jethro was the unofficial, self-proclaimed mascot of the Chestnut Diner, belonging to everyone and no one. Virginia Woof was his new best friend, a Pomeranian-husky mix who looked exactly like a fox, an occasional visitor to the diner. The two of them met when Quinn took care of Gin for her owner, Hugh Pugh.

"Hey, Jethro." Quinn stooped to give him a friendly thump on his side, then greeted Virginia Woof. "Hello, Gin. How are you this fine morning?" Gin lifted her chin and sat in a regal pose awaiting Quinn's expected boop on her snout.

That little ritual out of the way, Quinn pulled open the diner door. She was surprised to see the Retireds already at their regular table. With the addition of Hugh Pugh to their ranks, Quinn was still getting used to their new seating arrangement at the long table in back. It used to be more like *The Last Supper* with Wilbur, Herman, and Bob with their backs to the wall, and Silas and Larry at either end. But now, Bob was in Larry's place at the end, and Larry and Hugh—as the junior members of this senior group—sat with their backs to the diner, clearly the less-desirable locale. Much harder to see and be seen. Larry and Hugh were the most amenable to this hierarchy, luckily. Both had recently lost their spouses and were less interested in the comings and goings at the Chestnut Diner. They simply craved easy companionship and a reason to get out of bed every morning.

"Geez, guys," Quinn said with a good-natured smirk. "Don't you have houses of your own?"

"Of course we have houses of our own." Herman, literal loveable Herman, stared at her with his trademark quizzical gaze. He always looked like he was learning everything for the first time, and making no sense of it. Like Jethro attempting the study of electronics. A Martian confronted with an abacus. A mailbox researching opera.

"Ah, Herman. Don't ever change," Quinn said.

The Retireds all had mugs of coffee in front of them even though the diner hadn't officially opened for the day. Unless the door was locked, however, hours of operation meant nothing to them. They'd often sit at their table from breakfast through and long past lunchtime, pontificating, arguing, eating, greeting all the other diners, and being greeted in return. In the course of a week, almost the entire town of Chestnut Station had made an appearance of some kind at the Chestnut Diner. What else was there to do?

Larry jumped up to give Quinn a quick hug. Larry had lost his wife several months earlier, but grief still oozed off of him. He needed company and human touch the way an astronaut needed air. He broke Quinn's heart on a regular basis, and she hugged him long and hard without really meaning to.

"Honestly. Get a room," Silas said with fake indignation.

Quinn pulled away from Larry. "Jealous?"

"You know it, sister!" Silas laughed and winked at her.

Wilbur waggled his mug at her.

"Can't I even put my purse down?" Quinn scolded, then noticed the coffeepot right in front of him. She offered a melodramatic sigh, then topped off his coffee. While she was bent down, Wilbur gave her a peck on the cheek.

"Thanks, darlin'," he said in his cement-mixer voice. "Wanted to make sure you felt needed."

"That's so kind and passive-aggressive of you, Wilbur." Quinn topped off everyone's coffee.

Before heading to the back, she set the pot in front of Hugh. She rested a hand on his shoulder. "How are you doing, Hugh?"

"I'm doing okay, Quinn, thank you for asking. Taking it one day at a time. Gin helps, but I know she misses Creighton too."

Quinn resisted the urge to say gin might help them all, and was a tad surprised that jokester Silas hadn't already jumped in with a liquor joke of his own. Instead, Quinn said, "Gin's such a doll. I love how she and Jethro have bonded."

"Yeah, he comes over and spends the night sometimes." At Quinn's raised eyebrows, he quickly added, "Oh, I checked. He's been neutered."

"Haven't we all," Silas said.

"On that disturbing note, I suppose I should get to work."

As Quinn headed to the back, Bob smoothed back his never-mussed movie-star hair and called, "Hey, can you make sure Jake is making an *egg white* omelet for me? I think he slips in whole eggs just to see if I notice."

"Will do." Quinn doubted that Jake would ever purposely screw up an order for one of the Retireds. Even when he made everything precisely to their specifications, they always found reasons to complain. Multiple reasons. But that never stopped Jake from taking the offending item back to the kitchen, dousing it in green chili or chocolate sauce, depending on the perceived transgression, and then carrying it right back out and serving it to them again, usually to wild acclaim and heartfelt thanks for his stellar customer service. It was a trick Quinn used all the time now too.

On her way through the dining room, Quinn stopped to nudge one of the "hitchhiker paintings" back into alignment. They were not paintings *of* hitchhikers, but rather painted *by* a hitchhiker who'd traveled through town recently on her way to art school. She repaid Jake's kindness with art, practically life-sized renderings of scenes from the diner. There was an excellent one of Quinn carrying some trays of food, and another where she was looking pensive, leaning on the door between the kitchen and the dining room wearing her favorite apron that said, *There are two kinds of people I hate: 1. People who make lists ... 2. People who can't count ... 3. Hypocrites.* She almost didn't notice the artwork anymore, except when it was askew or when Loma teased her about it. There was also a very attractive painting of Jake cooking at the stove, with a nice view of his broad back and tight butt. Loma was convinced it would bring a lot of oglers into the diner and convinced Jake to give it a prominent spot. Even though Loma was Jake's ex-wife, she could still appreciate his many charms.

Quinn's favorite painting, however, was the one where Jake and Rico were sitting at the big corner booth eating slabs of pie. The artist captured the twinkle in Jake's eye and Rico's unfortunate curls. It was natural and homey and probably accounted for the diner's increased pie sales.

Quinn called a greeting to Jake in the kitchen as she went to clock in and grab her apron. She walked into the kitchen, dropping the neck strap over her head and tying the straps around her waist.

"The Retireds are here early," she said.

"Yeah. They can't get enough of me, I guess."

"I'm sure that's it." Quinn repinned her name tag in the center of the bib front of her apron instead of on the left side. "Oh, speaking of always being here…my mom said I should thank you for hiring that part-timer because those twelve-hour shifts were killing me."

"Don't get too attached to her." Jake flattened some hash browns on the grill, where they sizzled. "I don't think she's long for this place."

"I haven't even met her yet! What did she do?"

"Failed the diner lingo test."

"Oh, for Pete's sake. You should grade that thing on a curve." The door chime tinkled, and Quinn moved toward the dining room, shaking her head at Jake's inscrutable test. She'd been told it had driven several of his employees away, but she herself had aced it. A list of arcane phrases to memorize for no reason was well within her wheelhouse.

Quinn gave an inward, completely silent groan when she saw the new customer was the town's chief of police, Myron Chestnut. She thought her groan had been completely silent, that was, until he glanced at her and scowled. Yep, he still hated her for reasons unknown. She'd asked everyone, even Rico-who-couldn't-tell-a-lie, but nobody knew.

He clapped his bony hands on the backs of Silas and Hugh, then reached across and shook hands with the rest of the Retireds. He chatted with them until taking his favorite table in the center of the diner. Most police officers liked a seat in a corner with visual access to an entire room, but not Chief Chestnut. He wanted to be in the thick of things, always campaigning, it seemed, for the mayor's job when he retired from the police force.

Quinn poured his coffee while he removed the *Chestnut Chronicle* crossword from his shirt pocket, where he had folded it precisely, creases razor-sharp.

The only thing that redeemed Chief Chestnut in Quinn's eyes was his love of the crossword puzzle. He was an avid crossword puzzler too, like she was, but Quinn was convinced he'd drop them like a smoking hot potato, never to pick one up again, if he knew she was the one who created them. That was how much he hated her.

When she returned to take his order, she noticed once again that he was the rare bird who completed the Downs before the Acrosses. So contrary. So avant-garde. So weird.

* * * *

After the lunch rush died down, around two thirty, Loma strode into the diner, all curves and attitude. She and Jake embraced, performed their customary fake argument about Loma not being careful about her diabetes—"I need my sustenance, you know that!"—and Jake not dating enough—"How will I ever get a date when you're always mauling me in public?"

When they were finished, Loma kissed him square on the mouth, then turned to Quinn and shouted, "Let's go! I got on my walking shoes, and I've been looking forward to this secret field trip all day!" She held up one foot to show Quinn a bedazzled slip-on sneaker.

"Secret field trip? Where are you two going?" Jake asked. "And won't those shoes be visible from space?"

"It's not really a secret, but I didn't tell Loma the specifics because she wouldn't know where I was talking about anyway and she'd start asking a zillion loud questions." Quinn looked pointedly at Loma.

"Me? Loud? And ask a zillion questions? When do I do that? Why would you say such a thing? And where are we going, anyway? Are you just tryin' to make me curious?"

Quinn and Jake began laughing.

"Who made you like that?" Loma narrowed her eyes at Quinn and crossed her arms, hefting her bosom high—her power move.

"Get outta here, both of you." Jake snapped a towel four feet away, but Loma jumped like it had landed.

"Is that how you treat your customers?" she said.

"When was the last time you paid for anything here?"

Loma linked an arm through Quinn's and said, "Let's get gone before he starts adding up my tab."

* * * *

On the drive, Quinn told Loma about the Quit Claim Deed and her mother snapping at her about it.

"Georgeanne? I can't picture her snapping back at a snapping turtle who's chomping on her toe!"

"I know, right? But she did. It even surprised my dad. And then, get this…when I went to look at the deed again to GPS the roads that bordered her property, it had disappeared."

"What's the big deal with the property? Why does it freak her out so much?"

"I don't know if it freaks her out exactly, but she sure wishes that deed had never made an appearance, which I don't understand. What's so hush-hush about her dad giving her a piece of property anyway?"

"You'd think she'd appreciate it." Loma glanced around the empty fields surrounding them. I'd love a little plot of land out here." Loma struggled against her seat belt to angle her ample torso toward Quinn. "Maybe it was supposed to be a surprise for you. If your parents never built a house or developed the land, maybe they wanted you to."

"Maybe. That's what I said too." Quinn thought that was a real possibility. Maybe she'd ruined their plan by finding the deed. After all, she was fairly certain she'd ruined everything else with her OCD. Her parents worried about her constantly now. Maybe this was just one more thing. "But I would have thought my dad would have theoretically been in on this plan, but he looked as surprised as I did." She slowed down the car. "I think there's a pull-off coming up soon. I think we're close."

"Close to what?" Loma looked out at the emptiness.

"Close to my mom's property. I remembered it was between County Roads 34 and 68 on County Road DD—"

"Double D?" Loma hefted her bosom again.

"When we were in high school, we thought it was hilarious to call it Boob Boulevard."

"Memorable at least."

"Ah, here it is." Quinn veered across the yellow line and off the road at a large turnout on the opposite shoulder.

"This is it? Where are we?"

"This is the edge of Camp Chestnut."

Loma craned her neck trying to see whatever it was she was supposed to be seeing. "Where Boy Scouts make lanyards? Fat camp? Outward Bound Adventure fifteen miles from town so it's not too scary?"

"None of the above." Quinn got out of the car. "Camp Chestnut was a Japanese internment camp during World War II."

"Oh my." The smile slid off Loma's face as she stepped out and met Quinn at the front of the car.

Pointing a finger, Quinn said, "That's the only original building left. An old guard tower they restored. The rest of the buildings were torn down in the fifties."

Loma shaded her eyes and looked at the top of the guard tower where Quinn had pointed. "Did you guys come out here on school field trips?"

Quinn shook her head. "There was barely a passing mention of it. I remember asking Mom and Dad about the guard tower whenever we'd drive out here, but they just said it was a guard tower. I assumed there was an old jail out here. I made up this whole story in my head about it, like a territorial prison from the eighteen hundreds."

"Did your parents not know, or did they just not want to say?"

"They had to have known. But what can you say to a kid about one of the most egregious civil rights violations in American history?" Quinn waved vaguely to the right of the guard tower, farther along the road. "I hear they've turned the site into a museum, making the history more visible. I haven't been to it, though. They did it all while I was living in Denver."

"Is that where we're headed?"

"Not today. Mom's property is across Boob Boulevard. I don't really know how big it is, but it's bordered on this side by Double D, County Road CC on the other side of it to the south, County Road 34, which we already passed, and County Road 68, I think, which is farther on down."

"So we're here to survey it?" Loma asked with a smirk.

"Well, not officially. I don't own a sextant."

"Kinky."

"You ready?" Quinn locked the car doors and crossed to the road.

"Think there's snakes out there?"

"In September? I doubt it." Quinn had no information about snakes on the Colorado prairie but knew Loma would be standing on the hood of her car if she thought there would be anything slithering out there, plotting to scrutinize her bedazzled shoes.

They checked for traffic, even though they hadn't seen one car since they'd left Chestnut Station, crossed the road, climbed down the drainage ditch, and up again until they were on flat land, presumably owned by Georgeanne.

September in Colorado was a glorious time to be outdoors. The days were warm but not too hot under puffy clouds and azure skies, while nights were cool and crisp, a reminder that change was in the air. The migratory miller moths of summer made way for the grasshoppers of early autumn.

Quinn and Loma trudged due south, lifting their feet high over the cheat grass and yucca, and walking around the sporadic, scraggly clumps of sagebrush dotting the landscape.

Loma kept a wary eye out for snakes while bemoaning the state of her already-filthy bedazzled sneakers.

"What did you expect? A sidewalk?"

"Would that really be too much to ask?" Loma stopped to take photos of wildflowers still in bloom. "These would be great to naturalize that empty space at the house I'm redoing."

"The Texans?"

"Yep. They told me they're not into yard work, so I've been looking for good native plants for year-round color."

"Hope they like purple." Quinn glanced around. Everything blooming seemed to be purple. "That sumac turns red, I think." Quinn pointed to a bush spreading low to the ground.

The property, as most of the land out here, was flat and had been left natural. It didn't look to Quinn as if it had ever been farmed or developed in any way. There were occasional stands of evergreens here and there, as well as enormous cottonwood trees, easily a hundred years old, maybe even older. The leaves were just beginning to change, turning several different shades of green with a gradient yellow at the tips. If they were lucky, in just a few weeks all the trees would be a glorious blaze of oranges, yellows, and reds. If they were unlucky, they'd get a freeze soon, and their glorious autumn would last for eight minutes and sport a monochromatic palette of several dismal shades of brown.

Quinn walked forward but had turned her head to speak to Loma, who lagged a few steps behind. Her foot kicked something and she shrieked, jumping back toward Loma, who began shrieking too.

Loma bounced around from one foot to the other, sure Quinn had led them into a rattlesnake den.

Quinn and Loma held on to each other, scanning the ground around them. Finally Quinn's shrieks turned into giggles, and Loma clamped her mouth tight.

"What?" Loma whispered, sure the snakes could hear her.

"It's just a ball or something. I kicked it out from under that scrub oak. It just startled me." Quinn tried to peel Loma's hands from around her torso, but Loma's grip was tighter than an Edwardian corset. Quinn shimmied underneath Loma's arms.

"So, no snakes?"

"None that I can see." Quinn picked up the wooden object she had kicked and held it in her palm. "Oh, it's not a ball. It's flat on the top and bottom."

Loma stood beside her and studied it while keeping a wary eye on the ground for anything slithery. "Looks like it had been painted at some time. Pretty faded now, though."

Quinn used a fingernail on a fleck of paint that blew away in the breeze. "Red, black, maybe some white. Kinda looks like a cartoony face. Wonder what it was."

"A doll?"

"Maybe." Quinn turned it to the bottom and squinted. "What's that look like to you?" She held it out to Loma, who studied where Quinn was pointing.

"A signature?"

"Who signs a doll?"

"The artist? Maybe it was art."

Quinn shrugged, and they continued walking, Loma with her eyes out for snakes and Quinn now gently rolling the wooden object from hand to hand.

After a while Loma asked, "What exactly are we looking for?"

"We're not looking for anything. I just wanted to see what was out here. What's the significance of this property, how it relates to my mom."

"And?"

"And I have no idea." Quinn veered toward a sprawling rabbitbrush, only three feet tall but spreading its gray-green stems at least five feet in all directions. "Here's something yellow for your Texans' garden."

Loma went to its left side and squatted to take a couple of close-ups of its masses of tiny yellow flowers crowded in clusters at the top of each branch.

"What will you do with all these photos?" Quinn asked.

"Take them to my guy at the Botanic Gardens. He'll know what they are. And sometimes he gives me cuttings."

Quinn began to follow her until Loma swatted her away. "You're in my light." Quinn pivoted and went around the bush to the right, being careful to keep her shadow away from Loma's photo. "It's so pretty when this yellow bush grows right up next to these purple spiky flowers." She squatted next to it and framed up a nice picture of the two plants on her own camera. Maybe if Georgeanne saw how pretty it was out here, she'd be more excited about owning this property. Quinn made incremental movements to capture what she hoped was the perfect photo, in the course of snapping dozens.

She dropped to one knee when she found an exquisite purple bloom, the biggest and showiest of the bunch, unfortunately growing at an imperfect angle. Reaching with the index finger of her left hand, she pulled the stem just an inch or two toward a bright yellow cluster of flowers from the bush and posed them together. After she snapped a quick series of photos, she wondered about the unnatural way the purple stem was growing and peered down into the center of the vegetation.

Quinn gasped and scrambled to her feet. She stood for a minute, staring down, mouth gaping, then said, "Loma? Can you come here a minute? But walk carefully." Quinn thought she'd kept her voice calm, but she clearly had been mistaken because Loma shrieked.

"I knew there were snakes out here!"

"It's not a snake. Hush up and come here." When Loma sidled up next to her, Quinn dropped to one knee again, and using one careful finger, pulled back the purple spiky flower stem.

Loma shrieked again.

Chapter 4

"Is that what I think it is?" Loma asked, holding Quinn as a shield in front of her.

"If you think it's a human skull, then yes." For Loma's sake, Quinn made an effort to control herself and not let her mouth race like her mind was racing. The image of Emmett Dubois's dead body in the diner from a few months back, and the more recent crime scene aftermath at Hugh Pugh's house filled Quinn's senses. Again? This couldn't be happening again. She and Loma took tentative, shuffling steps, kicking up tiny clouds of dust.

"That's somebody's head," Loma said, still wielding Quinn like a shield between the skull and her bedazzled sneakers.

Quinn began chanting quietly at first, then louder and louder. "Not a dead body, not a dead body, not a dead body." She fisted her hands at her sides, knowing that her OCD monster was going to try to take control of the situation any minute now. She closed her eyes, clearly hearing Mary-Louise Lovely's voice in her head, walking her through the FADE technique. *Focus on what's going on.* Another dead body. No, just a skull. A long-dead body. *Ask what your OCD monster wants you to do.* I don't know. I don't know! Quinn's vision began to narrow to a pinprick, and she knew she was hyperventilating. *Decide if it's helpful.* Definitely not. *Establish two or three things to do instead.* Breathe. I need to breathe. She took deep, gulping breaths, then forced herself to slow down and inhale deeply. Her vision began to clear.

"Are you okay?" Loma finally loosened her grip from Quinn's arms and took a step backward.

Quinn heard the concern in Loma's shaky voice and turned, grabbing Loma in a bear hug. In her brain, Quinn pictured this as a reassuring move, but when she felt Loma gasping for breath, she knew it was quite possibly the opposite of reassuring.

Loma shook off Quinn's grip, filled her lungs to capacity, and stepped forward. She squatted down in front of the skull, letting the breath slowly abate. After a few moments, she stood and said, "Not a dead body, but definitely part of one."

Quinn joined Loma, but remained standing, in front of the skull. As she stared down at it, studying the purple spiky flower growing at an angle through the empty eye socket, she became aware she was doing her finger thing.

Loma watched Quinn's fingers for a bit, then grabbed her hand and used it to pull herself back up. "Hey," she said softly. "It's okay. It's just some old bone. Probably from a cow or something."

Quinn thought she knew a human skull when she saw one, but admittedly hadn't seen many. None up close in a field, certainly. "You're right. I'm sure it's nothing."

They stared at each other.

"You know that's a human skull, right?" Loma said after a while.

"Obviously."

"So what are we gonna do about it?"

Quinn took a deep breath and remembered some of her criminal justice classes and everything Rico had taught her over the years about his police work. She doubted he'd ever stumbled on a human skull in a field either, however.

The shock had worn off, and her curiosity finally kicked in. "We should call Rico. But I want to look around a little bit first."

"What about disturbing the crime scene?" Loma said.

"Who said this is a crime scene?" At Loma's expression, Quinn added, "And even if it is, if that bleached bone tells us anything, it's that it's been out here for a long time. I'm not going to mess with a potential crime scene. I just want to see what else might be out here. The minute I call Rico, we'll get kicked out of here. Besides, you know Rico doesn't have any help. Chief won't come out here, Donnie is useless for anything other than writing jaywalking tickets—"

"Fine." Loma threw up her hands. "You've convinced me. We're newly licensed forensic anthropologists. You go do your OCD thing."

"My 'OCD thing?'"

"Yeah, like that grid you made of Hugh's papers we had to organize that time. You had a...system. Pretty specific, as I recall."

"I always have a system."

"Then you go, girl. I'll be your anchor point."

"My 'anchor point?'" For all her shrieking, Loma was suddenly getting very much into this.

"Yeah. If I stand here, you'll know exactly where we found the skull and you can expand your grid from here."

"Impressive." Quinn took a deep, satisfying breath and felt herself get taller. *My OCD monster might want me to unravel, but I know what I need to do.*

"I haven't watched forty-seven million hours of forensics shows with you and not picked up something." Loma planted her feet, just behind the purple spiky plant. "I'll protect it, and you'll be able to see me wherever you are." She aimed her phone straight down, framing the flower and the skull in the center of the photograph. Then she took a close-up of the eye socket and showed them both to Quinn. Artistically creepy.

Systematically, methodically, Quinn walked a slow grid, scanning the ground. One hundred paces to the left of where Loma stood. Five paces up. One hundred paces back toward Loma, plus another one hundred more, past Loma to the right. Another five paces up. Two hundred paces to the left, five paces up, two hundred across. Quinn kept it up until Loma looked as tiny as one of Grandpa's toy army men.

When she came back, Loma was sitting on the ground. "Took you long enough."

"Long enough for you not to be afraid of snakes anymore?"

Loma shrugged. "If they were gonna attack, they would have by now. What did you find out there?"

"Lots more bones. And over there by that tall bush"—Quinn pointed to the left—"some buttons that look to me like they're from a man's shirt. And over there"—she pointed in front of them a bit to the right—"a pair of eyeglasses." While she was talking, she called Rico.

"Eyeglasses? Do you think they could have been—"

Quinn held up one finger. "Rico? Care to go on a little hike?"

Chapter 5

When Rico got to the property, he had Chief Chestnut and Junior Deputy Donnie Garfield in tow.

Quinn and Loma repeated their story to an attentive audience, interrupting each other, adding details, correcting factual minutiae.

"I think it must be someone from the camp." Quinn waved in the direction of the guard tower, barely visible in the distance. "Maybe someone was shot while they were escaping. Oh!" Quinn dug the faded wooden ball from her backpack. "Maybe someone stealing this! I found it just over there."

Chief Chestnut plucked it from her hand. "A croquet ball? Doubt it."

Quinn plucked it back. "It's not a croquet ball. See how it's flat here, and here?" She made it a point to hand it to Rico, who inspected it.

"That's definitely not a croquet ball," Rico said. "But I also can't imagine anyone getting killed for stealing it. I'll run it by CBI, though."

"It's just a theory," Quinn said with a pout she immediately regretted. "I found some other stuff." She pulled Rico behind her and led him to the eyeglasses she'd found. Rico planted a small flag as a marker, then she led him to the buttons. They had to squat near some sagebrush. "The buttons are mostly here, but some are over there, and there," she said, pointing. After he marked them, she peered under the bush. "Does that look like fabric to you?"

Rico dropped to his knees and leaned closer, following Quinn's pointing finger to a tangle of something in the middle of the gnarled branches. "Yes. Looks like it might have been plaid."

"If it's a shirt that got hung up and tangled on the branches, that would explain the buttons around here. After all that time out here, a shirt would eventually disintegrate, wouldn't it? Except this part that was a bit protected by the bush." Quinn straightened up, but her balance wobbled and she grabbed the closest branch for support. A handful of sprigs ended up in her fist. The aroma of camphor and Christmas billowed around them.

Rico helped steady her, then planted another marker flag. "Did you find anything else?"

"A bunch more bones scattered around. I'm guessing animals got to the body and dragged the bones away, but once they were picked clean, they'd have no more reason to disturb them."

"Probably." Rico gave her a side shoulder hug. "Nice job with your grid, by the way."

"Really? I was afraid you'd be mad at me for messing with a crime scene."

"You think this is a crime scene?" Rico surveyed the area.

"I don't know."

"Me neither. But out here in the elements, I doubt there's any real evidence you could have disturbed after all this time." Quinn started to speak, but he cut her off. "I know you were careful. I trust your grid."

Scanning the ground as they walked, Quinn and Rico trudged back to where Loma waited with Donnie and Chief Chestnut, who was on the phone.

"I understand that, but I am not interested in pursuing ancient history." Chief Chestnut listened, then said, "That's fine. Investigate all you want, but leave the Chestnut Station PD out of it." As he slid his phone back in his pocket, he said to Rico, "CBI wants to come out and take a look."

"Who's CBI?" Loma asked.

"Colorado Bureau of Investigation. Like the FBI, but for the state," Quinn explained.

"You girls get along now. You're not needed for anything else." Chief Chestnut gave them a dismissive flutter of his bony hand.

"You realize if it wasn't for us...*girls*...you wouldn't know anything about this." Loma pulled herself up to her full five feet, two inches, crossed her arms under her bosom, and gave Chief Chestnut the full impact of her power pose.

He didn't even seem to notice. "Yeah, thanks a lot," he said as he began walking away. "C'mon, Donnie. Rico, you coming?"

"I'll wait here for CBI. Point everything out to them, if you don't mind."

"Suit yourself."

"You're welcome!" Loma called after him.

"Save your breath," Quinn said. "Chief Chestnut doesn't like to be anywhere near crime, or potential crime. It might mean he'd have to do some actual work once in a while."

"It isn't that he doesn't want to work. He just doesn't want anyone to think there's crime in Chestnut Station," Rico explained to Loma.

"You save your breath too, Rico," Quinn said. "One of these days you're going to have to quit making allowances for that sorry excuse of a crime fighter and take over as chief of police around here. You do all the work anyway."

Rico smiled at her. "Actually, I think you did all the work out here today. When are you going to get back on that horse and apply to the academy again?"

"You went to the police academy?" Loma asked her.

Quinn shrugged. "Kinda."

"You can't *kinda* go to the police academy. That's like *kinda* being pregnant. You either are or you aren't. You either went or you didn't."

"Well, then I guess I went. But it didn't last long."

Loma waited expectantly for more information.

Quinn sighed. "That's when they diagnosed my OCD. I'm sure I told you this." Quinn knew she hadn't. "I had an…incident."

"An incident?"

"During my interview with these three muckedy-mucks in the department, I got so nervous when I didn't know the questions they were going to ask me that I started counting the holes in the acoustic ceiling tiles."

Loma raised her eyebrows. "Why would you know what they'd ask you? You ever interview with them before?"

Quinn sighed again. "No, but for the sixteen years before that, I always knew what every one of my teachers and professors were going to ask. It was the first time I ever felt completely and utterly out of control. None of us realized when I was growing up that all of my weird little ways to stay in control were actually the hallmarks of my OCD. When the script was flipped so completely on me and I didn't know what to do, I freaked out. Plain and simple."

"Nothing simple about it, Quinn," Rico said softly.

"I guess not." Quinn locked eyes with Loma. "You're the first person I ever told that story to. Rico, my parents, and my therapist know, but you're the first person I've actually told."

"I'm honored," Loma said seriously.

Quinn spat out a sharp, rueful laugh. "Not sure it's an honor. A burden, most likely."

"Girl! The only thing that's burdensome about you is when you don't let me eat doughnuts."

* * * *

After CBI got to the property and they were politely dismissed, Quinn dropped off Loma back at the diner, where she'd left her car. She had plans to show her photos, except the last couple shots of the skull, to her contact at the botanic gardens.

Quinn headed home.

When she got there, the house was empty. "Dad must still be at work," Quinn said to Fang while she changed clothes. "But where's Mom?"

Fang answered with a slow bubble that broke on the surface of the water.

"I see. And when will she be back?"

This time Fang didn't answer, just made some languid circuits of his bowl.

In the kitchen Quinn placed Fang's bowl on the table and decided to help Georgeanne by getting dinner ready. She checked the weekly menu stuck with a bright pink flamingo magnet on the front of the refrigerator. The square for tonight's dinner was blank. "Maybe they had some function tonight."

Fang didn't respond.

"I guess I'm on my own." Quinn rummaged through the refrigerator to see what she had to work with. She placed some chicken breast, tortillas, and a red bell pepper on the countertop. "Fajitas it is."

Next she opened the pantry and shut it just as quickly. Georgeanne had randomized the spices again. Quinn knew she'd asked her mother to do so, at Mary-Louise Lovely's request, but she still had to take a deep breath and close her eyes. After a long exhale, she inched open the pantry door and peeked in. Sesame seeds next to cumin. Cinnamon on top of tarragon. Paprika not only upside down, but next to Chinese five-spice powder. And the taco seasoning was nowhere to be found. She slammed the pantry door shut.

Quinn stared down at the fajita ingredients on the counter. With slow, jerky movements, ears and face hot, she returned them to the refrigerator and sat next to Fang at the table, wallowing in her failure. Or was it success? She hadn't alphabetized the spices, after all, but maybe that was because she almost couldn't bear to look at them. Failure or success, she'd lost her appetite.

After Quinn wallowed for a few more minutes, Georgeanne bustled through the kitchen door with a pizza.

"You're here! Good. I was afraid I'd have to eat this alone. I'm starving to death, but still probably couldn't eat this entire thing. Or at least I shouldn't."

Quinn jumped up to take the pizza while her mom struggled to remove her sweater. "What kind is it?"

"Your favorite...fig and ricotta." Georgeanne had found a kindred spirit over at Mario's Pizza. Mario had a secret menu just for Georgeanne that was longer than his real menu.

Not wanting to hurt Georgeanne's feelings, Quinn didn't tell her that her favorite pizza was black olive and sausage. "Where's Dad?"

"He had a work thing tonight. Some training for his agents. We can have a girls' night. Maybe watch a chick flick later?" Georgeanne stopped with her arms in midair as she reached for two plates. "You didn't already eat, did you?"

With a furtive glance at the pantry, Quinn assured her, "Nope. Not yet."

"Oh, good." Georgeanne placed slices of pizza on plates while Quinn poured drinks. "What have you been up to today?" Georgeanne bit the point off her slice.

"You probably wouldn't believe me if I told you." Quinn tore off two paper towels and handed one to Georgeanne. At Georgeanne's raised eyebrows, Quinn said, "Loma and I found some old bones."

"Old bones? What kind of bones?"

"I'm not sure, but we think they're human."

"Human bones? Where? Out on that property she's renovating?"

Quinn squinched her eyes shut. "No." She felt her mother staring at her. "Out on that property of yours. Or near it, at least."

Georgeanne dropped her pizza to her plate, where it landed upside down with a *sploosh*. She stared at Quinn. Both of them were decidedly more pale than when they sat down. "Okay, spill it. What are you talking about?"

"Loma and I went out to look at the property I saw on that deed."

"Why?"

"I just wanted to see what was out there. And Loma was looking at wildflowers."

"And?"

"And while we were out there, we stumbled on a skull." Georgeanne blanched, so Quinn quickly added, "It was bleached white, Mom. It's been out there for years, probably decades. Not gross or anything. Not like—" Quinn stopped herself before she compared it to finding the dead man facedown in his biscuits and gravy at the diner. "Just old, dry bones."

Georgeanne stared at her for a bit, then scooted her chair back. She said, "I guess I'm not hungry after all," and hurried from the kitchen.

Quinn heard her parents' bedroom door close. She absentmindedly lifted the slice of pizza to her mouth but placed it back on her plate without taking a bite. She'd lost her appetite again.

She wondered what was going on with her mom. Georgeanne wasn't typically squeamish, so her reaction to news of old, bleached bones didn't make sense to Quinn. Unless it was again about that piece of property. There was absolutely nothing interesting about that property, unless you counted the bones and the CBI agents now crawling all over it. But Georgeanne had been weird about the property yesterday, before Quinn told her about the bones. Quinn glanced uneasily toward the hallway leading to her parents' bedroom.

Did Georgeanne know something about those bones?

Chapter 6

After Quinn cleaned up the kitchen, she retired to her bedroom, where she stared at Fang, becoming hypnotized by the slow, methodical way he moved his ruffly fins.

Not being a forensic anthropologist, she'd had no intention of investigating anything about those old bones at the time she'd left Rico and the CBI crew at that property earlier. But she simply couldn't make sense of Georgeanne's reaction. After much thought, it was clear to Quinn that Georgeanne knew more than she was letting on. But about what? The bones? The property? Why was she so nervous, and why would she clam up like that? Georgeanne never clammed up about anything. Curiosity and her interest in everything she encountered was what made *her* so interesting.

Quinn had expected Georgeanne to be maybe grossed out for a second if she thought it was a dead body, but bones bleached by time and weather weren't particularly gross. They were definitely startling and stressful, as attested by Quinn and Loma's own reaction when they found them, but not gross.

A more typical Georgeanne-type response would have been to ponder whom the bones belonged to and to express sadness for their family and loved ones. But to go pale and rush from the room? That was unexpected and out of character.

The skeleton was in good hands with the CBI, though. Quinn thought about that wooden thing she'd found. She tapped Fang's bowl. "I'll go ask them about that at the internment camp museum. Maybe they know what it is."

She pulled her computer onto her lap and searched *Camp Chestnut internment*. Up popped photos and the museum website, which she perused.

She read all the pages on the site, learning everything she could. Then she clicked out of the search engine and brought up her crossword software. It was obvious to her that the death had something to do with the Japanese internment camp, but since she couldn't do anything about that, she decided to create a puzzle with that at its core. INTERNMENT CAMPS had fifteen letters so it went right in the center. With PRISONER in the northwest corner and JAPANESE in the southwest, it was another subliminal message to Chief Chestnut.

Even "ancient history" deserves closure, regardless of what Chief Chestnut said.

INTERNMENT CAMPS PUZZLE

ACROSS

1. A pop of red, say, on a couch
7. Quick kiss
11. In the past
14. Swamp, or a town in England
15. Woody's son
16. Daughter in "Family Guy"
17. Book and movie genre
18. One longing for freedom
20. Agency concerned with fuel standards
21. Cain and Abel's mom
23. Long chair
24. Almost never wins the poker pot
25. People who sacrifice for the greater good
26. Famous uncle
29. Twitter handle for a communication company
30. End to mat, bet, and let
31. What do cows do to have a cow
34. HBCU in SE US
38. Egregious civil rights violations
41. Type of salmon
42. What's a cow who can't have a cow?
43. Opp. of ant.
45. "Would you like a hot dog ___ hamburger?"
46. Blog feed initials
47. Cat or fabric
51. Agency that protects rights of employees
52. Tolerated
53. Ugandan President, played by Forest
54. Body image, for short
57. People interned at Camp Chestnut
59. Rough fights, often drunken
62. Kidney or bladder malady, for short
63. What do u do when u ROTF?
64. Controversial novel by Nabokov
65. Homer's neighbor
66. Forensic examiners
67. Vera Greenberg is a great one

DOWN

1. First black player selected to the Davis Cup team
2. Comes after a clip
3. Countess of Grantham
4. One of the conts.
5. Nonprofit operating independently, for short
6. Shake a fist at
7. Beats rock but not scissors
8. Make an oopsie
9. Hackneyed phrase
10. Food satisfying Jewish dietary law
11. Procedure where fluid is removed from uterus, for short
12. Honkers
13. Fairy tale baddies
19. Crew need
22. C, D, or B12
24. Catherine, the last of Henry VIII's wives
26. Comes before span
27. River in Tuscany
28. Erratic flyer
30. Exponential increase
32. VIP at the Co
33. Number in commandments or countdowns
34. "Salt, ___, Acid, Heat"
35. Arison, Johnson, or Talai
36. Major city in Minn.
37. Employs
39. What some of these clues are
40. Fiddler or ghost
43. "Let's take the ___ route"
44. Songs that frequently change pitch
47. Like some gumbo and jambalaya
48. Subside or lessen
49. Type of fatty acid
50. Early leader in civil rights movement, ___ B. Wells
51. Physicist Bohr
54. Nincompoop
55. Choir voice
56. Russian ruler
58. "___ sez to my friend, I sez..."
60. Stewart who wants to know if you think he's sexy
61. Mahershala in Hollywood

Chapter 7

On her next day off, Quinn convinced Loma to go with her to visit Camp Chestnut and tour the museum. Quinn drove the same county road they'd been on the other day—and Loma made the same "double D" joke—but instead of using the pull-off, they drove a bit farther and turned left through the main gate.

They got out of the car in the small gravel parking lot and entered the museum building.

A gray-haired man with red suspenders stretched taut over his big belly sat behind a small desk near the entrance. When he stood, he hitched up his pants, and Quinn saw he was also wearing a belt. Obviously a fail-safe system. "Good morning," he said. "Have you been here before?"

"Nope, first time for both of us." Quinn saw his name tag and added, "Robert."

He gathered up some tri-fold brochures, opening the one on top. "This here's the layout of the museum. Lots of exhibits, as you can see, and over thataway there are some computers and other audiovisual displays. You can listen to stories from people who were interned here, in their own voices."

"That sounds interesting," Loma said. "And sad. Is it sad? I don't like to be too sad."

"It is sad, but I don't think it's *too* sad for people to face. It's something everyone should know about, regardless." He opened the other brochure. "And this is the map for outside. You can go around and see where the old buildings were." He tipped his head to a donation box. "And if you feel disposed, you can drop a few bucks in there so we can get busy on our plans for re-creations of the buildings. It'll give us more space to display more of the artifacts we have in storage and to talk about all of it."

"None of the old buildings are still standing?" Loma asked.

"Only that one guard tower I showed you," Quinn said.

"That's right." Robert nodded. "But you can go up in it if you want. Get a good look at the camp from a bird's-eye view."

"Oh, I'd love that," Quinn said.

"You're lucky it's such a nice day. You can walk around out there and look at the kiosks too. There's one that tells you about everything that used to be out there. Inside here it's more about the people, and out there it's more about the camp itself."

They paid their admission fee and meandered around the exhibits. Robert called after them, "If you have any questions, there's always some of us docents hanging around. Just ask."

There were only a few other visitors besides Quinn and Loma. Everyone spoke in quiet, respectful voices. Some of the information she'd read on the website was included in the exhibits.

"That's awful." Loma pointed to a display with several black-and-white photos and oversized text explaining that after Pearl Harbor was bombed, everyone was so concerned about the "yellow peril" they decided to round up everyone of Japanese ancestry in case they were spies. "Look at that. They were only given six days to get ready to go. They had to sell their houses and everything."

"For pennies on the dollar. Same with any businesses they owned. Can you imagine?"

They shuffled silently through the exhibit until Loma gasped. "Quinn, look at this. These families were forced to live in horse stalls for months until these camps were built!"

Quinn read the informational poster about how many internees were housed at the Santa Anita racetrack in California. "How degrading to treat American citizens like that," she murmured.

"Says here the government told them these camps were for their own protection, but I think that barbed wire and those armed guards pointing weapons at them beg to differ." Loma's jaw tightened as she pointed at the photo.

The more they saw and read, the more Quinn felt ashamed she hadn't known about Camp Chestnut, having grown up less than twenty miles away. Why wasn't this part of the Chestnut Station school curriculum?

There were ten relocation centers around the United States, which imprisoned 120,000 people, most of them American citizens. About 7,500 lived here at Camp Chestnut.

"The average age in the camp was seventeen. Those kids had to say the Pledge of Allegiance in school every day. Can you imagine?" Loma said.

Quinn shook her head. She studied the oversized photos: the schoolrooms; the barracks where several families lived together; many sad-faced children and worried adults waiting in lines.

Robert wandered by. He stood looking at the exhibit, hands jingling the coins in his pocket. "It's a bit overwhelming, isn't it?"

"Terrible," Loma said.

"But it wasn't all bad." At Quinn's raised eyebrows, he said, "The Japanese families made the best out of a terrible situation. They are a resourceful people." He pointed to some other photos in the exhibit. "This was like any other small town in America. It was actually bigger than Chestnut Station, which is the closest town to here. They had a post office, but the mail was censored—"

"So aside from the barbed wire, the armed guards, and the censored mail, it was just like Chestnut Station." Quinn failed at controlling the sarcasm in her voice.

"I know," he said quietly. "But they also published a newspaper, had Boy Scout and Girl Scout troops, and they could take art, dance, and music classes. The adults had work to keep them busy and to earn a little money. They grew most of the food for the camp." He saw their faces. "It wasn't ideal, but like I said, they made the best out of a bad situation."

"Liberty and justice for all," Quinn said.

"After 9/11 and the Patriot Act and all that hysteria, this could have all happened again." Loma scowled.

"That's why we got this museum together. No American citizen should ever be treated like this again." He looked at Quinn and Loma, who were visibly shaken by what they'd seen. "Why don't you two go get some fresh air. Now would be a good time to take a look up in that guard tower. Don't worry. There's nothing there but the view."

They took him up on the idea and wandered outside, passing a couple of picnic tables. The gravel path had markers and small kiosks under protective roofs that also provided shade as museumgoers stopped to read the information describing the buildings that had been in the camp. They followed the markers to the guard tower. After they read the brief information listing the dimensions of the seven towers, how they'd rebuilt this one to the same specifications, and how not one person had ever tried to escape, they climbed the four stories to the top.

The docent was wrong, though. There *was* something up in the top of the octagonal-roofed tower—large Lucite-covered maps of the area in each direction showing the surrounding property with notations of the property lines and ownership.

Loma leaned against the railing, taking in the view while she got her breath back from the steep climb. On all sides, the prairie looked similar. Flat land dotted with the scrub oak, sagebrush, and occasional pine or cottonwood sentinel standing at attention. The wildflowers all looked muted from here, the spindly gray-green stems and the colors of the flowers invisible at this distance. But tinges of the coming autumn began to punctuate the patchwork palette in the distance. "You know, if you didn't know we were standing at the top of a guard tower, this would be a lovely place for a wedding," Loma said.

"Weirdo."

"I'm just saying."

Quinn studied each map, trying to get her bearings. To the east and to the north, the maps showed the camp inside the walls and where the fields had been for the crops. To the west, the camp property seemed to end at County Road 34. To the south, County Road DD, the road they drove in on, seemed to be the border of the camp property. Once she determined what she was looking at and where she was exactly, Quinn looked at the overlays. She made her way to all four maps, her frown getting deeper with each one.

"You look like somethin' smells bad up in here, but I'm going on record as saying—"

"Look at this." Quinn pointed to a name on each of the maps. "They own all of this, in every direction."

"Chestnut Family Trust. Is that Chief Chestnut?"

"Yep, must be. But look at this." Quinn walked over to the map on the south side. "My mom's name is nowhere on there as owner of that property."

"Maybe it's in your grandpa's name."

"But still, this only shows the Chestnuts as owners, not his name either." Quinn gave a royal sweep of her arm. "Look at this land, Loma. The Chestnut family owns all of this? That's crazy."

Loma studied the map. "Could be this map isn't who owns the property now, but who owned it when the camp was built. Chestnuts started the town way back when, right? Maybe they gave this piece to the government for the camp. I don't see any dates on this."

"Maybe you're right. Or maybe I don't really know where Mom's property is. Maybe I misread that deed."

Loma leaned close to the maps to see them better. "Some of these smaller lots aren't labeled. One of them could be your mom's."

Quinn joined her and squinted at the small lots she indicated. There were several all around the area, many looking like spikes and wedges poking into the perimeter of the Chestnut property. A weakling's finger jabbing into the sturdy torso of the Chestnut family's empire. She checked her bearings again. "I don't think so. None of them are past Double D Road."

"You said yourself you might have the location wrong."

"I might, but not that wrong." Quinn ran her hand over the map. "It bugs me that they're not all labeled."

"They're too small on these maps. Rest assured, though, somebody knows who they belong to. How else would they collect taxes on them?"

"You're probably right. Geez, I hadn't thought about the property taxes people have to pay on all this land, especially the Chestnuts. It must cost them a fortune."

"I wouldn't worry too much about them." Loma used her finger to underline the label. "Chestnut Family Trust." She emphasized the last word. "Pretty sure they're doing just fine."

"Probably." Quinn moved to the railing and took a deep breath of the earthy September air. "It smells so nice out here."

"As lovely as it is," Loma said, "I gotta tinkle, so I'm going back to the building. You coming?"

"Yeah."

When they got back to the museum building, Loma went one way to the restrooms, while Quinn stopped at an exhibit that caught her eye. There was a large, colorful poster of some dolls that looked like a robust, colorful version of the wooden thing she found.

The exhibit explained they were *Daruma* dolls. Usually made of a special type of Japanese paper, these dolls had no bodies. Everything was painted—usually in red, black, and white—except for the eyes, which were intentionally left blank. It was up to the owner of the doll to paint in the eyes. When you decided on a specific goal in life, you painted in one of the eyes. You worked toward your goal every day, and when you achieved it, you got to paint in the other eye.

Loma joined her. "Those are cute."

"I think that's what I found out on the property the other day."

Loma squinted. "Maybe."

Quinn read some more of the text, then laughed. "I'll have to tell Mary-Louise Lovely about these." She read the text out loud. "*Daruma* dolls are reminders of the Japanese idea of the *Ganbaru* spirit. Life is full of challenges and obstacles that will trip you up, but it's your job to get back up and keep moving forward. The doll embodies this popular Japanese proverb: *Nanakorobi yaoki.* 'Fall down seven times, stand up eight.'" She looked at Loma. "That's exactly what my therapist and I were talking about the other day." She read the rest of the text. "No matter how tired or discouraged you are, you keep going. The end is when you see your wish fulfilled by your hard work, grit, and endurance. *Daruma* dolls are built to automatically bounce back when knocked over."

"I had a four-foot-tall inflatable clown toy like that when I was a kid," Loma said.

"So did I!"

At the same time Quinn said, "I loved it," Loma said, "I hated it."

"You loved it?" Loma said. "Why?"

"No matter how often or how hard you punched it, it popped right back up. BOP...SPROING...BOP...SPROING." Quinn mimicked a boxer. "I loved the consistency of that. Just like with crosswords, you always know what will happen. Only one answer, no matter what."

"That's what I hated about it! It never did anything different."

Quinn looked back at the photographs of the *Daruma* dolls. She walked over to Robert, sitting again at the desk at the entrance to the museum. "Excuse me, but do you have any of those *Daruma* dolls in the exhibit?"

He shook his head. "Not historical ones. But we do have some in the gift shop."

"Thanks." Before they left the museum, she bought one for Mary-Louise Lovely.

On the drive back to town, Quinn said, "Now that I've seen that camp, I don't think that skeleton belonged to a detainee. I mean, the camp had a barbed-wire fence all around it, and did you see that there were a total of seven guard towers? That was a prison, plain and simple. Sure, they may have had a few amenities, but those guard towers guaranteed that nobody was going out on picnics or jogging or anything outside that fence."

"But if someone was escaping—"

"The kiosk at the guard tower said nobody ever escaped."

Loma rolled her eyes so hard her head and neck rolled too. "Girl? You think they'd publicize how many people they shot during escape attempts?"

"But the museum didn't try to whitewash or sugarcoat anything else. Why wouldn't they tell the truth about that?"

Loma thought for a moment. "Maybe they are."

"And if there were never any escape attempts, and if all that land belonged to the Chestnut family, did a Chestnut have something to do with that skeleton? It might just be a coincidence that the victim was found there, but who knows? What better place to dump a body than on undeveloped private property where nobody goes?"

Quinn appreciated Loma not mentioning that the same would be true if that land belonged to Georgeanne.

Chapter 8

Quinn dropped off Loma at the rich Texans' house she was remodeling. "Can I come in and see what you've done?"

"Sure. Just be careful. You're gonna want me to remodel your house too."

"Well, duh. But I'm not a rich Texan. And I don't own a house."

Loma unlocked the door and ushered in Quinn, who released a drawn-out, "Wow."

The great room had come a long way since the night they'd laid out all those wet papers on the bare subfloor in order to help determine who killed Hugh Pugh's husband.

"This looks great, Loma! If I hadn't helped knock it down, I'd never have believed there used to be a wall with a rotten floor over there."

"I sent photos to the Texans, and they're loving it so far. I think I'll be working on this house up until I'm set to retire, what with all the changes they keep wanting."

"That's good, as long as they don't want you to put that wall and rotten floor back in."

Loma's phone rang, and she checked the caller ID. "Speak of the devil."

"Your rich Texans?"

She nodded.

"I'll get out of your hair, then. I've got some things to do anyway."

Loma blew her an exaggerated kiss, then answered her phone. "Well, howdy pardner, how's things in the Lone Star State?"

Quinn got back in her car and pondered why she'd told Loma she had some things to do this afternoon. Really, the only thing on her agenda was a big, fat nothing burger. What waited for her at home, however, was that non-alphabetized spice rack. She did not need that shouting at her the rest of the day.

She passed the *Welcome to Chestnut Station* sign at the edge of town, which got her wondering about the Chestnut family all over again. She knew that Chief Chestnut's however-many-greats-grandfather had settled this town in the early 1800s. She knew that Myron Chestnut grew up here and had been the chief of police since Quinn was in junior high school and had been on the Chestnut Station PD before that. But she knew nothing of the Chestnut family history in between.

If those bones didn't belong to an internee during the war years, was it possible they'd been there before 1940? Or more recently? And did they have something to do with the Chestnut family just because they were found on their property?

Those were a lot of unanswerable questions, but her curiosity revved into overdrive.

Clearly, there was something Georgeanne didn't want her to know about that property, but what? Did it have anything to do with Chief Chestnut or his family? Many times in the past, Georgeanne had admonished her not to grouse about things Chief Chestnut said or did, presumably because they were friends, both having grown up in Chestnut Station together. They'd been friends, that much was clear, though they'd drifted apart somewhat over the years, as happens to adults with busy lives.

Georgeanne and Myron were as different as two people could be, and Quinn always marveled at the fact they had been so close. They seemed incompatible to Quinn, although in her eyes, Chief Chestnut seemed to be incompatible with everyone. Where her mother was warm, friendly, and curious about people, Myron was prickly and short-tempered. Perhaps their friendship was more random, begun with happenstance. When you lived in a small town, after all, you didn't get to pick from a wide assortment of friends. You were often just thrown together by circumstance: age, grade in school, proximity of houses.

Quinn considered her lifelong friendship with Rico. They were thrown together in kindergarten, but they'd just clicked. Immediately. The two of them seemed to have more similarities than Georgeanne and Myron did, but they had some fairly substantial differences too.

Where Quinn was neat, organized, and always had a plan in mind, Rico was much more go-with-the-flow. And where Quinn understood the value of a white lie to spare someone's feelings, Rico decidedly did not. She'd learned not to trust him with any secrets, and she'd learned the hard way never to ask him if her hair or an outfit looked okay, because he'd tell her exactly what he thought. No sugarcoating, no tiny fib to protect her ego. He was the rare human who always—*always*—spoke the truth. Most often Quinn didn't really want the absolute, completely unvarnished truth. But sometimes she did. When that was the case, she knew to ask him a point-blank question, and whenever she saw his nose twitch like a bunny, she knew he had something he had to say, some truth to spill.

It's quite possible people would wonder why they were such fast friends, just as she wondered why her mom and Chief Chestnut were. The answer was perhaps as simple as *because they were.*

Quinn stopped at the lone stoplight in town. Vera Greenberg, the publisher/editor of the *Chestnut Station Chronicle*, scurried across the street in front of her. Vera pulled off her slouch hat and waved it at Quinn.

"Hey, Vera. How are you?" Quinn called out her car window.

"Busy like a bee at a honey festival!"

When the light changed, Quinn drove a block, then turned left and ended up in the newspaper parking lot. She reached the front door of the *Chronicle* just as Vera did.

"Got a crossword for me?" Vera asked.

"Not since I emailed you the Japanese World War II one the other day."

"That was a bit of a heavier theme than I'm used to seeing from you."

"True. I've been thinking about Camp Chestnut lately. I didn't know much about Japanese internment camps before. Just the basics, in fact. Kind of embarrassing, really. But Loma and I went out there today and got quite an education."

Vera tugged on the door and waved Quinn in. "You could spend countless hours listening to those stories that the internees recorded. A fascinating and heartbreaking project."

"I can only imagine. We didn't do that. We were a bit overwhelmed."

"Make sure you go back and listen. Personal stories in their own voices delivered with the gentle patina of time. Beats a history book any day." Vera dropped her bag on her desk, perhaps the most cluttered in the entire newsroom, although all four desks in there were piled high with papers, books, folders, and half-empty coffee cups. The "most cluttered" award might be a four-way tie. "Not to be rude," Vera said, "but why are you here? I have an interview to get ready for."

"I was hoping I could look through the back issues of the paper. Can I do that and not be in anyone's way?" Quinn didn't see anyone else in the newsroom, but she wanted to be polite.

"Yep. Nobody needs to get back there much, but if they do, they'll kick you out. Reporters ain't shy! Looks like they're all out, anyway. Make yourself at home. Computer should already be on. Before you start, though, be a doll and get me some coffee."

"Sure."

"And what's that thing you're doing with your fingers?"

Quinn looked down. She hadn't even realized. "Oh, nothing." She didn't want to explain her finger thing to Vera. And even if she did, Vera certainly didn't have that much time. To save them both, she changed the subject. "No sugar, right?"

Vera bustled away while Quinn filled a clean mug for her from the half-full pot on the warming tray and delivered it to her desk. She stared at the mess to determine the least precarious place to set the mug. Finally she used the keyboard to slide everything away from the edge of the desk just far enough to allow space for the mug.

When Vera got back to her desk, she gave Quinn a shout and tipped her mug in the air. "Thanks, doll!"

Quinn jiggled the computer mouse at the desk in the far corner of the newsroom. The computer lit up and opened immediately to the *Chronicle* archives. Quinn remembered that summer when she and every teenager she knew had been hired to digitize the archives. The task was relentlessly nonstop, with three shifts working twenty-four hours all summer long. They had started with the most current issues and worked their way backward. The job was so tedious and had taken forever, but now it was such an excellent resource. And if she were being honest, she'd admit it had been great fun to work the midnight to 8 a.m. shift with a few of her closest friends while the entire town was asleep. She smiled at the memory. She'd eaten her weight in free pizza that summer.

She was glad Vera hadn't asked what she was researching because she didn't know how to logically explain she wanted to dig into the history of the Chestnut family.

There were many ways to search the archives, but Quinn settled on typing *Myron Chestnut* into the search bar. A zillion hits, every single time an article mentioned anything police department–related.

She thought for a minute then typed, *Myron Chestnut, Chestnut Station High School.*

Bingo. The first article was about his graduating class. There weren't many seniors that year. Out of curiosity, Quinn scanned for her mom's name but didn't see it. She checked the date and realized Chief Chestnut was a year ahead of Georgeanne.

The article was just a roundup of basic information for each graduate: name, parents' names, GPA, what their plans were after graduation, the inspirational quote they chose for the yearbook.

It dawned on Quinn that she was reading about eighteen-year-olds just beginning the adventure of their lives, but they were now all close to sixty. Had their lives worked out the way they wanted? Did those dreams to become nurses, farmers, teachers, to travel the world, to play professional baseball ever come true?

She reflected on her life when she had graduated from Chestnut Station High School. She'd expected to be a Denver police officer after getting her degree in criminal justice. She hadn't expected to have a mental health crisis that eventually forced her to move back home to her parents' house, depressed and broke, to accept work in a diner offered, she suspected, out of pity.

She wasn't sixty yet; she still had twenty-nine years to turn her boat around. The only question was, would she? Could she?

Quinn forced her eyes back to the article on the screen in front of her. She read the paragraph for Myron Chestnut. Parents, Beany and Donald Lee Chestnut. Beany? What kind of name was that? Quinn thought it had to be short for something, Beatrice maybe? Bernice? Bernadette? Quinn returned her attention to Myron Chestnut's information and was a little surprised to see he had an above-average GPA. She was also surprised he hadn't listed law enforcement as a career goal, instead saying he wanted "to farm, get married, and raise a passel of kids." Odd, since Chief Chestnut didn't seem to be the warm family type. He'd never married, as far as she knew. But more importantly, how many kids constituted a passel?

Knowing his parents' names gave her a search opportunity to circumvent all of the articles about police business over the years. She typed in *Beany Chestnut*. Not much came up, not even her real name. Was it possible her parents actually named her Beany?

Beany won a ribbon at the county fair in 1968 for sewing. She took home first prize for a lovely shirtwaist dress she'd made for herself, and third place for matching outfits she'd made for her kids. Quinn barked out a laugh when she saw a photo of Myron, who looked to be seven or eight, standing next to his sister, Marion, a couple of years older, wearing sailor suits with shorts. It verged on Buster Brown territory, and he did not look pleased.

The only other mentions of Beany in the paper seemed to be related to committee work—PTA, church, and civic stuff. The most unusual was a drive she spearheaded to decorate as many of the chestnut statues around town for each holiday as possible. That effort, Quinn knew, survived to this day.

The chestnut statues were probably the only thing anyone knew about Chestnut Station, but nobody knew—or they claimed they didn't know—exactly how they got there. Even though the town had been named after the Chestnut family who settled here, at some point in the 1950s, statues of chestnuts—the actual nut—popped up all around town, seemingly overnight. They were made of every type of material you could name: wrought iron, wood, bronze, plaster. There was even a stained-glass one that Public Works had to build a roof over so it wouldn't get ruined by hailstorms or high winds. The chestnuts were all types too: roasting over an open fire, fuzzy on the tree, cracked open, just the shell, just the nut. Large, medium, and small. Realistic muted colors, neon, and everything in between. Decorated for every major holiday, and many Quinn had never heard of. Santa beards for Christmas, menorahs for Hanukkah, leprechaun hats for St. Patrick's Day. Independence Day flags, heart-shaped glasses for Valentine's Day, all kinds of outlandish fascinators for Kentucky Derby Day, and plenty of silly nonsense for Beer Can Appreciation Day.

Quinn wondered if Beany was still around to see the fruits of the idea she had planted all those years ago. Would she be tickled by the idea or horrified by how outrageous it had become?

Next, Quinn looked up Myron's dad, Donald Lee Chestnut. Pages and pages of articles loaded. She started reading them and was surprised to find out Donald Lee and her own grandfather, Bernard Dudley, had been friends. Many of the articles linked their names, as if they were constantly together, joined at the hip. Apparently they were both a bit on the wild side, troublemakers to some extent. This was shocking to Quinn, as she'd never known her kindly, white-haired grandpa to be wild, unless teaching her to play cribbage and taking her out for ice cream was considered wild.

She read story after story about the two of them, some of the articles including another man's name, Odell Nilssen. All of them reckless, often hilarious stories of leading snipe hunts and encouraging cow tipping on unsuspecting city folk who came through town. There were reports of them breaking into people's houses and rearranging their furniture or making a snack for themselves in the middle of the night. How they never got shot was a mystery to Quinn.

The articles were full of whimsy and small town charm, most carrying the same byline. It was probably easy filler in a town where not much real news happened, and lighthearted enough that people were probably interested in hearing about their antics.

At one time, Donald Lee Chestnut had a dog he named "Help" so he could stand on his porch and call for Help. There was an entire article about it, complete with a photo of him wearing a slicked-back ducktail sitting on painted wooden porch steps with an arm draped around a shaggy white dog.

There were so many police blotter blurbs about them that Quinn lost count. She couldn't wait to ask Grandpa about all this.

The police blotter was a roundup of all the interesting—or maybe total—police reports over the course of a week or so. The *Chronicle*'s police blotter was a bit tongue-in-cheek and over-the-top. It was clear the reporter had fun writing it. It probably wouldn't have been much fun if it documented real crime, but these blurbs all had funny, punny, gossipy, alliterative, or rhyming headlines.

One said "Too Many Beans from Beany?" and reported that Donald Lee had been creating a ruckus because he didn't like what his wife, Beany, made for dinner. Apparently, Grandpa was there too, egging him on and laughing. The neighbor, Mrs. Washburn, complained that when Beany threw the contents of the skillet at Donald Lee, some splattered the roses Mrs. Washburn had been planning to take to Reverend Pinzer, who had taken a tumble down the church basement stairs and was laid up in the hospital for a few days. Beany offered to hose off the roses and drive Mrs. Washburn to the hospital, so she withdrew her complaint.

There were several blurbs along this same vein—Donald Lee Chestnut, Bernard Dudley, and Odell Nilssen creating mild havoc in town, which eventually led to a noise complaint by an exasperated neighbor.

But in one, Quinn read that Bernard and Donald Lee had been tossed in jail for assault. There were no real details; it could have simply been a half-hearted bar fight. It wasn't even clear to Quinn if they'd fought each other or someone else. Maybe it was just a misunderstanding, or a police officer who'd had enough of their hijinks.

But still, maybe it wasn't. Quinn wondered about all the reasons two men could get worked up enough to land punches. A woman? Both of them were married, so probably not. Money? A shift in their power dynamic? One of them disrespected the other somehow?

Quinn straightened the items on the newsroom desk while she mulled. Just as she had arranged all the pencils on the left side of the cup and all the pens on the right, a thought flitted through her brain. What if their fight had something to do with that piece of property? Maybe Donald Lee wanted the piece back that Grandpa owned. It was smack-dab in the middle of the Chestnut property, after all, assuming Quinn had her facts straight.

Maybe there was some dispute, and that's why neither Grandpa's name nor Georgeanne's showed as the property owner on the map at the museum.

People punched each other for a lot less.

Quinn went back to the archives.

The next article she came across was accompanied by a black-and-white photograph of a shattered wooden mailbox post, the top half with the mailbox still attached toppled to its side, the other half remaining stuck in the ground, jagged splinters on both halves. The article seemed to take a winking boys-will-be-boys stance about the fact that Bernard and Donald Lee were arrested for being drunk in public, barely mentioning that Donald Lee had been driving drunk and had crashed into the mailbox.

Quinn read the article twice to see if she'd missed something, astounded at the relaxed way drunk driving was looked at back then. She was glad it was handled more harshly now, and less wink-wink, boys-will-be-boys.

But this was the second time she read about Bernard and Donald Lee sitting in the Chestnut Station Police Department basement lockup.

If all of these escapades with Bernard Dudley and Donald Lee Chestnut were printed in the paper, she wondered how many more of their antics didn't get reported. There was a finite amount of newsprint they could devote to them, after all. There was other news happening in the world, even in Chestnut Station.

The final police blotter blurb she read was a report of Donald Lee breaking Grandpa's windshield from the inside of the car. "That can't be right," she muttered. "Broken from the inside?" Apparently, Grandpa was the one who'd made the police report in an effort to force Donald Lee to pay for it, but it sounded like Donald Lee counter-complained that Grandpa had socked him in the nose. The headline on this one was "Another Assault with a Dudley Weapon." Had the reporter just been waiting to use that because he liked the clever pun, or was there some truth to it? That behavior certainly didn't define the Bernard Dudley whom Quinn knew and loved. But it might explain why Georgeanne was acting so weird about everything. Maybe it was all tied together with whatever happened out in that field. Or perhaps the argument started with Grandpa's windshield and ended in the field.

If Bernard and Donald Lee had caroused and there was some kind of dispute over this plot of land, it wasn't out of the realm of possibility that something bad might have happened out there. Maybe there was some connection with why the property was in Georgeanne's name. Maybe that's why Georgeanne didn't want Quinn to bother her grandfather with questions about it, so she didn't stir it all up again.

But stir up what, exactly?

Quinn pictured Grandpa down in the basement of the police station, where she'd visited Jake so many times, and where Georgeanne had brought brownies to Hugh Pugh not too long ago. Did Georgeanne know Grandpa had been locked up down there? Quinn thought about requesting the police report, but she didn't want to ask Rico for it. If it unearthed anything important, then he'd be hard-pressed to keep it to himself. Rico's nose would twitch like a bunny, and who knew how far the information about Bernard would travel? Could he still get in trouble for something that might have happened so long ago? Quinn didn't particularly want to be the one to bring it to the world's attention.

"Assault with a Dudley Weapon" niggled at her, though.

Quinn became aware she was doing her finger thing, but for how long she wasn't sure. She'd been daydreaming she was back up in that guard tower, and like a movie camera, she was limiting the field of vision smaller and smaller until she could see Grandpa sitting in that jail cell.

Chapter 9

After dinner Quinn pulled Dan aside and whispered, "Can you find that deed for me? Something's weird about the way Mom's acting about it, and I want to look at it closer."

Dan studied her face. Quinn knew he was trying to determine if she was in an OCD spiral or not.

"I'm fine, Dad. You saw her too." She hoped her father couldn't see how desperately she was focused on trying not to obsess about Bernard, the spice rack, the desk, its contents, and the pile of books resting on top.

After a bit, Dan nodded.

"It's probably in your bedroom," Quinn said. "She knows I wouldn't snoop around in there."

Thirty minutes later, Quinn sat on her bed with the five-page document in her hands. She waved it at Fang. "I got it!"

Fang seemed to be less excited about the discovery.

She snapped a photo of each page with her phone, just in case Georgeanne whisked away the paperwork again.

Quinn used her computer to look up the definition of a Quit Claim Deed. After reading it three times, she tried explaining it to Fang. "It sounds like it's a really informal way to transfer property without any guarantees from the seller. This part seems important, though." She read to Fang from the website, ending with, "A thorough title or property record search should be completed in all land transfers." She looked at Fang. "Did you get all that?"

Fang stopped swimming and blew a bubble at her.

"I think it just means the property is given as a gift, but not necessarily from the person who actually owns it? But that makes no sense." Quinn read the definition again. "I guess it's like giving someone a gift certificate for a car. It's a nice gesture, but if the person can't drive or get insurance, then it's kind of useless. So for property, until the title is sorted, basically this is just a piece of paper." She flipped through the pages. "Five pieces of paper, actually."

She read through the rest of the pages, slowly and carefully. Her mom's name and address were listed as the "grantee," the property description and location was specified, then "for a valuable consideration, in the amount of one dollar ($1.00), given in hand and other good and valuable consideration, the receipt and sufficiency of which is hereby acknowledged as of June 15, 1979."

Quinn giggled. "Grandpa charged Mom a dollar for the property?" She flipped to the second page and swallowed her giggle.

On the line for the grantor's information was written "Myron Chestnut."

She frowned at the paper, then frowned at Fang. "Chief Chestnut gave Mom that property?" Gathering the pages while scrambling off her bed, she called, "Mom? Mom! Come look at this!"

"What are you hollering about?" Georgeanne rinsed a mixing bowl and set it in the dish rack.

"Look at this!" Quinn thrust the pages at Georgeanne, who began drying her hands on her apron.

"What's all the excitement?" Dan asked as he came into the kitchen. His smile faded when he saw what was in his daughter's hand.

"Quinn wants me to read something. Read it for me. My hands are wet."

Dan cleared his throat, which he did when he was uncomfortable, and reluctantly took the papers from Quinn.

"Look at page two," Quinn said.

Dan read out loud what Quinn had pointed out to him, but made no further comment. He handed the papers to Georgeanne, who shot a baffled look between the two of them. She read it to herself, then silently handed the packet back to Dan before returning to her dirty dishes in the sink.

"Mom, did you hear that? Chief Chestnut gave you property...not Grandpa."

Georgeanne spun around and waved a spatula at Quinn. Soapsuds flicked Quinn in the face and she blinked, but not before she saw the fury in her mother's face.

"I told you to let this go. I specifically told you to drop it. In fact, I purposely hid those papers from you." Georgeanne's eyes widened, and Quinn didn't think it was possible, but Georgeanne became even angrier. "Were you searching my things? Shame on you! That's not how I raised you, you should be ashamed of—"

"I gave the papers to Quinn," Dan said quietly. The pages hung limp from his hand.

"Then you should be ashamed too!" Georgeanne tore off her apron and flung it to the floor. As she left the kitchen, she yelled, "This isn't right. None of this is right!"

Dan hurried after her, leaving Quinn alone in the kitchen. She picked up Georgeanne's apron and hung it back on the hook. She finished washing and drying the dishes, wondering about her mother's anger and her words. What wasn't right? Something about the deed? It was such a simple document, how could it be wrong? Just names and locations.

An hour later, Quinn found herself staring into the pantry at the spices. She had no memory of alphabetizing them.

Chapter 10

Quinn left early for work the next morning, in a clumsy and completely transparent attempt to avoid her parents. Rico came into the diner for lunch as usual, but before she could tell him how mad Georgeanne had gotten at her last night, he jumped in with news of his own.

"So, the CBI collected all the bones and everything else you found in that field, and then they did a pretty extensive site investigation of their own out there."

"Did they find anything new?" Quinn slid into a chair at his table.

"Nope. Seems you were pretty thorough." Rico grinned. "Big surprise, eh?"

"Have they done any testing?"

"Yeah, they were excited to get started, since it's not something they see every day. They estimate the victim was a man between thirty-five and forty-five years old, but not of Japanese descent."

"So, a guard." She plucked a French fry off his plate.

Rico shook his head. "There would have been a report if a guard had disappeared. They also don't think the bones have been out there for seventy-five years."

"So my theory that it was someone from the camp doesn't work. Is there a missing person report that matches?"

"Nope. There's not much else they can do."

"A cold case, then."

"More of a nonexistent case, despite the unfortunate bones."

"How did he die?"

"Undetermined. No obvious cause of death." Rico took a bite of his burger, then maneuvered himself in his chair to pull out something from his pocket. "CBI kept the eyeglasses you found, but they didn't want this." He handed her the faded wooden *Daruma* doll. "Do you want it?"

Quinn nodded, rubbing her thumb across the flat top of the doll. "They won't be doing any further investigation?"

"Nothing they can do. They've closed the case."

Rico finished his lunch, then handed Quinn some cash. "I've got to get back. You can have the rest of my fries."

She pocketed the cash, then absentmindedly nibbled at the fries. The case didn't seem closed to Quinn. The refrain she'd tried to tamp back all last night came roaring back at her. What did Georgeanne know? What wasn't she saying?

With her mother angrier than she'd ever seen her before, Quinn knew there was something more to that property. Something more her mother knew. And the way she'd told Quinn not to talk to Grandpa about it, probably something more he knew too.

There were many things in Quinn's life these days that she felt compelled *not* to do, but right now she was overwhelmed by the one thing she felt she absolutely *must* do.

She had to find out about that property, and how it, Georgeanne, and Grandpa were related to those bones.

Chapter 11

Quinn didn't particularly want to go home after work—more avoidance—so she walked over to the newspaper office, where she caught Vera locking up for the night.

"I was hoping I could look through the archives again," Quinn said.

"Sure. You still have your keys?"

"You haven't changed the locks since I was in high school?"

"Why should we? I'm not entirely sure we even need to lock up at all."

"You do have that nifty new coffee machine. That's probably worth something."

"Worth more than all the computers inside, that's for sure." Quinn's raised eyebrows made her add, "Sentimentally, at least." Vera unlocked the door and waved good-bye to Quinn. "Have fun. What are you researching, anyway?"

"My grandpa. We have his old desk, so I've been going through his stuff. Turns out, I don't know much about him. Seems he had a rich, full life before I was born. Who knew?"

Vera laughed. "I've heard stories about Bernard. Quite a character. Hope you don't dig up too many family skeletons. Don't forget to lock up."

Family skeletons are exactly what I want to dig up, she thought.

The coffeepot was empty, so Quinn followed the machine's cryptic instructions to brew some more. She measured and ground the coffee beans, tamped, pushed, and pulled all the levers and buttons, and ended up with a cup of coffee that tasted exactly like the coffee at the diner. She vowed never to mention this to Rico or word would certainly get back to Vera that she didn't appreciate her expensive coffee station, although it would be fun to set up some blind taste tests and publicly prove her theory that a more expensive brand of coffee or apparatus did not make the actual beverage taste any more delicious.

With her coffee in hand, Quinn settled at the computer in the back of the newsroom. She sent her dad a quick text. *I'm at the newspaper. Probably be late. Is Mom still mad?*

Not sure, he replied. *I'd ask her but she's not speaking to me.*

Good luck to us both. If you need to get out, I just made some of Vera's fancy coffee.

I'll stick it out here. I deserve to be in the doghouse. Shouldn't have given you those papers.

I woulda found them eventually.

True.

She sent Dan a kissy face emoji along with some praying hands.

Quinn picked up where she'd left off earlier in the archive, but after hours of searching, she only found two more places that mentioned Grandpa: one when he was trying to sell his car in 1980, and the other when Georgeanne and Dan got married a few years later.

Smiling, she read the article about the festivities. It was an autumn wedding, and Quinn was reminded that her parents' anniversary was coming up next month. She never knew what to do to help her parents celebrate. They certainly didn't need her to buy them anything. She'd probably use the old standby…getting all dressed up, maybe springing for a facial or mani-pedi for her and Georgeanne, then taking them to dinner at a fancy restaurant in Denver. But not too fancy, as she was still trying to save up enough money to move out and relaunch her life, which would probably be a better gift for them anyway, come to think of it.

She scrolled through more of the archive, eventually ending up at a blurb about her birth with the headline, "Georgeanne and Dan Clan Began—Carr Girth Results in Star Birth." Quinn had never seen nor heard about this, making her believe Georgeanne had not taken kindly to the town giggling about her girth.

Probably why she'd never heard this story before.

She scrolled back through some of the blurbs and articles until she came to one that mentioned Bernard and Donald Lee's occasional cohort, Odell Nilssen. Quinn input his name in the search bar, and many citations popped up. The first article dealt with his position as procurement officer at Camp Chestnut. She did some mental math and didn't think that would make him a contemporary of either Bernard or Donald Lee. She did some further digging and realized there was an Odell Nilssen, Senior, and an

Odell Nilssen, Junior. It must have been the junior who'd hung around with Bernard and Donald Lee.

But Quinn became interested in this procurement job that Odell Nilssen, Senior, had held. If he was dealing with supplying the internment camp, perhaps he had something to do with those *Daruma* dolls. She searched for more information about Odell Nilssen, Senior, and found his name associated with Nilssen Imports and Exports, still in business today. It was in San Francisco, so an hour earlier than it was in Colorado. She checked the time, but figured the main offices would be closed. She took a chance and dialed the number on the staff listing for someone in the warehouse. Maybe they were a twenty-four-hour operation.

"Yeah, this is Joe."

Quinn was taken aback that her plan actually worked.

"Anybody there?"

"Oh, I'm sorry, I didn't really expect anyone to answer," Quinn said.

"And yet someone did." Joe didn't sound too upset to be talking on the phone.

"On the first ring too."

"I'm on my break."

"Then why'd you answer the phone?"

"Honestly? It startled me. Truth be told, I'm always a little nervous in the warehouse by myself."

Quinn hadn't been nervous in the newsroom by herself until this very minute. She glanced around at the shadows. "I don't blame you."

They were quiet a moment.

"While I like the company, is there some reason you called? And please don't say the call is coming from inside the warehouse. You're not an ax murderer, are you?"

Quinn laughed. "Nope. Just a waitress."

"Oh, calling to take my order?"

"I'd be happy to take your order, but I'm afraid your food would be cold long before it got to you. I'm in Colorado. I'm calling to get some information about what your company did during the war years."

"Which war?"

"World War Two. Specifically, if you imported something called *Daruma* dolls from Japan."

"Import something from Japan during the war with Japan?" Joe laughed. "Doubt it."

"Oh, duh." Quinn thought for a minute. "Would it be possible to talk to Mr. Nilssen? Maybe he imported these dolls before the war. I understand he was the procurement officer at an internment camp in Colorado."

"I don't know anything about that, but I think you're out of luck because Nilssen died years ago."

"Oh. What about his son, does he work there?"

"That deadbeat? Nah, he's out in your neck of the woods someplace, last I heard. Nilssen didn't want him anywhere near this place."

"Bummer."

"Listen, I don't know if we have corporate records that go back that far, but if you call back, ask for—oh, wait, I'm sitting right in front of a computer. Hang on a sec. Let me see how far back the database goes." Joe clattered on a keyboard. When he came back on the phone, he said, "Sorry. We only go back to 1963."

"Again, bummer. But thanks for your help. I'm sorry I used up your break time."

"Nah, now I'll just start the clock again. Union rules. If we had a union, that is. Hope you find whatever it is you're looking for."

He disconnected, and Quinn said, "Me too, Joe. Me too."

Since that was a dead end, and there was nothing more online about her grandfather, and sufficient time had passed that Georgeanne would be in bed, Quinn locked up and trudged the two blocks back to the diner parking lot, where she'd left her car.

Chapter 12

Despite a caffeine-fueled sleepless night, Quinn was again up and out early the next morning, in full avoidance mode. After she snuck outside, she realized how cold it was this early on a late-September morning and tiptoed back in to get a coat. It wasn't this cold yesterday morning, or even last night. She knew it would warm up in a few hours, but for now, shirtsleeves wouldn't cut it. Autumn was definitely making an appearance.

Just as she began to reverse out of the driveway, Georgeanne rushed out the side door, bathrobe and arms flapping.

"Uh-oh. This can't be good." Quinn put the car in park and rolled down her window while her mom ran to the car.

Georgeanne placed both hands on the door frame and leaned toward Quinn. Instinctively, Quinn leaned back.

"You don't need to sneak around. I'm not mad anymore."

"You're not?" Quinn wanted to believe her but was not fully committed to the idea, perhaps because at that moment Georgeanne resembled a crazy person with her robe askew and sporting a luxurious case of bed head.

"Well, I'm a little mad. But you don't have to stay out all night and sneak out in the morning."

"Okay. Thanks, Mom. And for what it's worth, I'm sorry I made you so mad."

Georgeanne patted Quinn's arm. "I know. And I'm sorry I yelled like that."

"But Mom—"

"Quinn, I know it's hard for you to let things go, but I'm asking you to let this go. Don't bother your grandfather with questions about that old property. Please?"

Quinn exhaled. "I promise. I won't ask Grandpa about that old property."

"Thank you." Georgeanne gave Quinn's arm another pat, then straightened. "Oh, and I unalphabetized—is that a word?—the spices for you. I'll be glad when this little exercise Mary-Louise Lovely is having you do is over. I'm having trouble finding things. I like the spices in alphabetical order."

"So do I, Mom. So do I."

* * * *

When the breakfast rush slowed, Quinn pulled up a chair at the Retireds' table. "What can you old-timers tell me about my grandpa, Bernard?"

Silas glanced around the table. "Don't see no old-timers here."

"Teenagers in the springtime of our youth," Larry said.

"Macho lads in their prime," Hugh said.

"Peak of freshness, just waiting to be plucked from the tree of life," Bob added with a flourish.

"At least until we look in the mirror," Herman said to hoots all around.

"What do you want to know about Bernard?" Wilbur finally asked. "And why don't you ask him yourself?"

"I'm actually looking for ammunition against him. I've lived my whole life thinking he was this angelic, sweet old man, and I come to find out he was one of Chestnut Stations' main hellions."

Wilbur, Larry, and Hugh convulsed with glee. The three of them began stories about Bernard, but before they got more than a sentence out, one of the others would remind them of another story as a topper.

Herman, Bob, and Silas apparently hadn't known Bernard, so they kept quiet, simply laughing at the stories, Herman with his typical quizzical expression visible as he tried to work through what was true and what was hyperbole. When would he learn it was almost all hyperbole with these guys?

This storytelling competition among the Retireds went on long enough for Quinn to take care of two of her other tables and refill all the coffee mugs at the Retireds' table. Many of their stories Quinn already knew from the newspaper archive.

Larry finally calmed down enough to say, "A town hellion? That he was, my dear."

"Along with Donald Lee Chestnut, as I understand it," she said.

"Yup." Hugh sipped his coffee.

Wilbur tore open a packet of stevia and dumped the contents into his coffee, even though it was half empty.

Larry made a design in the pool of ketchup remaining on his plate. "Okay. What gives, guys? What's the deal with Donald Lee? Why no funny stories about him?" Quinn asked. When nobody spoke, she said, "No more refills until you tell me."

Wilbur held out his cup. "Nothing really to tell. Donald Lee disappeared when Myron and his sister were young'uns. Lost touch with him."

Quinn cocked her head, then refilled his coffee as a reward and a bribe to keep them talking.

"I know for a fact he went to work on the Alaskan pipeline," Hugh said.

"For a fact." Larry nodded emphatically.

"For a fact," Wilbur repeated.

Quinn squinted at them. "For a fact?" That wasn't a particularly unique phrase, but it sounded funny to Quinn. Of course, much of what the Retireds said sounded funny to her.

"For a fact," they said in unison.

Bob was clearly tired of a conversation he couldn't participate in about someone he didn't even know, so he changed the subject and began talking about a play he'd done once called *Facts Don't Matter*. It didn't take too long for Quinn to realize his story was less about the play and more about the ingénue he lusted after.

Quinn left them to it. As she worked the rest of her shift, she thought about the stories the men had told about her grandfather. They seemed to enjoy Bernard's antics, maybe even admired him for them. But why did they barely include Donald Lee in their yarns? As she got to know the Retireds better, she knew that underneath their bluster lurked kind and generous men. It was entirely possible they didn't talk about Donald Lee out of respect for Myron. Myron was, after all, the chief of police in Chestnut Station, a position worthy of at least a modicum of their esteem, and when Donald Lee abandoned his family, they must have seen firsthand how painful and difficult it was for Myron, his mother, and sister.

* * * *

After work, Quinn had just enough time to get over to the courthouse to talk to someone in the county clerk and recorder's office about the quit claim deed. She had a twinge of guilt about Georgeanne, but she'd only asked Quinn not to talk to Grandpa about the property, not anyone else. She knew it was quibbling about the *letter of the law* versus the *spirit of the law*, but that was on Georgeanne. She knew she should be more specific if she wanted more from Quinn. After all, she knew what Quinn was made of.

"Can I help you?" The woman behind the desk rose and came to the counter toward Quinn. She was four-foot-nothing, and about as wide as she was tall. Her face was etched with a web of wrinkles large and small, some around her mouth deep enough to hold a pen.

"I hope so. You're not on your way out, are you?"

The woman pointed at the clock. "Nope. Got twenty more minutes, so make it good." She smiled at Quinn. "You're Georgeanne and Dan's girl, right? I'm Sandy."

She grinned so broadly that Quinn could see each of those wrinkles was really a well-earned laugh line. Quinn liked her immediately and vowed to smile more.

"Nice to meet you. I'm trying to figure out something about a Quit Claim Deed of my mother's." She brought up the photos of the paperwork on her phone. "Can you tell me anything about this? I'm not sure I understand these papers."

Sandy scrolled through the photos, turning the camera and pinching to enlarge the images. She pointed to one of them and said, "Well, I can tell you that this deed was never recorded. The signatures aren't complete, and it was never, what do you call it...notarized."

"Oh, I just assumed that was because we only have a copy."

"Let's just see, shall we?" She motioned Quinn around the front counter so she could see the monitor on her desk. Sandy plopped down in her office chair, earning a little hiss from the pneumatic lift.

Quinn watched as she pulled a yellow sticky note from the side of her computer and lifted up the reading glasses that hung on a chain around her neck. Without putting the glasses on, she held them like magnifiers in front of the note. Quinn saw it was her password. Sandy typed it in. Quinn wondered how many times a day she must perform that particular ritual. Surely it must be often enough to have memorized the password by now. Or maybe the county clerk's office was one of those places where the passwords got changed every day. Probably not, if the password included the words "BroncosFan7" like Sandy's did, and not a string of random letters, numbers, and special characters.

Sandy saw her watching and stuck the note back on the monitor. "Whoever thought someone with a bad memory should be forced to have a computer that goes to sleep after only five minutes should be shot." Her fingers clicked over the keyboard. She tilted her head to read the screen. "Nope, that property is still in the Chestnut family's name, not your mom's." She used her tiptoes to walk her chair farther off to the side so Quinn could see better.

Quinn squinted at the screen. "What exactly am I looking at?"

"It is hard to see on the computer." Sandy crossed the room to a bank of oversized leather-covered volumes. She searched, smiling when she found the one she wanted. She pulled it out, plopping it down on a big worktable in the center of the room. She flipped through some pages, then beckoned to Quinn. "Here's that property." She used her finger to trace a rectangle on the oversized map in front of them. "You can see it's still Chestnut land. All of this is." She traced a perimeter that almost doubled the area. "Used to be Chestnuts owned all this too."

"Wow. That's a lot of land," Quinn said.

Sandy shrugged. "That's why Chestnut Station got named after them. Sad what happened, though." Sandy's sunny smile turned into a black frown, exposing a new set of wrinkles.

"What?"

"Government took it for the internment camp. You been out there lately? They've made a neat little museum."

"I was out the other day. What do you mean, the government took it?"

"They just swiped it. Mind you, sometimes the government pays for easements and rights of way, but not always, and not always for a fair price. In this case, they never even compensated the Chestnuts for it at all." Sandy used her whole arm to flop the book closed.

"They can do that?"

"Honey, the government can do anything it wants to." Sandy smiled again, but it was more rueful than jolly. The effect was the same on her wrinkles, though.

"I guess that's why Camp Chestnut and the museum sits in the middle of all their land. They have maps up in the guard tower. I was looking at them the other day." Quinn developed her own black frown. "I can't believe the government can just scoop out a chunk of someone else's property willy-nilly like that."

"They even have a highfalutin name for it…eminent domain. Shameful business. I don't know how some people can sleep at night." Sandy thought for a moment. "But I guess—what's his name?—Samuel Chestnut never compensated the Utes or the Arapahos for stealing their land, either. Doesn't make it right, though, no matter who does it." She struggled to heft the volume back to the shelf. Quinn hurried to assist.

When they finished, Sandy grinned brightly again. "I'm just glad that Chief Chestnut's family got at least part of that property sorted after Donald

Lee went to Alaska back in the day. That would have been a double tragedy for them." She glanced at the clock. "Is that all you needed?"

"Yes, thanks." She turned to leave, but then pivoted back. "Sandy? Can I ask a favor, though, before I go?"

"Shoot."

"Could you please not mention any of this to my mom? It's…well, it's kind of complicated."

Sandy stared at Quinn, her face a stony mask. But then she grinned and nodded. "You were never here."

Quinn let out a relieved breath. "Thanks so much!"

As she left the building, she wondered once again what circumstances could possibly make it legal or ethical to steal land in order to imprison American citizens. But like Sandy said, was it any worse than Chief Chestnut's ancestors stealing the land from Native Americans in the first place?

Chapter 13

A few days later at the diner, Quinn, Jake, and Rico were having a late lunch. The only other diners were a couple of lovebirds at a table in the corner who had been feeding each other bites of chocolate lava cake for at least forty-five minutes, and Abe the handyman at a table near the window sitting with an overalls-clad farmer Quinn didn't recognize. Abe had his tool belt puddled on an empty chair. She'd known him since she was a girl, as he was friendly with her mom and dad. She'd been fascinated by his rough, gnarled workman's hands, something she'd never seen before in either her father or her grandfather. Abe did all the household repairs the Carrs had ever needed. Georgeanne had gotten to the point where she never even bothered to ask Dan to fix something. It wasn't that Dan was incompetent; he just had zero interest in buying a garage full of tools and learning how to use them, especially when Abe already owned the tools—probably better ones than Dan could even buy—and he relished the challenge. "I shouldn't deprive him of the joy," Dan always said.

Abe and his friend had finished their lunches and had been murmuring in low voices occasionally punctuated by loud laughs. Clearly old friends catching up. Quinn had left a pot of coffee on their table before sitting down to her own Cobb salad lunch with double the bleu cheese. She'd have to remember to overtip her waitress.

Quinn hadn't been able to stop thinking about the man left to die in that field. "It's so unfair that they might never know who that poor man was. His family will never get closure because—despite what everyone says—somebody missed him at some point."

"There's no missing person's report, though." Jake took a big bite of his BLAT sandwich, then wiped his chin where some of the avocado oozed out.

Quinn waggled a wedge of tomato spiked on her fork at him. "Just because they couldn't *find* a missing person report doesn't mean there *wasn't* a missing person." She glanced at Rico. "Right?"

Rico's nose twitched, and he looked away.

"Spill it," Quinn said.

"What do you know?" Jake asked him.

Rico refused to meet their eyes, so Quinn knew she had to ask the exact question they wanted to know the answer to.

"Is there news about the identity of the victim Loma and I found in that field?"

Rico pushed his plate away. "Yes."

Quinn and Jake leaned forward expectantly.

Rico sighed. "CBI determined the dead man was Donald Lee Chestnut, Chief's father."

Quinn gasped and almost choked on a bite of salad.

"How'd they figure that out?" Jake had a skeptical tone to his voice.

"Donald Lee had a nasty break to his arm when he was a kid and it never healed right. Plus, those glasses you found, Quinn. Chief saw a picture of them in the report, then went to Denver to check them out in person."

"Didn't you show them to him at the crime scene when I gave them to you?"

"He'd already left by then, remember?"

"Why didn't you make it a point to show him?" She glared at him with a harsh squint.

"You mean because it was so obvious out there in the field that they belonged to his father?" Rico mirrored her annoyed expression.

Her expression softened. "Yeah, I guess that wouldn't have made sense. But it would have saved CBI some time."

Rico rolled his eyes at her. "Woulda, coulda, shoulda."

"How's Chief Chestnut taking it?" Jake asked.

Rico shrugged. "Based on what he says, it was 1973 when Donald Lee disappeared. Chief was thirteen, his sister a couple of years older. Chief says his dad was a drinker. Probably went out to celebrate his upcoming escape to Alaska with a bender and ended up out there, which sounds like a logical scenario to CBI too. No signs of trauma or obvious cause of death. They found remnants of his pants and shirt scattered around. So old nobody wants to pursue it. Not even Chief. Case closed."

Quinn remembered the shirt buttons she found under that sumac bush. "It's so creepy he was out there for so long that his shirt just disintegrated."

"I had a fascinating talk with the forensic anthropologist who worked on it," Rico said. "She was telling me about the stages of decomposition—"

"Ahem." Jake had a spoonful of cottage cheese halfway to his mouth. "I'm eating here."

"Sorry." Rico turned to Quinn and stage-whispered, "I'll tell you later."

"Yeah, you will." Quinn cleared her plate and Rico's, then met the lovebirds at the cash register, where they stood closer than conjoined twins, ready to pay.

Rico waited until they had gone before ambling over to write his lunch amount in the ledger Jake kept for him under the front counter. He slipped a five-dollar bill in Quinn's apron pocket as a tip.

It felt weird to Quinn to accept Rico's money since they'd been friends for so long. But not so weird that she didn't continue to do it with a grateful smile.

After Rico left, she stopped by Abe's table. "You guys doing okay? Need anything else?"

"You kicking us out?" Abe asked, using one of his gnarled hands to smooth back his thinning hair.

"Of course not," she said with a smile. "You two stay as long as you like. *Mi casa es su casa.*" Quinn waved a magnanimous hand across the diner.

"*Mi casa es su* greasy spoon, you mean," he said with a laugh.

Jake called out, "Hey! Our spoons aren't greasy. The plates, though…"

Abe laughed. "My mistake. I'll edit my Yelp review." He turned back to Quinn. "We're catching up. Haven't seen this son of a gun since he pulled up stakes and headed out Burlington way."

She glanced pointedly around the dining room. "Don't think we'll need to turn the table anytime soon."

The man in overalls said, "I wouldn't mind a piece of that chocolate cake I saw you bring out earlier."

"As long as you don't expect me to feed it to you," Abe said.

The man's blustering response bordered on homophobia, so Quinn headed to the kitchen before she said something that would cause her to lose her tip.

She brought a piece of chocolate lava cake to the man, then she and Jake took advantage of the lull to clean and prep for dinner.

When Quinn had to handle the breakfast and lunch shifts, she could hardly stand to do dinner prep. But with Rachel, the new waitress, covering dinner, Quinn was delighted to clean and get the dining room ready for her. She just wished Rachel were as conscientious with her cleaning and prepping after dinner for Quinn to open the next day. Maybe Jake was right, and Rachel truly wasn't diner material. Some people were suited to slinging hash at a diner, and some weren't.

Quinn mused that maybe she should volunteer to spend a shift with Rachel and teach her—really teach her—how to handle the Chestnut Diner. Quinn was self-aware enough to realize that only one of them would truly appreciate the training. But she'd keep the offer in her back pocket just in case.

As Quinn finished with the floor, Chief Chestnut stormed into the diner waving his crossword puzzle. He stomped past Abe's table to the big corner booth, grumbling that the diner was the only place he could get some peace and quiet from all the reporters, "ghouls" he called them. "Pie," he barked at Quinn without even a glance in her direction, much less a "please" or "thank you."

She plated half a piece of chocolate silk and half a piece of peach, but before she could deliver it, Jake intercepted. "I'll take it over."

Quinn gladly relinquished it, not wanting to spend any time in Chief Chestnut's orbit, especially with his mood so foul. As soon as the thought flitted through her mind, she felt guilty. The man had just found out his father had been dead in a field twenty miles from home all these years. She should cut him a bit of slack.

Jake placed the pie in front of Chief Chestnut and slid into the booth across from him. "Hey, I heard about your dad. I'm sorry."

Quinn noticed Abe wave one of his gnarled hands at his friend to shush him so he could turn and listen to Chief's conversation with Jake. Subtlety was not Abe's strong suit.

Chief Chestnut stabbed a bite of the chocolate silk pie and shrugged. "Nothing to be sorry about."

Quinn walked over with a fresh pot of coffee and poured a cup for him. Chief Chestnut didn't acknowledge the coffee. Or Quinn. "Until this one"—he jerked his head at Quinn, as if she were a bronze statue on display—"found those bones, I would have bet my life that he took off to spend New Year's with some other woman, or he went on a bender and tried walking home."

"From where?" Quinn asked.

He ignored her. "Celebrated his upcoming emancipation from his boring, undesirable family, got drunk, lost his way to the bus station. Maybe got rolled for his wallet."

"But there was no sign of trauma, I thought," Quinn said.

He ignored her again. Took a big bite of the peach pie.

"I see you've thought about this a lot," Jake said.

"Not really, but I've had a lot of years to think about it here and there. Even when my dad was around, he wasn't really around. Couldn't be bothered to get me to my Pop Warner practices, even made me miss a game once and got me kicked off the team. I wasn't very old, but I was already tired of all the drama he made us deal with, Mom especially. Clearly theirs was not a storybook romance. Unless the story was written by the Brothers Grimm. Ha." His single-syllable laugh had no mirth to it. He took another bite, then shrugged, chewing thoughtfully. "He left us to work in Alaska. I couldn't really complain. We were poor, but Mom was happier after he was gone. No more drama. No more police-blotter stories for the neighbors to laugh about. Everything about the household was lighter and less tense." He held his fork in the air. "For a while, I wondered why there was never any contact from him, not even a postcard." He stabbed his pie a little too forcefully. "Good riddance."

"Even if he wasn't the best dad, I'm sorry this happened," Quinn said quietly.

In response, Chief Chestnut held out his cup to her to be topped off.

She and Jake left him to work his crossword puzzle. Quinn noticed it was the internment camp one. *Oh, well, there goes my record of subliminal clues to the rescue.* Clearly she didn't need to steer Chief Chestnut's improbable investigation toward the internment camp.

Quinn hung around acting busy while Chief Chestnut at his table, and Abe and his friend at theirs, remained in the diner. She knew Jake had work to do in the kitchen, so to help out, she could hang around until he was done, or until Rachel showed up for work, whichever came first.

Chief Chestnut finally slid out of his booth, having eaten his pie, finished off a pot of coffee, and completed his puzzle. He was noticeably calmer now, despite all the coffee—crosswords had that effect on people—but he still flung a handful of singles on the table instead of paying like a polite person. He walked past Abe's table, offering a token greeting before leaving.

As the door chimed his departure, Quinn had already scooped up the money and was on her way to the cash register. Nearing Abe's table, she heard the two of them discussing Donald Lee's death. Abe's back was to her, and when she was within a couple steps of him, she heard him say, "If I were Chief, I'd look into Bernard Dudley for the murder. Remember how the two of them would go at it?"

Quinn skidded to a stop just past their table, face twisted in outrage. She turned to face Abe. "What did you just say?"

Abe had the decency to redden. "I'm sorry, Quinn, and maybe I shouldn't have said that, but it's common knowledge your grandfather and Donald Lee had some history."

"Having history and killing someone are two vastly different things. You and Jake have history. You and your friend here have history. You and my *parents* have history, for Pete's sake. I hope that doesn't mean you're going to kill any of them." She noisily cleared their plates and cups. *Mi casa es not their casa anymore.* "I hope you won't be gossiping about my grandpa in the future. You know it's going to get back to my mom, right? Idle chatter like that about her father would break her heart, and you know it."

"I know," Abe said quietly. He watched her clear the table, then added, "But, Quinn? I won't be the only one thinking it. You should prepare yourself. And Georgeanne." He stood and hitched his chin at his companion, indicating it was time to go.

Quinn tossed their dishes into a bussing bucket and stomped to the kitchen with it. She proceeded to slam the dirty dishes into the dishwasher.

"Whoa, whoa, whoa! What's going on?" Jake stepped away from the prep table, wiping his hands on his apron.

Angry tears pricked at Quinn's eyes, but she blinked them away. "Abe had the gall just now to say that my grandpa probably killed Chief Chestnut's dad!"

"What? He said that to you?" Jake started out to the dining room, a vein in his forehead suddenly throbbing.

"They're gone." Quinn slumped against the counter.

Jake joined her, leaning against the counter shoulder to shoulder. "It's absurd, I'm sure," he said. "I don't know your grandfather, but I do know you and your parents, and there's no way any of you descend from murder stock."

"Bernard is my mom's dad. He just moved back to town, into that new assisted living place on the other side of town." Quinn appreciated Jake's confidence in her genetics, but didn't feel like sharing the information she'd found in the newspapers about all the times Bernard had ended up sitting in the Chestnut Station jail. "Thanks. I'm sorry. I'm probably overreacting." She finished loading the dishwasher, more gently now.

"You reacted completely appropriately, I'd say. It was a lousy thing for him to say. I'd have punched him in the face." Jake moved back to the prep table and picked up his knife. "You want to clock out and get out of here?"

"No. I'm not done out there. I'll be fine." She placed her fingers on the carotid artery in her neck and jokingly said, "I think I'm out of stroke territory. Touch and go for a minute there, though."

As Quinn went through her entire diner checklist, systematically cleaning and organizing everything for the third time, Abe's words echoed in her head: *I won't be the only one thinking it.* His enormous tip didn't make his words any easier to swallow. She mulled over that article about Donald Lee and her grandpa with the headline, "Assault with a Dudley Weapon." The fact that Donald Lee had been identified and nobody in law enforcement was interested in pursuing it any further didn't alleviate the funny feeling she had that Grandpa might actually have had something to do with all this. She hated the idea of it, but reluctantly admitted to herself there was a lot of circumstantial evidence. Windshield fight. Assault with a Dudley weapon. Weird plot of land in Georgeanne's name—but not officially, for some strange reason—right in the middle of the Chestnuts' land…maybe even right where the bones had been found. Based on the newspaper blurbs, it was clear she didn't know her grandfather like she thought she did. Was this yet another thing she didn't know about him? Did Abe know him better?

One thing was certain, though. She wouldn't be creating a crossword to subliminally convince Chief Chestnut to investigate her grandfather for Donald Lee's murder.

Quinn slipped into Jake's office for some privacy and called the assisted living home her grandfather had moved to.

"Bonneville Care. This is Rosemary. How may I help you?"

"Hi, Rosemary. This is Quinn Carr. I've been calling every day to find out when I can visit my grandfather, Bernard Dudley. His caregivers wanted to give him time to settle in before he had visitors?"

"Ah, Miss Carr. Let me check for you."

Quinn listened to a slow orchestral arrangement of Led Zeppelin's "Immigrant Song" that was oddly soothing.

"Miss Carr? You can come anytime. His care team says he's adapting perfectly well and is ready for visitors."

"Oh, that's great news! Can I bring him dinner?"

"Let me take a look at his chart… I don't see any dietary restrictions. But no guarantees he'll want it."

"Why not? Isn't he feeling well?" Quinn asked with a worried voice.

Rosemary chuckled. "No, nothing like that. But tonight is Fiesta Night. Taco bar, fajitas, make-your-own-nachos, virgin margaritas."

"That sounds delicious. Maybe I'll eat there."

"You're absolutely welcome to. It's an eight-dollar charge for guests. Dinner runs from five until seven thirty."

"I'll see you between five and seven thirty then." As Quinn hung up, she heard the diner door chime. She hurried out, hoping to finally meet Rachel, the new waitress. She called out, "I'm so glad to see you!"

Instead, Quinn heard Wilbur's gravelly voice. "That's something I never hear."

"You just saw us"—Hugh checked his watch—"four hours and seven minutes ago."

"I could have sworn the two of you owned actual houses where you actually live." Quinn smirked at them.

"But they don't have actual food in them," Hugh said.

"You're here to eat? Again?" She held out menus to them. "Someday you should investigate that big building a couple streets over with the neon sign that says *Groceries*. I think if you go in there and ask them real nice, they'll sell you actual food for your actual houses where you actually live. Maybe even give you a tour of the place."

Wilbur removed his straw boater and plopped into his regular seat. "What can we say? Jake's a genius at the grill."

Quinn pointed to the sheet of specials paper-clipped to the menu. "He's a genius at meat loaf tonight."

"Don't rush us," Wilbur grumbled. "We just got here."

"You're always here. Don't tell me you need a minute to commune with a menu you've known by heart since the Stone Age."

"Can't we just take in the ambience of this classy establishment?" Wilbur waved a hand at the paintings on the wall.

"Yes, of course. Ambience your little hearts out. But first"—Quinn sat with them—"explain why you both lied right to my face and told me you knew *for a fact* Donald Lee Chestnut had run off to Alaska to work on the pipeline."

Wilbur and Hugh looked at each other, then at Quinn. The men spoke simultaneously.

"Everyone said that."

"It was a fact."

Quinn stared at them. "Just because people say something doesn't make it a fact." She hoped Abe understood that. "You old farts should know that better than most."

"Well, I know one young fart who should get me some iced tea."

Quinn narrowed her eyes at Wilbur. He narrowed his back. Quinn leaned forward, keeping slitted eye contact. So did Wilbur. She only stood up when Wilbur winked at her and said. "Great googly-moogly, I love you, kid. Didn't have much hope for you when you started here, but I'll grant you, you give as good as you get."

Quinn left them reminiscing about all the waitresses that had come through the Chestnut Diner over the years. She wanted to ask them what they thought about Rachel, the newest, but before she could, Jake cut her loose.

"Go ahead and clock out. I'll take care of things 'til Rachel gets here."

She handed him Wilbur's iced tea. Quinn had resisted leaving earlier, but now she had a date with her grandfather. "Are you sure?" She had her apron untied and was hurrying toward the time clock before he even got the chance to nod.

Chapter 14

Before she drove over to the Bonneville to see Grandpa, she called Georgeanne. "Hey, Mom. I called to see if I could finally visit Grandpa, and they said yes!"

"I know! Great news, huh? I was over there earlier."

"I'm going to have dinner with him."

"He'll love that, but I hope you're in the mood for Mexican. He couldn't stop talking about that make-your-own-nacho bar."

"Then we'll definitely have something to talk about because I've been thinking about it ever since Rosemary mentioned it. I don't think I'll be out too late. Laters."

Quinn signed in with Rosemary at the front desk and followed her directions to Grandpa's unit on the second floor. She'd never been there before but was so pleased by what she saw. Residents played cards and lounged with books in the fully stocked library. Shelf labels pointed to locations for all the major fiction genres and subgenres, plus a robust nonfiction section. Soft tones emanated from a piano being played somewhere. Beautiful comfortable furniture was utilized in nooks and crannies. Large windows overlooked a tranquil landscape dappled by the setting sun. Laughter and the low murmur of voices. Ornate woodwork she was happy not to have to dust.

She passed a small room that doubled as a convenience store for the residents. As she slowed her pace to glance at the interior, an elderly woman whom Quinn assumed to be a resident beckoned her inside. "Hello! Are you in the market for a greeting card? Candy? Tissues? Deodorant? Red Bull?"

"You sell Red Bull here? Do the residents drink that?" Quinn asked incredulously.

"No, but we make a killing on visiting grandkids." She gave Quinn a melodramatic once-over. "Which it looks like you are."

"Guilty as charged. Not a fan of the energy drinks, however." Quinn glanced around the merchandise and saw a package of the sugared peanuts Grandpa liked. "I'll take some of those, though."

"Who are you visiting?" The woman took the peanuts to the register.

"Bernard Dudley. My grandpa."

"He's new. You'll be wanting a card too."

She said it with such authority that Quinn's feet automatically moved to the tall rack of greeting cards, the majority of which were of the "Welcome to your new home" variety. Equally prevalent were holiday-themed and get well cards. Quinn scanned a few of the cards and plucked out one that said, "New home, new beginning, new adventure." After the woman rang up her purchases, Quinn borrowed her pen and wrote, "New peanuts. Love, Quinn."

She thanked the woman and headed up the stairs. The beautiful mahogany woodwork made her stop at the top and peer at it, rubbing her hand across its intricacies. She straightened up and saw the number for Bernard's room just beyond…could it be? She couldn't take her eyes off the stainless-steel wonder as she walked past it. She hoped it wasn't a hallucination.

She knocked on Bernard's door. When he opened it, she squealed. "Grandpa! You have a soft-serve ice cream machine right outside your room?"

"I had them install it just for you." He winked, then wrapped her in a hug and walked her back out to the machine. "Want some? Chocolate or vanilla. Or both."

"Of course I want some, but I'll wait until after dinner. Like a grown-up."

"Pish. No grown-ups around here." He rested his head of wispy white hair against her temple. "Tell you a secret. The older you get, the less you have to behave like an adult. One of the perks of old age." He plucked a bowl from the upside-down pile, expertly filled it with a chocolate and vanilla swirl, and handed it to her.

"Looks like you've done this before."

"Couple of times." Bernard grinned and handed Quinn a plastic spoon.

"Couple hundred times, you mean."

"That's another perk of old age. You don't have to keep count of how many times you visit the ice cream machine. Not that most of us could remember, anyway."

"All you need to remember is how much I love soft serve." Quinn handed the card and peanuts to Bernard before attacking the ice cream.

They stood next to the machine. Bernard read the card and laughed. "Thank you." He kissed her on the forehead, tickling her with his walrus mustache, stiff as a housepainter's brush, then picked up his bowl of ice cream.

"You've always loved ice cream, Georgie. Ever since you were little. Every Sunday your mother and I would push you in your stroller to the Rexall, where they had the soda fountain. We'd have a treat, then rush home to put you to bed so we could watch Ed Sullivan."

Quinn swallowed a bite of chocolate ice cream, but it was hard with that lump in her throat. "Grandpa, I'm Quinn, your granddaughter. Georgeanne is my mom."

Bernard looked flustered, then ashamed. "I know who you are, Quinn. You're my granddaughter."

The way he said it made Quinn think that he was firming it in his memory. Placing another brick in his wall and smoothing the mud around it so it would stay put. She took his hand and led him back to his unit. "Show me your room! I'm dying to see it." She spoke brightly, a bit too loud. "Do you like it here?"

Bernard smiled at her. "I do like it here." He opened his door and ushered her in. Immediately to the left was his bathroom: toilet, sink, and shower. A few steps forward, the short hallway opened into his combination sleeping and living area. He had a twin bed against the wall to the left, a couple of easy chairs, some shelves, and a desk under the window overlooking the courtyard in front. Some tall aspens were turning golden, and an enormous ash tree had several hues of reds already.

"Grandpa! It's great! And what a beautiful view."

Bernard joined her at the window. "And when those leaves drop, I won't have to rake them up."

"Even better."

They settled into the two easy chairs and finished their ice cream. Bernard told some long, rambling story about something funny that happened at breakfast. Quinn tried to follow but couldn't tell if it had happened in the past few days or when he was young. Regardless, it was entertaining.

"I'm glad you live in Chestnut Station, Grandpa, so I can visit you all the time."

"I'm glad too, Geor—Quinn." He glanced up at the clock on his dresser. "Yippee. Dinnertime. Hey, you want to stay? Guests are always welcome."

"I'd love to. What are they having?" She hated the idea of testing him, but also thought she should.

"It's Mexican Fiesta Night," he said excitedly. "Tacos, nachos, fajitas. Even margaritas. Hey, are you old enough to drink?" Without waiting for her to answer, he slapped his forehead. "I'm such a ninny. Of course you are! I went to your college graduation." He shook his head, chuckling.

Two tests passed. Good for you, Grandpa.

"It's still ten minutes until five, though. Can I ask you something before we go down there?"

"Of course."

"You knew Donald Lee Chestnut, didn't you?"

"I did. Troublemakers, both of us. Raised more than our share of hell." Bernard told her a couple of the milder stories she'd read about in the newspaper archives, then a melancholy look passed over his face. "But we had a falling-out."

"That's actually what I wanted to ask you about."

He nodded and stared into space. Quinn could see the memory flickering through his brain. "We were in my car listening to the ball game on the radio because it was raining. Donald Lee got mad since the Cubs were losing so bad and he punched my windshield so hard it cracked. And then he had the nerve to refuse to pay for it. Said the Cubs should pay for making him so mad, or at the very least, it was *my* fault for making him listen to the game in the first place. I said to him, I never twisted your arm and you can get out and walk home anytime you want—we were out at the ball field shagging flies—so he did. Walked all the way back to town in that rain. I drove past him four times just so's I could run puddles and splash him, I was so mad."

"Sounds like you were both pretty mad. At least you got mad about something important, though. I got mad at Rico once when we were kids because he said he didn't like dipping his French fries in ketchup. Why that made me mad, I'll never know. I didn't talk to him for two days."

"The important thing is you talked to him again." Bernard shook his head sadly. "Nothing's more important than friendship. I can't believe ours was over because of a stupid crack in a window. I never talked to him again. He was a pistol, but it was an important friendship."

An important friendship. That was an interesting phrase, she thought. "Was that the only time you fought?" Quinn held her breath, already knowing the answer to this question, hoping he'd tell the truth, but also worried about that truth.

"Oh, heavens no. We fought all the time."

"I've never heard any other stories of you fighting or getting in trouble before."

Bernard made a noncommittal noise that Quinn couldn't quite decipher. She tried a different line of questioning. "Did you run around with a guy named Odell Nilssen?"

"Odell Nilssen. Haven't thought about him in ages." Bernard got a far-off look on his face, visiting the past. Abruptly he snapped back to the present. "Never liked that guy." He picked up his spoon and collected the last few drips of melted ice cream, slurping it down.

"How come?"

"I don't know. Just seemed shady to me. Went into real estate and tried to get me to jack up the price of the house when we sold it to you and Dan—I mean, your parents. He was trying to run some scam on the bank and told me we'd all get rich if we'd just go along with him. Of course I said no, and then he had the nerve to strong-arm me to sign him as my Realtor when your grandma and I were looking for a house in Denver." He looked out the window and got that far-off gaze again. "He and Donald Lee were tighter, a bit closer in age." Bernard glanced over at Quinn. "You know he up and left his family, Donald Lee did, went to work on the pipeline. Folks say he made a ton of money, but I don't know. For a long time after, every time I'd see Donald Lee's kid—Myron, his name was—wearing his old parka, I'd think it was Donald Lee coming to apologize, but he never did. Never apologized for being a Cubs fan neither."

Quinn chuckled, even though she knew the sting of losing a best friend. That's what she was so afraid of when Rico suggested they should date a while back. She knew it was a potentially explosive and stupid idea. Luckily for both of them, there were no sparks, no romantic chemistry, and they knew they were destined instead for a lifelong friendship.

Quinn was glad Bernard didn't seem to know about Donald Lee's death. She sure wouldn't be the one to tell him, but that didn't mean she wouldn't try to explore any culpability he might have had in it. If there was going to be gossip spreading through Chestnut Station, she wanted to be ready for it.

And now there seemed to be another viable candidate. If Odell Nilssen, Junior, was some shady real estate guy, maybe Donald Lee's death had something to do with the property the Chestnut family owned. Maybe Odell, Junior, was more than shady. Maybe he was a murderer. Joe, the warehouse guy at Odell's father's company, came right out and said Odell, Senior, had wanted nothing to do with him. If your own father didn't trust you, then who would?

Before she could ask any more questions, Bernard had launched into a story about trying out for the Yankees when a scout—the brother or uncle or twice-removed cousin of his neighbor down the street—came through town. "We named your mother Yogi, after Yogi Berra."

"Grandpa," Quinn said softly. "My mother's name is Georgeanne." Quinn expected him to pause, then reorganize and refile the contents of his memory. He simply looked at her quizzically. "Of course it is. Broke my heart when George Brunet got traded to Baltimore. He wasn't the best, but he was entertaining. You know," Bernard leaned in, "he didn't wear underwear."

"I did not know that." Nor did Quinn know who George Brunet was and why she—or anyone, for that matter—should care about his undergarment situation.

"Said he didn't want to have to worry about losing them."

"Why would he have to worry about losing his underwear? Is there something I don't know about the national pastime?"

"Had another whole career down in Mexico. Pitched until he was in his mid-fifties."

Quinn listened to Bernard ramble on about George Brunet's life story. She wondered how much he was making up, or confusing with someone else. Her mind wandered to Yogi Berra, someone from baseball she actually knew something about. Well, one thing anyway. He was famous for saying goofy things. Bernard was always quoting him to her and cracking himself up.

She interrupted his story with a Yogi Berra-ism. "Hey, Grandpa, you can observe a lot just by watching."

Without missing a beat, Bernard said, "The future ain't what it used to be."

"Baseball is ninety percent mental and the other half is physical."

"Always go to other people's funerals; otherwise they won't come to yours."

Quinn wasn't sure if that last one was his or Yogi Berra's. *At least he can remember these, even if he can't remember what he named his own daughter.* "Wanna go stuff our faces with nachos, Grandpa?"

"I'll race you."

Bernard showed her the way to the dining room. They passed an elevator, and Quinn asked if he wanted to take it. "Nah, that's for the old folks," he told her.

At dinner they filled their plates and sat at a table with an interesting assortment of people: a woman so hard of hearing she said "eh?" to everything, even sentences she herself spoke; a man who'd spent his career working in zoos, handling animals large and small; a woman who'd curated the traveling exhibits at the Denver Art Museum, many of which Quinn remembered visiting; a fascinating man Quinn would love to spend more time with who had a shady, colorful past making a fortune by running Three Card Monte schemes and hustling pool; the mother of two boys who both played in the NFL.

Rounding out their table was a woman who kept interrogating Quinn as to whether she had paid for her meal. As she became more and more agitated, Quinn finally called over one of the servers and made a show of handing her a five-dollar bill and saying, "Please make sure to give this to Rosemary as payment for my dinner." That seemed to calm the woman down enough that she could enjoy the virgin margarita Quinn had fetched for her.

A short time later, Rosemary bent to whisper in Quinn's ear while dropping the cash back in her lap. "Thank you for playing along with Mrs. Benson. She used to work in a women's prison, kind of a stickler for rules."

Grandpa will never be bored here, she thought as she slipped the money back in her purse.

Quinn refilled everyone's plates with a requested dab more of this, and a smidge of that, and was happy to do it. These were Bernard's new friends, after all.

She found herself in a conversation with the mother of the NFL players. "Did you know there's a Loch Ness monster that lives in Flathead Lake in Montana?" she asked Quinn.

"I did not. But wouldn't that make it a Flathead Lake monster?"

"That's what they want you to think," the woman said, tapping her temple.

"What?" Quinn had already lost the thread of this conversation.

"But that's nothing compared to all the secrets the government is keeping out at DIA." The woman swigged the remains of her virgin margarita, making Quinn wonder if it really was devoid of tequila. Luckily, the woman turned to the zookeeper to pitch her airport conspiracies and let Quinn off the hook.

Quinn had heard all the funny conspiracy theories about the Denver International Airport. Constructing a facility twice the size of Manhattan that went two billion dollars over budget made it impossible for gullible people not to believe some unnamed government entity had built a secret bunker underneath it all to house the headquarters of the Illuminati, or extraterrestrials who'd crash-landed on earth, or where the Nessies of the world could swim unencumbered by paparazzi taking grainy photos of them when all they were doing was simply trying to live their best lives.

Nothing would convince conspiracy theorists otherwise, certainly not facts or logic.

When they'd eaten their fill and guzzled enough virgin margaritas to float to Cabo San Lucas, she escorted Bernard back to his room. He gave her a running commentary on the residents and staff they encountered along the way.

"That was so much fun, Grandpa. Thank you for letting me join you."

"Letting you! I'm thrilled you wanted to hang out with an old geezer like me."

Quinn thought of the Retireds. "Dude! There's nothing I like better than old geezers. But I have to go now. See you in a few days?"

"Counting the minutes." Bernard must have noticed the guilty look that flashed across her face. "I'm not *really* going to be counting the minutes. I'll be busy with a ton of activities. And you met those people, right? That was just one table of characters in this place. I have a bunch more to meet!" He pulled her in for a hug. "Don't you worry about me, Georgie. I'm fine. This is a good, safe place for me. You come by when you can, and tell Quinn not to be a stranger, okay?"

Quinn pulled away and blinked back the tears that threatened to spill. She didn't trust her voice, so she simply nodded, kissed him on the cheek, and hurried away.

All the way home, Quinn debated how much to tell her mother about Bernard's condition and how many times he'd confused her with Georgeanne. By the time she pulled into the driveway, she knew she'd tell Georgeanne everything. She had probably seen the same confusion anyway. Besides, if they both knew where his cognitive baseline was, then they'd both be able to keep a watchful eye on him and alert his medical team if they noticed a precipitous decline.

Dan and Georgeanne were at the kitchen table playing Scrabble when Quinn walked in. She told them about her visit, still a bit uncomfortable with Bernard's confusion. After a bit of hemming and hawing and more than a few glances in the direction of the spice rack, she turned to Georgeanne and told her about him confusing the two of them occasionally.

Georgeanne absentmindedly moved around the Scrabble tiles from the draw pile. "Yeah, I saw a bit of that too."

Quinn didn't really want to but told her the rest. "Probably the weirdest thing Grandpa said was that he and Grandma named you Yogi, after Yogi Berra." Quinn cast her eyes downward. "I'm sorry to tell you that, Mom, but I thought you should know."

Instead of the sadness Quinn expected from her mother, Georgeanne let out a huge laugh. "That's absolutely true."

Dan and Quinn both raised their eyebrows.

"It didn't officially get on my birth certificate, though, thanks to an alert nurse. Apparently she came into my mom's room to make sure that was the name she actually wanted."

"Let me guess," Dan said. "It was not."

"Nope. It seems Mom thought they'd decided on Mary—"

"Yawn."

Georgeanne shot Quinn a look. "Which was my grandmother's name—"

"Sorry."

"But Dad would have none of it. Claimed they'd never discussed names. So they had a long discussion there with the nurse as arbitrator, and compromised on Georgeanne, after some baseball pitcher Dad loved."

Quinn laughed. "George Brunet. I got his complete life story tonight."

"That's him. Broke Dad's heart when they traded him to Baltimore. Dad loved that Brunet didn't wear underwear. I must have heard a million times growing up that he didn't want to have to worry about losing it. I always wondered—"

Quinn and Georgeanne spoke in unison. "Why he'd worry about losing his underwear."

Dan had his phone out. "Says here George Brunet pitched until he was in his mid-fifties. Ended his career down in Mexico."

Suddenly Quinn felt much better about Bernard's cognitive abilities. "I guess Grandpa doesn't forget everything!"

Quinn let them get back to their game and headed to her room. Before going to bed, though, Quinn texted Mary-Louise Lovely. *Hope you're having fun at your conference. Just wanted to tell you I came home tonight a little upset from my visit with my grandpa and wanted nothing else but to alphabetize those spices. But now I don't. I'll tell you all about it when you get back.*

Chapter 15

The next day at the diner, Quinn was intent on fishing for information about Bernard and Donald Lee. She had been up all night, her brain a whir of activity and her nerves abuzz, trying to understand their relationship. Her monster wouldn't let her drop the idea that Bernard absolutely could have been involved in Donald Lee's death. The more she fought against it, the stronger her monster got.

She finally got the opportunity to plop herself down at the Retireds' table and ask Wilbur, Larry, and Hugh why her grandfather and Donald Lee got in so many fights.

The three men shrugged and continued eating while they answered.

"They both drank a lot," Hugh said, crunching his bacon.

"That they did," Larry agreed. "Probably accounted for ninety percent of the liquor store's revenue."

The men laughed.

Silas said, "That reminds me of a joke. Three men walk into a bar—"

"Heard it," Wilbur said.

"How do you know? I didn't even get started."

"We've heard all your jokes, Silas."

"More than once," Bob said.

"More than twenty times," Larry said.

The men burst out laughing at the look on Herman's face, trying to calculate how many times he had heard Silas's jokes and the rate of jokes per minute if they'd heard them all more than twenty times. It wouldn't have been a surprise to Quinn to see Herman's hair begin smoking from the exertion.

"Focus, boys. Bernard, Donald Lee, fighting," Quinn said.

"They accused each other all the time of cheating at cards," Hugh said.

"All the time," Larry said to Wilbur's nods.

"And they bet on every stat you can think of—and some you can't—at every baseball game," Wilbur said.

"And old Bernard, boy howdy, he did not like to lose, did he?" Larry said.

Wilbur stole a glance at Quinn before saying quietly, "No, he did not."

As the men spoke, Quinn felt her finger thing begin. All of those statements sounded like possible motives to her. She quickly changed the subject, trying to find other alternatives. "Do any of you know Odell Nilssen?"

"Junior or senior?"

"Junior," Quinn said.

"Yeah, I know him," Bob said. "Wouldn't trust him as far as I could throw him. Why?" He looked sharply at Quinn. "He do something to you?"

The Retireds all snapped their heads to look at Quinn. They were meerkats, every one of them in protection mode. How she loved these coots.

"No, no, nothing like that. I just heard he used to hang out with my grandpa and Donald Lee."

"You stay away from Odell Nilssen." Wilbur shook a finger in her face. "Trouble sticks to him like stink on a skunk."

She wanted to ask more, so much more, but just then Chief Chestnut came in demanding pie and a quiet place to work his crossword. She did not want him to know what they had been talking about so she scrambled from the Retireds' table. She knew better than to interact with him any more than to ask what kind of pie he wanted. To make sure the Retireds wouldn't continue the conversation where Chief Chestnut could hear, as she walked away she dropped a stealthy Silas bomb on them. "Hey, Silas, tell the boys that joke you were telling me the other day."

After she delivered Chief Chestnut's pie, she couldn't help but wonder what it was like for him to grow up thinking his father had just abandoned him to go to Alaska.

She couldn't put herself in his place even for a minute. Her dad would never do such a thing, and based on the stories she'd heard over the years about her parents' upbringing, they wouldn't have been able to believe it of their parents, either.

Georgeanne and Chief Chestnut both grew up here. Georgeanne and Myron were friends. Quinn wondered if they ever spoke of Donald Lee's disappearance. Maybe that's why her mom felt a bit protective of Myron. When Quinn had been frustrated with Chief Chestnut in the course of his non-investigations into the murder at the diner and the death of Hugh Pugh's husband, Georgeanne had shushed her, not willing to hear any bad talk about her friend Myron. It had baffled Quinn then, and it baffled her now.

Asking Georgeanne about it might set her off like it did when Quinn asked her about that quit claim property deed, and Quinn absolutely didn't want to open that can of worms again.

But who else was there to ask about that time in Chief Chestnut's life?

Jake came up behind her. "If you keep washing that table, you'll wear away the Formica."

Quinn jumped. "Oh, sorry."

"I've been wondering too." He tipped his head in Chief Chestnut's direction.

She was almost positive Jake wasn't wondering whom she could speak with to determine if her grandfather was somehow involved in Donald Lee's death. "Wondering what?"

"How he's doing. He acts tough, but it must be weird finding out your dad has been dead in a field so close by all these years."

"I'm sure it must be. I wonder if he has anyone to talk to."

"He has a sister, but I don't think she lives around here."

"He's such a hard nut to crack, no pun intended. I'd love to talk to someone who knew him when he was a kid. Someone other than my mother, that is. Oh, speaking of my mother"—Quinn turned to face Jake—"I just found out from my grandpa she was almost named after Yogi Berra!"

Jake laughed. "That's rich. Parents have such cool, humiliating stories about their kids. I wonder what my mom goes around telling people."

Quinn glanced at Chief Chestnut, still hunched over the crossword. "I wonder what his mom would tell me."

"Chief's?"

"Yeah. She had an interesting name too. I saw it in the paper... Beany. I think it was short for something."

"So, not her Christian name?" Jake said with a smirk. "And she still has it, by the way. She's alive. Lives in a nursing home in Arvada. Chief was talking about it not too long ago. His sister was in town, and they were going to visit."

"Why in the world would you remember that?"

"Because it's just down the street from the Regal Pig, this restaurant I've been dying to try."

"The Regal Pig? How many Michelin stars does it have? With a name like that, half a dozen I'd expect."

"You scoff. Their barbecue is so good it should rule a country, according to their website."

"Why haven't you been yet?"

"Don't get to Denver much. And Arvada is clear on the other side."

"Can't be more than a couple hours from here," Quinn said.

"Round trip plus stuffing my face would be half a day. And unlike you, I work seven days a week."

"Don't blame that on me. You're the one who won't hire a weekend cook."

"Do you see anyone beating down the door to work here?"

"My mom would work here in a heartbeat."

Jake looked thoughtful.

"I was joking! Remember when she took over the diner?"

"I remember it was the only thing people could talk about for weeks. Maybe I'll give her a call."

"*Oy vey.* What have I done? Okay, but just be sure to stock up on Funfetti cake mixes. She likes to make casseroles with it." Quinn didn't dare tell him how much she liked Georgeanne's Weeknight Funfetti Casserole. She'd be mocked mercilessly for her immature palate. Of course, being mocked by a guy who swoons over barbecue from a place called the Regal Pig shouldn't be more than a glancing blow to her feelings.

Between duties for the rest of her shift, Quinn did internet research to find out if Jake's memory was solid. She found several nursing homes in Arvada, but only one, Victorian House, in the vicinity of the Regal Pig.

She toyed with the idea of calling to see if Beany actually lived there, but she couldn't come up with a conversation that didn't make her sound sketchy. And she didn't want to alarm anyone at Victorian House and have them call Chief Chestnut about it.

No. She'd have to ambush Beany, catch her off guard.

Chapter 16

On her next day off, Quinn took a chance and drove to Arvada to see if she could talk to Chief Chestnut's mother. Passing the Regal Pig, which looked like a complete dive, exactly Jake's favorite kind of place, she took the next right turn, then a quick left, and found herself on the street in front of Victorian House, a sprawling two-story facility designed with gingerbread trim in ice cream colors, gables, and wide, inviting bay windows, the hallmarks, Quinn thought, of Victorian architecture. Or perhaps she just assumed they were hallmarks, based on the name of the care center.

The landscape was lush with many areas of seating. Several residents were outdoors, enjoying the grounds and the weather.

Quinn parked in the small lot and made her way up the sidewalk to the huge wraparound porch. Friendly residents on the porch waved and called out greetings to her, which she returned.

The automatic doors *whoosh*ed open, and Quinn found herself standing in a room that looked like the lobby of the fanciest hotel she'd ever been allowed in. Her grandfather's place was nice, but this was gorgeous. Probably had a fully staffed ice cream parlor tucked away instead of just a two-flavor soft-serve machine.

A woman stood and moved toward her from behind a cherrywood table. They both had graceful legs, but only one wore suede ankle boots. She held out her hand to Quinn. "Hello. May I help you?"

"I'm here to see Beany Chestnut."

"Very good. I believe she's outside." Alarm flashed across her carefully made-up face. "You didn't see her when you came in?" The woman hurried out the automatic doors to the porch and let out a breath. "Oh, there she is." She pointed to a small grotto, where a birdlike, delicate-boned woman sat knitting.

"I'm sorry I worried you. I didn't see her when I came in. Too busy admiring this place, I guess." Quinn felt it prudent not to mention she had no idea what Beany looked like, since they didn't even know each other.

"Have a nice visit." The woman *click*ed her way across the porch and returned inside.

While she walked toward the grotto, Quinn studied Beany, who was oblivious to her, intent as she was on her knitting. Beany looked somewhat out of place here. Whereas most of the women on the porch wore lots of jewelry and obviously didn't skimp on trips to the beauty parlor, Beany wore no jewelry and wore her hair in a simple bun at the nape of her neck. Her wire-rimmed granny glasses had slid halfway down her nose.

In an effort not to startle an elderly woman, Quinn quietly cleared her throat when she was about four feet away.

Beany looked up from her knitting. "Who are you?" She asked it in the way a child might, unguarded, not judging, not scared, simply looking for facts.

Quinn had already decided on, and practiced, her greeting. Enough facts, but not too many that Chief Chestnut might learn she had been here. "I know your son, Chief, er, Myron."

A grin split her face. "I'm always happy to meet a friend of Myron's. Is he here?" Beany peered around Quinn.

"No, I came alone."

Beany gathered her knitting into her lap and slid over on the bench, making room for Quinn, who sat next to her.

Quinn dropped her bag on the ground next to the bench, but not before drawing out a box of candy. "I hope you like chocolates."

"I love chocolates."

Quinn marveled as Beany managed to tell a long, rambling story about how her daddy used to bring home chocolates after work from France, which didn't seem right, while she proceeded to eat seven chocolates…all almost without taking a breath. Then she launched into an overwrought story about the stone bench they sat on and the grotto. The best Quinn could make out was there was some idea that maybe this was the very place Beany expected the Rapture to happen. "Mark my words, it's only a matter of time before I'll sail up to heaven to meet the Lord in the air. He'll say, 'Welcome home, Beanpole! I'm so happy you're here!' You can come too," Beany said to Quinn, leaning in close. "Anyone who sits on this bench." She dropped her voice. "I have it on good authority."

If there'd been a Mexican fiesta and a scattering of empty margarita glasses in front of her, Quinn could have been right back at the Bonneville with the conspiracy-minded mother of the NFL players.

Quinn let Beany ramble on and on about people, places, and events she was unfamiliar with. Apparently Beany had attended every birthday party ever thrown and was intent on describing each of them. Quinn's attention began to drift until Beany mentioned Donald Lee. "There was a storm that night, too. Bad one."

"Was that when Donald Lee disappeared?"

Beany nodded. "He said he had a present for Marion." Her voice trailed off, and she seemed sad to Quinn, like he'd never had a chance to give his daughter that gift.

The storm passed from Beany's eyes, and she held out the chocolates to offer one to Quinn. "I always tried to give the kids great birthdays even when we didn't have much. Dollhouse, books, ukulele for Myron when he turned nine, brand-new bikes for both of them. Marion's had a basket. Hers was sky-blue. Myron's was red like a fire engine." Beany popped another bite of chocolate in her mouth. "Rode everywhere, the two of them. Never at home on summer days. Or on weekends. Sunup to sundown. They'd pack a sandwich and an apple, and I wouldn't see them 'til supper." She looked Quinn in the eye. "I always took care of things at home, but I worried about the little ones, whole town did. Watched out for 'em. Like Myron does now." Beany paused, another chocolate halfway to her mouth. "He shouldn't be around."

Quinn glanced around but didn't see the man she spoke of. In fact, she hadn't seen any men at all here. Quinn had definitely lost the thread of this conversation. Did she mean her son? "Myron shouldn't be around?"

"Better that way." Beany paused. "Never got his homework done. Marion did, but Myron only had his head in the clouds. Plenty of time for fighting, though. Gave as good as he got, I'm happy to say. Got that from me." Beany's eyes glassed over, and Quinn knew she was definitely in the past. "Took down a bull before he ever knew what hit him. A flea can bite a horse, don't you know."

Quinn nodded, not at all knowing, but it was clear Beany was proud of Myron's fighting prowess.

"Nobody ever did anything about it, though. Sometimes you just gotta take charge. Maybe that's what made him want to be a policeman. Marion should have been a policewoman, like that Cagney or Lacey. She loved that show."

While Quinn certainly understood Marion's love for *Cagney & Lacey*—because she shared it—she didn't understand the verbal leaps Beany was making, but nevertheless she listened politely and tried to keep up.

Beany ate another chocolate and then launched into a tale about touring a candy factory.

Quinn's mind wandered to what Beany had said about Myron. It sounded a bit to her as if Myron could have been responsible for Donald Lee's death. He got into a lot of fights, and Beany didn't think he should be around. She didn't seem scared of her son, though, since she was excited at the prospect of seeing him when she thought he'd come today with Quinn.

As she listened to Beany's prattle, she wondered how much of what she said was real and how much came from some fantasyland where she visited.

Quinn tried asking some gently probing questions about Myron and Donald Lee, but Beany brushed her off. "Marion knows Myron the best. Thick as thieves, them two." Surprisingly, Beany whipped out a cell phone in an attractive leather case, which she opened to a notepad and small pen. She scrawled two phone numbers on the pad, tore off the page, and handed it to Quinn. "Marion's home and cell number. But let's just call her up now, and we'll have a nice chat." Beany punched a number and listened for a bit before whispering to Quinn, "Not answering. She does that sometimes." She spoke into the phone. "Hi, Marion. A nice girl came to visit, friend of Myron's. Expect her to call you. Name's—" Beany looked at Quinn and asked, "What's your name?"

Quinn was so surprised and confused by this entire conversation she blurted, "Quinn." So much for staying on the down low. There was no way now that Chief Chestnut wouldn't know she'd visited his mother.

Beany turned back to the phone. "Expect a nice girl named Quincy to call you. Ta!"

Quinn could only imagine how many phone calls like this Marion, and possibly Myron, received over the course of a week. No wonder Marion let it go to voice mail.

A quiet chime sounded, and Beany jumped up like she'd been stung. Quinn was surprised to see just how very tiny she was. Beany's thigh was probably smaller than Quinn's arm. At five-foot-eight, Quinn had at least a foot on her. "Lunch!" she sang out, collecting her knitting and the box of candy—what was left of it, anyway—and shoving them into a bag next to her. "Ladies! Lunch!" Beany called excitedly to the group of women sitting on the porch.

Beany began to hurry away from the grotto, but turned back toward Quinn. "Come on! It's lunch!"

"Thank you for the invitation, but I'm so sorry, I can't join you today."

Beany scurried over to Quinn and shook her hand with gusto. "Thanks for the candy! Come see me anytime!"

Quinn watched her race-walk through the automatic doors, clearly ravenous after only eating three-quarters of a pound of chocolates. Quinn settled back into the grotto to catch her breath and further try to digest their conversation.

Before Quinn left Arvada, she stopped at the Regal Pig. She ordered the combo plate with brisket and pulled pork, which came with hush puppies, coleslaw, potato salad, and baked beans. When she finished, she felt like the Goodyear Blimp, but in a good way. She picked up the to-go order she got for Jake and steered her car toward Chestnut Station.

Chapter 17

She swung by the diner to deliver the barbecue feast to Jake. After greeting a lolling Jethro, she stepped inside, looking around. "Where's Rachel?" she asked Jake. "I was hoping to meet her today."

"Stepped out."

Quinn stared at him. "Did you really hire a new waitress, or are you messing with me?"

"Why would I mess with you?"

She gave him the side-eye. "Why, indeed?" She handed the bag of food to Jake, whose eyes widened when he saw the Regal Pig logo.

"Did you...is this...you got me..."

"Geez, it's just barbecue, not the Hope Diamond."

"Barbecue so good it should rule a country," he murmured reverentially. "You're the best! Let's dig in!"

"It's all for you, cowboy. I already ate my weight in barbecue."

He hugged her tight, then ran back to the kitchen to indulge in his banquet in private. Jake firmly believed it was never good for business if his customers saw him eating takeout from some other restaurant, especially when it was an item he had on the diner menu.

Quinn hung around, ready to handle any customers while Jake enjoyed his feast, at least until Rachel returned.

After a while, Jake wandered out to the dining room, wiping his face with a napkin covered in sauce stains, a goofy look of contented ecstasy on his face.

"Let me guess. You enjoyed it?"

"Rule a country," he declared. His eyes remained unfocused, and he meandered back into the kitchen.

Rachel hadn't returned yet, so Quinn went home.

* * * *

The house was quiet, so Quinn took a moment to visit with Fang. She placed her index finger on the glass. "How's your day been so far?" Fang swam to her finger and booped the glass with his puckered lips. Then he backed up and swam in place, fins and tail rippling majestically in the placid water.

"Do anything fun today?"

Fang released a big bubble that slowly made its way to the surface, where it popped.

"I had an interesting day too, topped off by a disgustingly enormous lunch." Fang swam quickly around the bowl.

"Are you? Okay, but just one." Quinn dropped one flake of fish food into the water.

Fang scooped it up almost before it hit. He swam another quick lap.

"Okay, fine, but that's it. And mind your manners." Quinn dropped another flake into the bowl. This time Fang let the flake drift down toward his mouth, and when it was close enough, politely gobbled it down.

Quinn placed his bowl on the windowsill so Fang could enjoy the autumn day, then propped her pillow up on the headboard and leaned against it. She dug out the scribbled note Beany had given her with Marion's phone numbers. If she couldn't get details about the relationship between Donald Lee and her grandfather from Beany, maybe Marion could shed some light.

Quinn went back and forth between the impossible idea that Bernard could have been involved in Donald Lee's death, and the more acceptable notion that he absolutely wasn't. But still, the idea niggled at her. The newspaper archives made it clear there was much she didn't know about her grandfather. She'd always heard that people mellowed with age. Was it possible Bernard had been a hothead when he was younger? Was the falling-out between him and Donald Lee important enough to trigger violence, even accidentally? She wished she'd had the chance to talk to Beany about it.

Quinn fiddled with the scribbled note. She dialed, but like Beany, got Marion's voice mail.

After the tone, she said, "Hi, Marion. I visited your mom today. My name is—" Before Quinn finished her message, Marion's number popped up. Quinn answered. "Hi, Marion. Thanks for—"

"Is my mom okay?"

Quinn's mind raced. "Yes, of course, well, I think she is. She was when I left."

"Are you one of her caregivers? Nobody calls me unless they have bad news."

"Oh. No, nothing like that." Quinn relaxed. "She's fine. I went to visit her. I'm the one she left you a message about. I'm a fellow *Cagney and Lacey* fan too."

"You're Quincy? I assumed she'd been watching too much TV. Last month she left me a message that Phoebe and Monica would be calling to get my cheesecake recipe."

"It's actually Quinn. Shall we start over?"

"Let's. First, are you Team Cagney or Team Lacey?"

"Ugh. Do I have to choose?" Quinn asked.

"Yes."

"But I love them both!" Quinn added a melodramatic whine to her voice.

"I do too, but I have a special affinity for Lacey because she's a mother."

"Funny, since you're making me choose, I was going to say Cagney because she's single, like me." Quinn paused. "But I have dark hair, like Lacey."

Marion laughed. "This is wild. I'm blond, like Cagney."

"So confusing!"

"Now that we have that cleared up, what did you need? I just have a little bit of time. I'm getting ready to teach a parenting class."

"Your mom mentioned you volunteered at a women's shelter. That must be so rewarding."

"Stressful, but yes, very rewarding."

"First, I've got to say, Beany is a delight, and that Victorian House seems fantastic."

"They take good care of her, and she seems to love it there. I feel bad I can't visit more, but Kansas City isn't a quick trip. Luckily my brother is close by."

Quinn could sense her growing impatience. Marion was nothing like her brother, though. Myron would have bit her head off by now. "So, the reason I went to visit your mom is because your dad and my grandfather, Bernard Dudley, were friends. I wanted to offer my condolences. To her and to you."

Marion made a noise that Quinn couldn't identify. A sigh? Cough?

"I'll admit it was quite a shock when Myron called me with the news. But Dad disappeared when we were just kids. Myron barely remembers him, and it's probably better that way."

Not a sigh or a cough. More like a dismissive harrumph. "It must have been awful to have your dad disappear right before your birthday."

"My birthday is in July."

"Oh. I must have misunderstood something Beany said. She told me there was a big storm the night your dad disappeared. For some reason, I thought thunderstorm."

"No, it was winter," Marion said. "So much snow we got a rare snow day from school. I remember because—well, never mind. Don't feel bad about not being able to keep up with Beany, she babbles a bit. I have real trouble following her stories most days. I'm never sure if what she's telling me actually happened to her or if it was just something she saw on TV. And if it did actually happen, I can't tell if it was last week or when she was a girl." Marion paused, then softly added, "It must be hard getting old."

Quinn thought of Bernard. "My grandpa is the same way." Quinn wasn't sure how to broach the subject about the falling-out between the two men. "Do you recall your father ever talking about my grandpa?"

"What was his name again?"

"Bernard Dudley."

There was silence on the other end of the phone, and Quinn hoped Marion was searching her memory and not plotting revenge.

"I remember he ran with some men, drinking buddies I assume, but they didn't really hang around the house. Sorry. And thank you for your condolences, but I don't really need them. Donald Lee has been out of our lives for such a long time that it seems like he's been dead all this time anyway. For Beany, though, it might be just yesterday. But I've really got to go now. We're talking about logical consequences today, and I'm afraid they'll take my phone away as the logical consequence for being late because I was talking on it." She chuckled. "And thank you for visiting my mom. I'm sure she really enjoyed it."

"She sure enjoyed the chocolates I brought."

"You brought her candy? Now I'll have no chance... You're her favorite daughter now."

Smiling, Quinn set her phone on the nightstand. She liked Marion about a thousand percent more than she liked Chief Chestnut. How did siblings grow up to be so different? As an only child, Quinn had no frame of reference. When she'd go to friends' houses to play, she always marveled at the sibling relationships she saw. Her friends would complain about their younger brothers (too bratty), older brothers (too aloof), younger sisters (too needy), and older sisters (too cruel), but Quinn never saw it. All she saw was companionship, someone to share confidences with, a playmate always at the ready, a buffer against parental scrutiny. Of course, she'd seen some of the obnoxious behavior between siblings too, but it always seemed to pass like a summer storm, leaving behind another link in the chain of shared experience.

Georgeanne poked her head in Quinn's room. "Hey, wanna go to Camp Chestnut with me?"

"Camp Chestnut? The internment camp? Why do you want to go there?" Quinn felt the back of her neck get prickly. Was her mom looking into the connection between Donald Lee's death and the museum property too?

"Helen McKinley is volunteering at the door tonight, and she and I need to talk about the piano recital coming up. She has eighteen students and wants to include Glenda Smith's fifteen. With my ten, that makes it much too big. But she says she has a plan. And she'd better, because we need to finalize everything."

Not so much investigating as using the museum to have an unrelated meeting. Got it. "Sure, I'll keep you company. I can poke around the museum some more while you're hatching your nefarious piano recital scheme."

"You kill me. You never did like recitals, did you?"

"Only the ones I was in. And only when I was finished playing."

Mock exasperation filled Georgeanne's entire being. "How did I ever raise a child with such disdain for concertos?"

Quinn laughed while she tied her Keds. "Concertos? Have you ever actually listened to your students play?"

She followed Georgeanne to the car, then immediately headed back to the house. "Brr. I'm getting my jacket. I keep forgetting how chilly it's getting to be when the sun goes down. Are you okay?"

Georgeanne flapped her heavy sweater at Quinn. "I'm toasty."

Quinn ran to her bedroom to grab her embroidered jean jacket. She noticed the *Daruma* doll sitting on her dresser and changed her mind, grabbing her beige car coat with the big pockets instead. She shoved the *Daruma* deep into one before hurrying back out to the driveway.

They headed out of town. The sun was down, and the lights of Chestnut Station twinkled behind them. Ahead of them, the world was inky, split faintly by Georgeanne's headlights.

"I'm always amazed how dark it seems away from town." Quinn gazed out her window, amorphous shapes along the shoulder of the road whipping by. She pulled her canvas jacket tighter around her.

"Even as a little girl, I loved the dark. Never afraid of it like some kids," Georgeanne said.

"Because you're Wonder Woman."

"More like Wondering Woman. Tonight, at least. Still not sure how to get everyone into that recital and not have it go on for six hours. And where in the world are we going to put that many people?"

"You'll figure it out."

Georgeanne made a noncommittal grunt.

Quinn returned her gaze to the hidden landscape rushing past her window. As she stared, she became Wondering Woman too. If Donald Lee was out in a field just like this in the middle of a snowstorm, why were no shoes or coat found? The shirt buttons were there, but wouldn't there be a zipper that had fallen off a disintegrated winter coat if there were buttons that fell off a disintegrated shirt?

Maybe Marion had it wrong. It was a long time ago, after all. She seemed sure about that snow day, but perhaps she was confusing it with some other event. On the other hand, those sense memories that got tied to traumatic events seemed to gel pretty firmly in people's brains. Having your dad disappear would definitely be traumatic, but Marion hadn't seemed all that broken up about it.

This might be the same thing with siblings, Quinn thought. *I don't have any so I can't really understand anything about it. I've never had my dad disappear. If he did, I'd be devastated. But I adore my dad. Both Myron and Marion seem ambivalent about Donald Lee.*

Her jumbled thoughts were interrupted by Georgeanne slowing the car to veer through the gates of the museum.

They greeted a bored Helen McKinley at the front desk. She perked up immediately when she saw them. "Finally! Real people. It's been dead out here today." She pulled out a yellow legal tablet full of scribbled notes.

"I'll leave you to hatch your scheme," Quinn said.

Helen started to say something, but Georgeanne waved it away. "Don't mind her. She's not a patron of the arts."

"I think we'll need to define our terms." Quinn laughed. "I've listened to some of your students play."

Helen wagged a finger half-heartedly in Quinn's direction. She had obviously heard this complaint from her family too.

"Oh, go educate yourself and look at the exhibits," Georgeanne said with fake annoyance.

Quinn jammed her hands in her pockets and felt for the *Daruma* doll. She wanted to ask Helen if she knew any more about the Japanese dolls, but didn't want to ask in front of Georgeanne. Instead, she said, "Helen, I heard there were some computers set up somewhere that had genealogy stuff and recordings of internees talking about their time here in the camp?"

Helen nodded vigorously. "Yes, over there. Fascinating stuff."

Quinn followed her finger pointing at two computers at a table with some vintage, vaguely militaryesque chairs. "How do I get on them?"

Helen rummaged for a set of sheets on a clipboard, then pushed it toward her. "Write your name and wait."

Quinn's brows knit together as she glanced nervously at the none-too-sturdy-looking chairs. "My real weight or my driver's license weight?"

"Wait," Helen said with a laugh and an eye roll. "While I turn them on." Helen ducked down behind the counter, creating clicks and whirs of machinery. "Your daughter is hilarious, Georgie."

"Isn't she just," Georgeanne said dryly.

Quinn shrugged. *Let them think I was joking and not worried about cracking my tailbone.* She pulled the clipboard toward her and signed in, noticing that the last person to sign in for the computers had done so more than a week ago.

She left her mom and Helen to figure out the logistics of their piano recital while she ambled toward the computers. A hand-lettered sign told her there were more computers upstairs, making her wonder if there was ever a time when all the computers in the museum were in use. An exhibit about the camp schools caught her attention, and she perused it on the way, suddenly realizing that school groups would completely take over this place. Then all the computers would definitely be in use. Listening to first-person narratives would probably be an excellent way for kids to learn this history, she thought. She hoped lots of them did.

When she tentatively pulled out one of the chairs, testing its strength and durability before she sat, the computer was up, no doubt helped along by Helen's machinations. The bright screen had a series of choices to click on. She read them all, becoming more and more disturbed that the list seemed random. "What's wrong with alphabetizing?" she muttered to nobody.

Deciding to listen to a woman's memories of attending the camp high school, Quinn, within just a few moments, became rapt at the recording and hypnotized by the black-and-white photos that accompanied the narration. She jumped when Georgeanne touched her arm.

"Ready to go?"

"Mom, have you ever listened to any of these?" Quinn's eyes were wide.

Georgeanne nodded. "They're fascinating, aren't they? They have something like eighty hours of recordings stored."

"You can search them, if you're looking for something in particular." Helen pointed to a search bar that Quinn hadn't noticed.

Quinn typed in *Daruma*, and a page of recordings loaded.

"What's *Daruma*?" Georgeanne asked.

"It's Japanese," Quinn said, not wanting to get into detail, but glad there seemed to be some information on the computers. With her mother waiting, she knew there wasn't time to scan it all tonight, and hoped it wasn't just a listing of generic internet citations because Quinn was almost positive she had already read all of those. Knowing she'd be back to take another look, she crossed her fingers she could find something that linked her *Daruma* doll to Camp Chestnut.

She'd kicked that doll for a reason. Now she only needed to figure out what that reason was.

As they walked toward the exit, Helen explained briefly about *Daruma*s.

"Interesting," Georgeanne said. She turned to Quinn. "And it looks like there are lots of recordings about them."

Quinn nodded, vowing silently she'd listen to every minute of them.

Chapter 18

During her next shift at the diner, Quinn put her evolving plan to learn about Donald Lee and her grandfather into action. She'd hatched it after her conversations with Beany and Marion didn't turn up any information about the falling-out the two men had.

After the Retireds had been thoroughly fed and watered, after the breakfast crowd dissipated, and after she'd brewed a fresh pot of coffee, she carried it over to their table. Instead of refilling everyone's cup, though, she set the pot in the center of the table, then slumped in a chair she'd slowly dragged over from a nearby table.

She sighed loudly and melodramatically.

Larry put his hand on her forearm. "What's the matter, Quinn?"

"Oh." Another loud sigh. "Nothing."

"Doesn't sound like nothing," Hugh said.

"Would you like to hear a joke?" Silas asked.

In unison, all the Retireds thundered, "No!"

Silas pulled a face, his feelings hurt. "I just wanted to cheer her up."

"Thanks, Silas, but I don't even think one of your jokes could help," Quinn said forlornly.

"Well, it couldn't hurt." He leaned toward her. "So...a guy walks into a bar—"

"No!" the men repeated.

"Just tell us," Bob said. "Maybe we can help."

"Yeah, just tell us," Herman said, reaching for the coffeepot.

Wilbur held out his cup and waggled it at him, but Herman didn't quite understand the subtlety of Wilbur's nonverbal request.

If you wanted literalist Herman to pour you coffee, you'd need to make prolonged eye contact while stating loudly and clearly, "Please pour six ounces of coffee from the pot in your left hand into the cup I'm holding in front of you." Herman didn't understand a waggled cup, or a vague, "My cup is empty," or even "I'd sure like some of that coffee." No. Prolonged eye contact. Loud, clear declarative sentences.

Quinn feared she'd start laughing if Herman held that pot much longer. He finally filled his own cup, and everyone turned their attention back to her. But not before Wilbur uttered an oath directed at Herman.

"Tell us what's troubling you," Larry said in a soft, kind voice to Quinn.

Her third dramatic sigh made Quinn a bit light-headed so she decided to plunge forward. "I think I've solved the mystery." She kept her voice low and serious.

"What mystery?" Hugh said.

She looked each man in the face, ending with Wilbur. "The mystery of who killed Donald Lee."

"Somebody killed Donald Lee?" asked Silas with surprise.

"Of course someone killed Donald Lee, you ninny," Bob said. "A person's bones don't just end up in some field. Sheesh."

"What are you talking about, Quinn?" Hugh said quietly.

"It's true," she said solemnly. "I know who killed him."

"Who?" growled Wilbur.

She stared him in the eye. "I think you know already."

Silas let out a little yelp. "Wilbur killed Donald Lee?"

The men looked around the table at each other, unsure of what exactly was happening.

Except Wilbur. He stared directly at Quinn until she got flustered.

"No, no, no," she said. "Wilbur didn't kill anyone—"

"That we know of." Herman laced his fingers behind his head and studied Wilbur.

This was not going quite the way Quinn had envisioned. "Let me start over. I've been thinking about all this, and now I know that my grandpa killed Donald Lee. They had some big argument about Grandpa's broken windshield, and he lost control. Something bad happened. I don't know what precisely, but it was bad." She tried to muster tears but failed. "My mom is going to be devastated." Quinn was ninety-five-point-seven percent sure her grandfather hadn't killed anyone, but she simply hadn't been able to shake that remaining four-point-three percent. She knew the Retireds well enough, she hoped, that they wouldn't let her go through the rest of her life thinking Bernard was a murderer. They might not know who was, but she felt confident that at least they'd tell her this.

There was a stunned silence around the Retireds table, then the men all began talking at once, a cacophony of voices. Quinn couldn't make sense out of any of it.

Wilbur banged a fist on the table so loudly it made Jake stick his head out of the pass-through window and ask what happened.

"Nothing," Quinn called, waving him back into the kitchen.

"Bernard Dudley didn't kill nobody," Wilbur said.

"Absolutely not," Hugh said.

"No way in hell," Larry said.

"How do you know?" she asked.

Wilbur stared at Hugh and Larry each for a long time before he answered. "Because we know the parties involved."

Quinn needed more information. "Grandpa and Donald Lee?" She leaned forward and whispered, "Myron?"

Nobody spoke.

"Who do you mean, Wilbur?" she prodded.

"I mean," he said slowly, "that we know the parties involved. Now, run along and get me some more toast."

From experience, Quinn knew this conversation was over. She emitted another dramatic sigh—only this time she meant it—and replaced her chair at the other table from where she'd borrowed it. While she was buttering Wilbur's toast, she heard the door chime. As she walked out with the plate, she saw Loma chatting with the Retireds.

"Land sakes, you men act like you're glued to those chairs. Don't you ever go home?"

"We like it here. Pretty ladies come in to visit us." Bob doffed an imaginary hat to her while the others, except Wilbur, murmured their agreement.

Loma curtsied in reply. "You certainly have good taste, I'll say that for you."

Wilbur stared at Quinn the entire way across the restaurant. She stared back, not sure whether she was annoyed with him or not. She always had a low-grade annoyance going because of one thing or another the Retireds did, but she couldn't decide if this was—or should be—in addition to her normal aggravation with him. Of all the Retireds, she understood him the least. They enjoyed a warm relationship full of teasing and good humor, but there was something just below the surface with Wilbur that she couldn't quite pierce. She wasn't sure anyone could.

When she bent to place his toast in front of him, he spoke in his low, gravelly voice. "Your granddaddy didn't go and kill Donald Lee. You put that thought right out of your mind this instant."

"But how—"

"Don't matter how I know. I just do." Wilbur crunched a big bite of his sourdough. When he saw the entire table, along with Quinn and Loma, staring at him, he sputtered toast crumbs. "And I didn't kill him, either." He used the back of his hand to wipe his mouth. "Everybody knows how much Donald Lee liked his liquor. He went on a bender out there celebrating his job on that pipeline, fell asleep in that storm, and never made it back to Chestnut Station, much less Alaska. Myron said so himself."

"Who's Myron?" Loma asked.

"Chief Chestnut," Larry answered.

"Ah," Loma said.

"Understood?" Wilbur asked Quinn.

Quinn studied Wilbur's face. While she didn't know everything about Wilbur, she knew he wouldn't lie to her, especially about something this important. Besides, she really didn't think her grandfather killed anyone. It was absurd. She nodded at Wilbur. "Understood."

The men began talking about the Broncos' chances of going to the Super Bowl as Quinn and Loma walked away.

"What was all that about?" Loma asked.

"You know they determined those bones in the field belonged to Chief Chestnut's dad, Donald Lee?" Loma nodded. "Well, I found out that Grandpa and Donald Lee had been close and then all of a sudden they weren't, some kind of fight."

Loma's eyes went full saucer. "You think your grandpa killed him?"

At Loma's raised voice, Wilbur called across the restaurant, "What did I just tell you?"

Quinn flapped a hand at him. "It crossed my mind, but not really," she said to Loma. "I still had to confirm it somehow. Wilbur and a couple of the other guys knew both Grandpa and Donald Lee, but I think they're not telling me something. So I pretended I was sure Grandpa did it."

"You devil, you." Loma grinned at her as she slid into the big back booth. "So now you know he didn't." At the befuddled look on Quinn's face, she added, "Don't you?"

"Yes, I guess, but I still don't know who did." Quinn glanced around the diner to confirm nobody needed her at that moment. The Retireds were still talking football; table five with the two couples seemed like they were doing some serious catching up with one another; table three with the four church ladies seemed to be oblivious to everything except their fund-raising project and the slices of pie they'd ordered. She slid into the booth across from Loma.

"Shall we get out the butcher paper?" Loma asked excitedly.

When Quinn and Loma had investigated a previous murder, they had spread butcher paper on the table of the very booth they sat in, and Quinn color-coded their thinking onto it. Apparently Loma had been even more impressed with Quinn's skills than she'd let on at the time. And she was fairly complimentary back then.

"No. This isn't like that."

"Girl, I know you. You have suspects in your brain."

"Suspect. Singular."

Loma leaned across the table as far as her bosom would allow. "Who? Don't leave me hanging."

"I'm thinking Chief Chestnut had something to do with it," she said quietly.

"Shut the front door! You think Chief Chestnut killed his own *daddy?*"

Quinn cringed but didn't dare turn around to see if the other diners had heard. Because of course they'd heard. Loma's everyday voice had the ability to be heard over the roar of a vacuum cleaner, but her *shut-the-front-door* voice shook pigeons off roofs from miles away.

"Shush!" Quinn tried to surreptitiously check to see who might be paying attention to their conversation. Nobody, she hoped. But as she turned, she saw fourteen pairs of eyes on them. Fifteen, when Jake peered out from the pass-through window.

"Nothin' to see here, folks," Loma said. "We weren't talking about *Chief Chestnut*, we were talking about someone completely diff—"

"Will you shut up?" Quinn pulled Loma from the booth and into Jake's office. She pushed Loma in ahead of her, then turned to look at the diners. All of them stared directly at her, except for one of the church ladies, who had her phone to her mouth.

"Betty, you'll never believe what I just heard at the diner…"

Bile rose from Quinn's stomach into her throat. *This is going to be bad,* she thought. *Very, very bad.*

Chapter 19

Quinn was wrong. It wasn't very bad. It was stupendously awful. Ghastly. Tragic. Ugly with a capital UGH.

Less than an hour after Loma uttered those words, Chief Chestnut stormed into the diner, seemingly more bony and angular than normal, and got nose to nose with her.

"You seem to have something to say to me."

"No, I—" Quinn's brain went blank. All thoughts erased. No opinions. No memory. No words.

"But it seems you had plenty to say when you told everyone in the Chestnut Diner that I killed my own father."

"I never said—" Quinn took a step backward. Technically she knew she did actually say that, but only in confidence to Loma, not the entire diner. It was surely a distinction Chief Chestnut wouldn't appreciate hearing. She let him talk, get it all out of his system.

"Thanks to you, my phone has been ringing nonstop and the entire population of Chestnut Station has trooped through my office." He thrust his phone in Quinn's face. "There's even a voice mail on here from someone at the *Denver Post*. Was that your doing?"

Jake came out from the kitchen and stood at Quinn's side.

"No, sir. I didn't call anyone. I don't—"

"Of course you didn't call anyone. You just climbed up on a table, shouted out your slander, and let the small-town grapevine go to work on your behalf."

Jake pulled Quinn back another couple of steps, then stood between her and Chief Chestnut. "What's going on, Chief?"

"Your waitress"—he spat out the word—"took it upon herself to tell the entire world that I killed my own father."

Jake turned to Quinn, his eyes wide. If his eyebrows raised any higher, they'd surely end up in his hairline. "Is that true?"

"No."

When Chief Chestnut began to bluster, Quinn interrupted.

"But I can see how everyone got that impression."

Jake made a noise deep in his throat while Chief Chestnut said, "Aha!"

"Chief Chestnut, please believe me. That's not what happened. This is all a huge misunderstanding."

"Tell that to my phone messages."

Quinn raised her voice, but she needn't have gone to the trouble. Everyone was engrossed, captivated by the conversation before them in the center of the diner. This was exactly why the Retireds and everyone else came to the Chestnut Diner, she realized. Here was where the news happened. The entire diner had turned in their seats and watched, as if it was the show at a dinner theater. *The Chagrined Waitress and the Furious Police Chief.* "Everyone, can I just say something? I don't know what—if anything—you heard, but there is absolutely no truth to the allegation that I—" Quinn paused here because she really did believe that Chief Chestnut might have killed his own father. She chose her words carefully. "That I proclaimed out loud…in this very room…to all the diners…that Chief Chestnut killed his father."

"That's not what I heard," called a voice from behind her.

She spun around but couldn't tell who spoke.

"Me neither," said another voice.

She whirled around the other direction, but again, couldn't determine the speaker.

A third voice said, "I heard it from my neighbor, who heard it from Betty—"

"Listen," Chief Chestnut said. "I don't care who you heard it from. I did not murder my father. The whole idea is ludicrous. I was just a kid."

"Thought you were a teenager, Chief." This time Quinn saw it was Abe the handyman who spoke. "And as I recall, you got into a lot of scrapes when you were"—he used air quotes—"just a kid."

Chief Chestnut's face went red, but from rage, not embarrassment. His lips curled into a snarl. Fists clenched. His eyes bored directly through Abe, then he whirled on Quinn until he was in her face again. "See what you've done?" he sputtered at her. Then he turned to Jake. "I'll be back the minute she's gone. And not a minute before." He stormed out of the diner, yanking on the door with such force Quinn thought it would pop right off its hinges.

The diner was silent for a moment, then every voice but hers and Jake's began speaking at once.

Quinn listened, becoming more discouraged with each word she heard. Everyone seemed to be discussing why or how Chief Chestnut had killed Donald Lee…not if. At least they weren't gossiping about her grandfather. She looked hopelessly at Jake.

He crooked a finger for her to follow him into his office.

I hope he'll give me a good reference, she thought as she pulled her apron over her head.

Chapter 20

"I'll wash this and get it back to you." She unpinned her name tag and waved the apron toward him.

"What? Why?"

"So it's clean for your next waitress."

"Don't be stupid. I'm not firing you."

"Then why did you call me back here?"

"Because I didn't want everyone to start asking you questions out there." Jake narrowed his eyes at her. "You realize what's going to happen now, right?"

Quinn stared at him, slack-jawed, still trying to wrap her head around the fact that she'd managed to hold on to her job.

"This town will divide into two factions—those who think he did it and those who don't. It's the only thing anyone will talk about. They'll talk about it here, they'll talk about it in church, they'll talk about it around their dinner tables, they'll talk about it at the hardware store. They'll talk about it—"

"Yeah, I get it. This is a small town."

"And it's the most excitement they've had—"

"Since the last murder."

"Well, yes. But this one isn't quite so scary. And it involves the chief of police."

"Jake, I—"

He held up his hand. "I know. Of course you didn't mean to do any of this. But now it's done. The question is, what are you going to do to fix it?"

Quinn stared at him. He broke eye contact with her and watched as she did her finger thing. Thumbs to fingers at warp speed. She fisted both hands and pressed them against her thighs. "I don't know. But I *will* fix it." Jake held his hand out for her apron and her name tag. "Your shift's almost over. Go out the back. I'll deal with everyone out there."

"But—"

"Just go. Figure it out. Go make a chart or something. Take the whole day off tomorrow too. Not just the morning."

Quinn nodded, then slipped out the back door.

* * * *

She walked halfway home—6,428 steps, to be exact—before she remembered she'd driven to work that morning, so she walked 6,428 steps back to fetch her car. She didn't want to go home yet because she didn't know what to say to her parents, Georgeanne especially. She was going to be furious when she found out what happened. *How many times has she told me to go easy on her friend Myron, and here the whole town thinks I accused him of murder?*

Quinn drove to the elementary school, all the students gone for the day.

She parked and wandered across the grass to the playground. The merry-go-round drifted in a slow path to the left, pushed by the slightest of breezes. The metal felt cold on her butt, even through her khakis, but it brought her back to some semblance of reality. Shifting her toes planted in the dirt caused her to sway from side to side, the rhythm methodic and comforting.

She felt her OCD monster stirring. Her breathing became faster, and she tried to remember what Mary-Louise Lovely had taught her. The FADE technique. She struggled to remember the acronym. She took three lung-expanding breaths, exhaling slowly after each one. She felt calmer, like maybe her brain would shift into gear again any minute now.

"Fade." Saying it once out loud didn't seem to help her memory. "Fade, fade, fade, fade, fade, fade, fade." But saying it seven times did.

"Focus on what exactly is going on." She picked up a pebble and tossed it from hand to hand. "I'm sitting in a playground afraid to go home." Another deep breath. True, but not really the point. Effect, but not cause. She tried again. "I said something in private to Loma, but she blabbed it to everyone with her stupid loud voice."

She threw the pebble where it bounced harmlessly off one of the swings. "Baba ghanoush." Another deep breath. "FADE. F is for focus... A is for... ask what my OCD monster wants me to do." She picked up another pebble and spoke to it. "He wants me to freak out about Loma, and my mom, and Chief Chestnut, and Donald Lee, and spiral into frantic, exhausting activity." She threw that pebble too, but didn't see where it landed. "D... decide. Decide if that's helpful. D should be for duh. It's never helpful."

Quinn gave a mighty push with her feet, then picked them off the ground, tucking them up under her on the base of the merry-go-round. She felt herself slowing and pushed off again, spinning herself faster and faster. She flung herself backward just like she'd done when she was a kid and watched the clouds spin above her until she felt queasy. Sitting up, she scuffed her feet in the dirt to slow down, finally coming to a stop. She inched her way to exactly the location where she'd sat previously, staring at the swings.

"No, it's not helpful," she whispered. "E is for establish." Deep breath. "Three things I can do to stay in control and not let my monster win." She stared at the swing set. *That's easy. Stuff my face with ice cream. Spend the rest of my life in my bedroom. Call Mary-Louise Lovely and have her tell me what to do.* Quinn came *this close* to pulling her phone from her pocket, despite knowing that her therapist would never tell her what to do. She flung herself backward again on the merry-go-round. "Three things, three things..." she muttered. She balled her fists when she realized she was doing her finger thing again.

The FADE technique was all about distraction. Distracting herself so the monster didn't take over.

She tried doing the description exercise Mary-Louise Lovely had taught her. *Clouds. They're white. Puffy. That one looks a little bit like Fang. Blue sky. Contrast with the leaves on the trees.* She sat up. *Swing set. Silver. Metal. Three swings. Black plastic seats. Chains. That one has been flung over the top to make it higher up. Probably by a bigger kid. Or one who wanted to prove how brave he or she was.*

Quinn cocked her head, staring but not seeing the swing set any longer. Brave. That was the key. That was the key to anything, really. Another deep breath. "I need to be brave. Prove one way or another about Chief Chestnut. He either did it, or he didn't. If he did, well, then, I solved another one. If he didn't, then I made this mess for him and I have to clean it up. That'll shut up the town."

And my monster.

* * * *

When Quinn got home, she already knew what she had to say to her mother. She began talking as she walked in the house. Before Georgeanne even turned around from the stove, Quinn was speaking. "I know you've already heard about what's going on, but I never meant for any of that to happen. I know you and Chief Chestnut are friends—and that's perfectly fine—but there is no love lost between him and me, so I'm going to figure this out because he either did it or he didn't and there's got to be a way to know one way or the other. I kinda think he did. But if he didn't kill Donald Lee, I owe it to him and to the whole town to clear his name. And for the record, I didn't say anything. I was talking to Loma, quietly telling her my theory, and she yelled it out loud in the diner. If you—and Chief Chestnut—should be mad at anyone, it's Loma. I know I am."

Georgeanne had been gazing at Quinn in silence, spoon dripping above the stew pot she'd been stirring.

After what seemed to Quinn like seven hundred years, Georgeanne finally said, "You do what you need to do," and turned back to the stove.

Quinn went to her room and collapsed on her bed in the fetal position, without even greeting Fang. She wasn't sure what she'd expected from Georgeanne, but that wasn't it. That wasn't quite true. Quinn was sure what she wanted from Georgeanne. She wanted her to be as outraged as she was with Loma and her indiscretion. Loma was loud, no doubt about it, but it usually only got her shushed at the movie theater. Most of the time it was fun. Loma and Quinn singing at the top of their lungs to the car radio. Loma laughing uproariously at some YouTube video. Loma telling funny stories whenever they were out. Injecting energy into any room, always the life of the party.

Until now.

Quinn sat up, swinging her feet to the floor. She picked up Fang's food and counted out his twenty flakes. "I'll do what I need to do, Mom," she whispered as she dropped a flake into Fang's bowl. She made a mental checklist as she watched him eat each flake.

Chapter 21

At dinner nobody talked about what was going on, but Dan made a valiant attempt to draw Quinn and Georgeanne into normal conversation. There was no anger, just an uncomfortable undercurrent of stress, things left unsaid, partially formed thoughts that shouldn't be uttered. He talked about his day at work, telling another funny story about an insurance claim he'd heard about. He talked about the linebacker the Broncos had just traded. He asked Quinn about the crossword she'd been working on. He asked Georgeanne how her piano recital plans were coming along.

All he received for his efforts were some short, lukewarm sentences with no details and no color. He might as well have been talking to Fang.

As soon as was reasonable, Quinn started clearing plates and began cleaning up, but both Georgeanne and Dan quickly told her they'd do it. Quinn didn't put up a fight and fled to her room, where she practiced her distraction exercises. She'd have to remember to ask Mary-Louise Lovely if describing every single thing in her room was truly an exercise to distract from her OCD behavior, or if she'd just managed to turn a promising therapy into yet another OCD behavior. She'd lost all perspective. Baba ghanoush. Yippee.

Loma had been texting and calling continuously, but Quinn had ignored each attempt at contact until now. She'd been thinking about it all day, so when Loma texted, *Are you mad?* Quinn didn't hold back.

OMG. SO MAD! She added thirteen angry face emojis just in case Loma had missed the shouty capital letters.

How many times do I have to apologize?

Quinn texted the "shrugging girl" emoji.

Then how will I know when you're not mad anymore?

Another shrugging girl emoji.

Loma texted the praying hands emoji.

Quinn didn't respond.

Loma texted five times in rapid succession.

Quinn.

Quinn.

Quinn.

You know I can do this all night, right?

QUINN.

Quinn stared at her phone without responding.

Listen, Q. I'm sorry I shouted like that, but c'mon! The Chief? Killing his own dad? It surprised me is all, and you know how I get. I'm sorry. This is coming out all wrong again. I don't mean for it to sound like what I did was your fault. At ALL. I'm just trying to get you to understand. I'm really, really, really, really, really REALLY sorry. Sorry x infinity. Please forgive me. What can I do to make it up to you?

When Quinn didn't respond to that, either, Loma texted one last time.

You have every right to be mad, but I have every right to try and get you to forgive me.

Quinn was miles away from forgiveness, so she turned off her phone and tried to go to sleep. That didn't work out so well, so she sat up in bed and stroked the wooden *Daruma* doll. She tried distracting herself by describing everything she noticed about it. It wasn't much. Roundish. Faded paint. Red here. Black there. Little white over here. Aged wood. Small lines and cracks. Miniscule writing on the bottom.

She squinted in one more attempt to decipher the signature of the artist, if that's really what it was. Maybe it was the owner's, like a kid scrawling their name on a toy, or like she did in high school when she wrote her name on all of her CDs in the ridiculously misguided notion that her parents might mistake her Smash Mouth, Vampire Weekend, or Red Hot Chili Peppers CDs for one of theirs.

The more she learned about the internment camp, the more important it became to her to try to reunite this little doll with its owner. People didn't sign their name on things unless they wanted—or expected—them back.

She swung out of bed and held the doll under the light from her bedside lamp, something she'd done a million times. She just saw the same thing—a little cartoon spider next to some indecipherable Japanese characters.

Dragging her computer to her lap, she pulled up her favorite search engine. She typed a *J* and immediately up popped all the websites that she'd already searched under *Japanese artist cartoon spider Daruma doll.*

Without clicking on any of them, she set aside her laptop and sighed. Her heart wasn't in it right now.

The only thing she could think about was how she was going to prove Chief Chestnut did or didn't kill Donald Lee.

Beany, his own mother, had said he was in a lot of fights. Why was he wearing Donald Lee's parka after he died? A trophy? And why did he give Georgeanne that plot of land? Did he know Donald Lee's bones were out there and he wanted to cast suspicion on her instead of himself?

Quinn slid open the drawer of her nightstand and pulled out a journal and three markers. She uncapped the purple one and gave it a sniff. Grape. She held it poised over a blank page, willing her hand to come up with a definitive plan of action.

Grapes might be willing to give you the benefit of their wisdom, but grape markers decidedly did not. No brainstorm. No flash of brilliance. No plan. No nothing. She capped the pen.

What's more, with the town divided, half of them wouldn't even be interested in talking to her, even if she came up with an investigative plan to go along with her vague theory.

Hopeless. It was all hopeless.

Chapter 22

Bleary-eyed, the next morning Quinn padded out to the kitchen, made herself a piece of peanut butter toast, and sipped a cup of coffee someone had already brewed. She hoped her mom and dad wouldn't come out before she'd finished because she was fairly certain she didn't want a replay of last night's awkward dinner. She gobbled her toast, topped off her coffee, and carried it back to her room to get ready for her therapy appointment in Denver.

She had extra time and wanted out of the house before her luck ran out and one or both of her parents made an appearance. She left early and swung by Rico's house, happy to see his car still in the driveway. She couldn't very well go talk to him at the station until all this blew over with Chief Chestnut.

Rico saw her walking up the sidewalk and waved her inside. "What brings you by so early?"

He was already in uniform, his necktie tucked inside his shirt between two of the middle buttons. She never understood that aspect of his uniform regulations. It did keep his tie out of his spaghetti, but it wasn't germane this morning. A plate of fried eggs and toast sat in front of him. He didn't bother getting up from the table.

"I wanted to ask you something." She moved his duty cap out of the way and sat.

"Let me guess. You wanted to ask how you always find yourself in these messes." Rico smiled at her.

"It's not funny. And it's not even my fault, not really. But no, that's not what I wanted to ask, thank you very much." She tossed him an annoyed look, then poured herself a cup of coffee and warmed up his.

"I'm sorry. I know you're upset, but this little storm will blow itself out soon enough." He took a sip.

She looked at him, incredulous. "You can't possibly believe that. You grew up here, you know how much everyone likes a good controversy. Who in their right mind would just walk away from that? But that's why I have to figure out whether he actually did it or not."

Rico's fork dropped limply toward his plate and hung from his fingers like a metronome. "I was afraid that's what you were going to say."

"I mean it, Rico. Logically, he either did it or he didn't. Right? I just have to prove it definitively one way or the other." She blew across the top of her coffee.

"How do you intend to do that?" Rico drained his cup, then used his last bite of toast to wipe the smear of egg yolk from his plate. He got up and poured himself another cup of coffee.

She continued blowing absentmindedly across the top of her mug. "Not sure. But I have a question for you."

"Fire away." He placed his dishes on the counter and turned to face her, leaning against the sink with his arms crossed.

"Aren't you going to rinse that?"

He glanced at his dishes, then at her. "That's your question?"

"I guess it's one of them." She gestured at the sink. "Aren't you? That egg yolk is going to be glued on by the time you get around to washing it."

He rolled his eyes by way of his answer but ran water and used his fork to scratch the egg yolk away. "Happy?"

"Ecstatic."

"What's your next question? Would you like to inspect my laundry?"

"Gross. No. I've been wondering. When exactly did Donald Lee go missing? Was it in the winter or closer to July?"

"Why? What are you getting at?"

"When I was talking to Beany—"

"You went to see Chief's mom? Does he know this?" Rico looked alarmed.

"I hope not, but yes, I went and had a conversation with her. She kind of rambles like my grandpa, but she made it sound like Donald Lee was getting ready to give Chief's sister a birthday present, but Marion said her birthday was in July—"

"You talked to Marion too?"

"Yes. Beany gave me her number. But anyway…Chief Chestnut said—"

"You talked to Chief about this? Directly? To his face?"

Quinn sighed. "He came into the diner after we heard those bones belonged to Donald Lee, and Jake and I gave him our condolences."

"Oh, well, he likes Jake."

"Anyway." Quinn drew the word out. "Chief Chestnut said it happened in the winter, Marion said it happened in the winter, but they were just kids and maybe they've forgotten. Beany made it sound like it happened in July."

Rico leaned against his spot at the sink again and recrossed his arms. "You think teenagers don't know the difference between winter and summer?"

"No, but...why wouldn't Donald Lee be wearing his heavy coat in a storm? And I didn't find any shoes out there, and I don't think CBI did, either. Did they?"

Rico stared into space, trying to remember. "No, not that I heard. But shoes and clothes could have been dragged off. I mean, his bones were scattered pretty far."

"But his shirt was there all disintegrated—"

"Stuck under a bush."

"And all the buttons had dropped off. But no big metal zipper off a disintegrated parka? And how long would it take before a big heavy coat like that would fall apart? I'm guessing lots longer than just a shirt."

Rico shook his head. "No idea. But maybe a coyote dragged it off to line her den or something."

"Maybe. But can you confirm what season it was?"

"Everything I've heard says it was winter."

"And no coat or shoes were found anywhere out there?"

"Not that I'm aware. I can check again, if you like."

"Thanks. Just text me. I won't be at work today."

A smile played at the corners of Rico's mouth. "Jake doesn't like you accusing the customers of murder?"

"Ha-ha. No. I have a therapy appointment this morning, and he gave me the whole day off." She paused. "Because he doesn't like me accusing the customers of murder," she said miserably.

Rico walked across the kitchen to where she leaned against the doorway. He wrapped his hand around hers. "Tell your therapist about your finger thing. You've been doing it since you walked in here."

Quinn looked down at her hands. She hadn't even been aware.

Chapter 23

On the way to Denver, Quinn had some time to think—about her therapy, about Loma, about Chief Chestnut.

She sat forlornly in the waiting room, the only patient there. If her life were a movie, she concluded, she'd be well into her Black Moment. Her OCD monster was in control, no matter how hard she tried to tame or distract him. She couldn't trust her best friend to keep her secrets. And she had no idea how to prove Chief Chestnut's involvement—or lack thereof—in Donald Lee's death all those years ago.

If her life were a movie, she'd probably walk out on it. Take her overpriced popcorn and Milk Duds and hightail it next door into the romantic comedy or even the western. This horror show she was starring in was not at all to her liking.

She pulled the *Daruma* doll from her bag so she'd have something to fiddle with while she waited. The last thing she wanted was for Mary-Louise Lovely to come out and see her doing her finger thing, or arranging the magazines yet again (she'd already fanned them in chronological order), or worse, grilling other patients about their problems. Quinn assumed she had learned her lesson about that, after she met a germophobe here and then made her problems a million times worse. She hadn't meant to do that, either, but she couldn't be sure it wouldn't happen again.

Quinn was once again staring at the bottom of the doll, completely engrossed in trying to decipher the markings, when Mary-Louise Lovely squatted next to her chair.

"What has so completely captured your attention here, Quinn?"

Quinn startled and held the doll out to her therapist. "I'm trying to figure out what this says next to the little spider."

Mary-Louise Lovely walked toward the window and held it in the sunshine streaming through. "Do you read Japanese? Because that's what that writing is. And it's not a spider, it's a mouse."

"A mouse?" Quinn jumped up and hurried over.

Mary-Louise Lovely used a fingernail to trace the tiny outline of the mouse she saw. Quinn squinted and moved closer.

"Oh! That's a crack, not a couple of little spider legs!"

Mary-Louise Lovely studied the *Daruma* before handing it back. "What is this, anyway? It looks old."

"I found it in a field across from that internment camp museum out near Chestnut Station. I'm trying to figure out if this is the artist's name and maybe, like, his logo or something. He probably made it while he was imprisoned at the camp. I thought maybe if I could track him down, then I could give it to one of his kids or grandkids." Quinn's ears and face suddenly felt impossibly hot. "It's a long shot, I know."

"But if anyone can figure it out, I'm sure you can. And it's a really sweet thing for you to do." Mary-Louise Lovely began walking toward her office. "Are you ready?"

Quinn took a deep breath. "As I'll ever be." She veered to grab her bag, then followed her therapist in. Quinn dug in her bag as she walked. "Oh, I almost forgot. I got this one for you." She handed Mary-Louise Lovely the *Daruma* doll she bought at the museum gift shop. "The thing about them is that they're little perseverance reminders, just like we talked about the other day. That saying of yours? 'Fall down seven times, get up eight?' That's actually a Japanese saying." Quinn proceeded to tell her everything she'd learned about *Daruma* dolls.

When she finished, Mary-Louise Lovely said, "Wow, that is cool. Thank you." She placed the gift at the edge of her desk and sat down.

Quinn began to put her faded *Daruma* into her bag. She looked at the bottom of it again as she sat down. "A mouse," she marveled. "I've shown this to everyone under the sun, and they all thought it was a spider too." She tilted her head. "Is this where we talk for an hour about the extended metaphor describing how only you seem to be able to show me the truth?"

Mary-Louise Lovely chuckled. "We can if you want, but I suspect it's just that my vision is exceptional. Always has been. But if you want to tell everyone what a great therapist I am"—she leaned forward, lowering her voice an octave and speaking slowly—"because I can see into your soul"—she straightened up again—"well, then, I won't stop you."

Quinn slipped the doll into her purse. "Nah, let's talk about me for a change."

"Much more interesting." Mary-Louise Lovely picked up her pen and pad and settled in. "So…I notice I haven't gotten any texts from you lately about the spice rack. How's that been going?"

"Badly. Can we do something different instead?"

"Of course. But why did it go so badly?"

"Because I couldn't let those stupid spices just stay in the wrong places."

Mary-Louise Lovely watched Quinn but remained silent. Quinn knew she was expected to elaborate, but she didn't feel like it. She also knew calling the spices "stupid" sounded petulant and childish.

When Mary-Louise Lovely realized Quinn wouldn't be more forthcoming, she said, "You seem angry and distracted. What's going on?"

Quinn picked at a hangnail. "I had a fight with my friend Loma."

"Do you want to talk about—"

"She got me in so much trouble, and now everyone hates me."

"Everyone?"

Quinn's eyes flashed. "Half of Chestnut Station, anyway."

Mary-Louise Lovely raised her eyebrows in a way that Quinn knew meant *I'm ready to listen if you're ready to talk.* And boy, was Quinn ready to talk.

"When I found that Japanese doll, Loma and I were out tromping in that field together. We also found some old bones, some old *human* bones."

Mary-Louise Lovely looked at Quinn with wide eyes. "Oh, my goodness! Are you sure they were human?"

"Absolutely. CBI—the Colorado Bureau of Investigation—even tested them. Based on some eyeglasses I also found out there, they determined the bones belonged to our police chief's father."

Mary-Louise Lovely's hand splayed across her breastbone.

"Right? Well, anyway, for…reasons, I mentioned to Loma that I thought maybe Chief Chestnut had something to do with it, and—get this—she blurted it out loud to the whole diner! Do you know how fast something like that spreads in a small town?"

"Like chlamydia in koalas?"

"I was going to say wildfire, but sure. Yours is more colorful." She cocked her head at her therapist. "Is that really a thing?"

"Yes. But go on."

Quinn sat back in her seat, ready for Mary-Louise Lovely to dissect Loma's behavior. "Can you believe Loma did that?"

Confusion flashed across Mary-Louise Lovely's face. "Let me make sure I understand. You're more upset about what Loma did than about stumbling on human remains?"

Now confusion passed across Quinn's face. "That happened a couple of weeks ago. The Loma thing just happened. Besides, they were just old bones, out there since the seventies." By her therapist's face, Quinn saw she still didn't seem to be getting it. "Bleached white? They looked like something from a movie set. I've seen an actual dead body and the aftermath of a murder up close and personal within the last few months."

Mary-Louise Lovely made a noise in her throat. "Yes, of course." She wrote something on her notepad. "We'll circle back to all that. So, what about this thing with you and Loma?"

"Isn't she horrible? How could she do that to me? It was so thoughtless. Don't you think so?"

They stared at each other for a bit. Quinn narrowed her eyes.

"You want me to agree with you, but you're trying to control the therapy. You know that's not how this works," Mary-Louise Lovely said. "And you don't need me to weigh in on a disagreement with your friend."

"But I'm the injured party here!" Quinn wailed.

"I understand you're feeling hurt by what Loma did, but is this really something you need me to help you sort through? We can spend your time here doing that if you'd like, but I'm wondering… Would that just be a way to put off talking about your OCD during this session?"

Quinn made a face. "You and your darn perfect vision peering into my soul."

Mary-Louise Lovely suppressed a smile.

"Fine. Let's talk about my stupid OCD." Quinn tried not to pout but thought she was probably unsuccessful.

"If you don't want to do the exercise with the spice rack, what do you want to tackle this week?"

Quinn stared at the floor. "I've been doing this thing with my fingers…" She didn't want to admit that the reason she wanted to work on her finger thing was because it was one of the few obvious, outward signs of her OCD that people noticed. And lately, everyone had been noticing. Jake, Loma, and Rico all mentioned it to her, but she was sure Georgeanne and Dan had taken notice, and who knew how many of the people in the diner had seen it too. She wondered suddenly about the Retireds. Surely they would have mentioned it, probably at length, but maybe their eyesight wasn't good enough to see something so subtle.

"Quinn?"

"Oh. Yeah. My finger thing." Quinn raised her right hand, then slowly touched thumb to each finger in turn. Then she did the same with her left hand. Then she began doing them in unison, then faster and faster, then like *the wave* in a sports arena. Finally she balled her fists and forced them into her lap. "I usually don't even know I'm doing it." She again stared at the floor.

"It's nothing to be ashamed of. I'm guessing you feel better when you do it? More in control?"

Quinn nodded but continued staring at the floor. "Until I become aware I'm doing it and don't know how long it's been going on."

"I can see how that might be disconcerting. And have people mentioned it to you?"

She nodded again.

"Look at me, Quinn."

She did.

"It's nothing to be ashamed of. It's no different from counting your steps when you walk, or alphabetizing the spices—"

"Which I'm also ashamed of, if we're keeping track."

"Let me rephrase. These are simply ways your brain has learned as a way of dealing with feeling out of control with your OCD."

"It's not my actual OCD?"

"They are so very closely linked it's hard to unravel them. We've talked before about how there's absolutely nothing wrong with any of these OCD-type behaviors. It's how you *feel* about them that becomes the problem. OCD is a feeling disorder, remember? Not a physical one."

"Well, then, I'm feeeeeling like I don't want to do any of it anymore."

"You know it's not that easy."

"I'm beginning to feeeeel that's true."

"What I'm hearing you say is that doing your finger thing, as you call it, makes you feel better and more in control until someone notices, or until you become aware you've been doing it unconsciously. And then you get embarrassed by it."

Quinn nodded.

"Let's do a little exercise. Come over in front of the mirror."

Quinn walked over to the full-length mirror hanging on the wall. "Mirror, mirror, on the wall, who's the OCD-est of them all?"

Mary-Louise Lovely let out a loud *pfft*. "You're such an overachiever. You're not even close."

Quinn laughed. "Are therapists supposed to say stuff like that?"

"Only the good ones." Mary-Louise Lovely adjusted Quinn's stance so Quinn's reflection was centered and the only one visible. "Okay, now do your finger thing the way you like, but while you're doing it, I want you to watch your hands and really concentrate on how it feels. How do your fingers feel? How do your thumbs feel? How do your arms feel? How do your shoulders feel? How does your neck feel?"

She stood silently, letting Quinn feel the sensations for a while.

"Now I want you to remain aware of the tactile sensation of it all, but also, tell me where and when you remember doing it lately."

"Just before I came here this morning, in Rico's kitchen." She cut her eyes at Mary-Louise Lovely, who tipped her chin, sending her attention back to the mirror. "He was the one who pointed it out to me. I didn't even realize." Quinn rolled her shoulders twice but kept feeling the sensations of her fingers and arms while she listed all the times and places she could remember doing her finger thing. She was shocked there were so many, but her therapist had the same sanguine look on her face when Quinn shook out her hands and snuck a peek at her.

"Okay, now I want you to put your hands in your pockets—"

"I don't have pockets. Women's clothes are so annoying."

"Just make fists then, down by your sides." Mary-Louise Lovely made her go through the same long list until she couldn't remember any more.

Quinn shook out her shoulders.

"We're going to do it one more time, but first we're going to do a little breathing exercise." She ran Quinn through a series of deep breaths with some calming imagery.

It didn't last long, but when it was over, Quinn said, "Wow. That was fantastic. I feel like melted ice cream."

Mary-Louise Lovely laughed. "First time anyone told me *that*." She had Quinn go through her list again while doing the finger thing. When she'd finished, she said, "This was just a way to increase your awareness that you're doing it and give you a different response so it's not just automatic." Mary-Louise Lovely glanced at the clock. "I want you to think about what all of those times and places have in common. Next time you know you'll be in a similar situation, do that breathing exercise, or just take a few deep, calming breaths and see if you can't remain aware that you're doing it." Quinn started to say something, but Mary-Louise Lovely waved her off. "You don't have to stop doing it. If it's something that calms you, makes you feel more in control, then there's no reason to stop. It's not the finger thing that bothers you. It's the not knowing you're doing the finger thing and having people point it out that bothers you. Right?"

"Twenty-twenty vision right into my soul, lady."

Chapter 24

Quinn was feeling calmer than she had in a long time. She'd had serious reservations about therapy, but was overjoyed now that she'd stuck with it. As she turned the key in her ignition, though, her serenity began to dissipate. She really didn't want to go home to the tension there, she couldn't face any insinuations and accusations from the residents of Chestnut Station that Bernard might be involved in Donald Lee's death, nor did she want to hear any theories about Chief Chestnut's potential guilt. She couldn't very well hang out with Loma, and Rico was on duty today. It annoyed her that her day off might be wasted.

"Where else can I go?" she murmured. Did she have any other business to attend to in Denver? Even though she'd lived in Denver for many years after college, she hadn't made friends or even any acquaintances she'd like to call and catch up with. She thought about her grandfather, and all the friends he'd left behind when he moved to Chestnut Station. Maybe she'd drive by his old house, for nostalgia's sake.

Grandpa's house. She opened up a search for Odell Nilssen's real estate office. She followed the driving directions and was sitting in his parking lot in twenty-three minutes, beating the time on the app, even though she wasn't convinced she was in the right place.

She glanced around the run-down strip mall in front of her. Sketchy marijuana dispensary with sketchy people loitering out front. Sketchy liquor store with sketchy people loitering out front. Sketchy massage parlor with furtive men scurrying inside. Sketchy payday lending establishment with heavily barred windows and doors. She was just about to double-check the address when she spied a sketchy door with peeling vinyl lettering: *Nilsse Real Off.*

As she debated whether it would be wise to enter the Nilssen Real Estate Office, she saw a perfectly non-sketchy-looking middle-aged woman yank open the door and stride in. She wore a sturdy, no-nonsense black handbag over one wrist that looked exactly like the one her grandmother used to carry. Quinn immediately felt a thousand times safer. Nothing bad could happen with a woman like that inside. After she formalized the details of her plan, Quinn followed her into the Nilsse Real Off.

The Real Off was, indeed, real awful, even worse than she'd expected. She had no control over the wrinkling of her nose, assaulted by the acrid stench of mildewed carpet, historical amounts of cigarette smoke that had seeped and settled into every nook and cranny of the concrete-block walls, all of it possibly mixed with the pungent aroma of unseen dead rodents. She hoped they'd remain unseen, that was.

She raised a delicate hand to her face, covering her nose and mouth, but trying to pretend she was simply shading her eyes, which made no sense as she entered a room darker, much darker, than the sunshine she longed to return to.

I'll just be here for a little bit, she told herself.

"Can I help you?" The grandmotherly woman with the sensible handbag spoke.

Quinn's eyes had adjusted enough to see, dismayed, that up close the woman looked extremely sketchy too. Garish fuchsia lipstick with a smear slashing across her yellowed teeth. Unfortunately dyed hair in every conceivable color, as if she was making her way through the grocery store do-it-yourself shelf of home hair color. And she was pouring herself bourbon into the coffee cup that sat on her desk, overflowing with paperwork.

The woman tossed back a slug from the mug, then cocked her head. "Do you need something, or you just gonna stare all day?"

"Oh, I'm sorry." Quinn shook her head, as if that would change anything. A human brain wasn't an actual Etch A Sketch, despite how often she tried. "It's just so sunny outside…and…so"—she couldn't come up with the right word—"in here."

The woman poured another shot, and a man came out from a hallway behind her holding out his mug. "It's about time you got here. I'm parched." When he saw Quinn, he was quick-witted enough to say, "You make the best coffee around here, Wanda."

Wanda rolled her eyes and tossed back another shot.

"And who do we have here?" The man placed his mug on Wanda's desk and held out his hand to Quinn. "I'm Odell Nilssen. Let me get you into one of my houses." His hair was thin, oily, and combed over. The rest of him was just thin and oily.

Quinn mentally pawed through her bag to see if she had enough hand sanitizer with her to warrant shaking his hand. She tentatively accepted his handshake. It was the first time she was happy to shake a limp fish like that. Less actual skin-to-skin contact. She swallowed hard, though. "My name is Quinn."

"Quinnnnn." Odell rolled it around in his mouth long enough that Quinn considered legally changing it the minute she left the Real Off. He ogled her like he was starving and she was a royal wedding banquet. "Here at Nilssen Real Estate, we're skilled in appraisals, and I'm here to tell you… you are priceless." He licked his lips cartoonishly. If he had a pencil-thin mustache, he would have twirled it.

Quinn choked down rising bile and got to the point. "I understand you were a friend of my grandfather, Bernard Dudley."

Odell barked out a laugh so loud it made Wanda spill a bit of her next shot of bourbon. "Dammit, Odell," she muttered. "Indoor voices."

"Bernard Dudley, good old Bernard." He smiled, showing his pointy badger teeth.

"So you were friends?"

His smile stayed, but he said, "Hated the guy," while he poured himself a triple, maybe quadruple, of bourbon. He motioned with the bottle. "Want a snort?" Quinn declined, trying to suppress a full-body shiver. He stared at her. "So you're Bernie's granddaughter." His eyes traveled up and down the full length of her again. She wished she'd thought to wear a layer of thermal underwear today. And all the rest of the clothes in her closet. "You know, the housing market goes up and down," he said. "But I bet you'll be hot forever."

"Gross." It just slipped out of Quinn's downturned mouth, causing Wanda to laugh using her outdoor voice. Quinn pretended none of it had happened. "You don't like my grandfather?"

Odell sipped his morning cocktail. "More like he doesn't like me. Wouldn't even consider signing a contract with me for a house he was selling in that armpit of a town we lived in." His smile was oily too.

Quinn ignored his dig at Chestnut Station. "What about Donald Lee Chestnut? Were you friends with him?"

Odell's smile slid off his face. He slammed back the rest of his drink. "Are you in the market for real estate or not?"

His change in demeanor scared Quinn, and she stammered, "No, I'm sorry to have bothered you," and race-walked back to her car. She saw

Odell standing on the sidewalk watching her, so she jammed the car into gear and fled. A few blocks away she pulled into a less sketchy strip mall and doused herself with hand sanitizer.

She calmed down on the drive home, but as she neared Chestnut Station, she still didn't want to go home, still couldn't face the gossip of the townspeople, and hanging out with Loma and Rico was still off the table. The museum. That would cleanse her palate after her encounter with Odell Nilssen. "I'll go listen to some more of those first-person accounts. Maybe someone will be around to talk about my *Daruma*."

When Quinn got to the museum, the weather was Colorado glorious—78 degrees, cobalt-blue sky with just a few puffy clouds, the tiniest of breezes. She sat on the bench of a picnic table, but with her back to the table, taking in and admiring the view of the grounds. The landscape was groomed near the outdoor exhibits, but left natural. Prairie grasses, native flowers, towering trees. The faint odor of skunk—or maybe it was a den of garter snakes—hung in the air, gentle on the breeze kissing her cheek. If the odor had been stronger, more pungent, she would have been on edge, but she knew you could smell a skunk from more than five miles away. Maybe more out here, where the scent could travel for a huge expanse unencumbered by buildings or competing with man-made smells.

She had the grounds to herself. With closed eyes, she listened to the sounds of the prairie. The trill of the meadowlark always made her smile. She could identify its song, but she wasn't sure she could pick the actual bird out of a lineup. Didn't matter, the song was the important part. She watched bright yellow goldfinches not much bigger than her finger perch and sway on top of the wild goldenrod that dotted the area. Bossy magpies, the biggest ones Quinn had ever seen, pecked divots out of the dirt searching for tasty earwigs, worms, and spiders. A bushy-tailed squirrel and a sleek chipmunk began an argument over a misshapen pinecone. It was one of the skinny kind, not the beautiful full pine cones you'd see in a Christmas craft. Instead of looking like a torpedo, it had grown into more of a *J* shape, with a dramatic bend.

The chipmunk, a fraction of the size of the squirrel—and not much bigger than the pinecone—had the benefit of speed and proximity to the ground to snatch and grab. But when the squirrel noticed the theft, it began chasing and chittering until the chipmunk dropped the prize. The squirrel grabbed it in his mouth and disappeared up a blue spruce so wide around at the skirt, it must have easily been a hundred years old. Quinn could only imagine how many pinecones regularly dropped out of that towering tree and wondered why the creatures felt they had to fight over that particular misshapen one.

Quinn thought about how much wildlife was out here. For every animal she saw, she suspected there were a hundred she didn't. There'd be whitetail deer, maybe antelope, coyotes, foxes, all kinds of birds, rabbits, raccoons, rodents...all of which would stake their claim on whatever would help them survive.

The squirrel, or perhaps a different one, Quinn couldn't tell, skittered down the spruce and dropped the misshapen pinecone on the ground before skittering back up.

The chipmunk stood on hind legs and scrutinized the situation, perhaps remembering the lesson about the Trojan horse from chipmunk school. He took some tentative steps toward the pinecone, sniffing it and the breeze, even risking a glance at Quinn to see if she might be involved in this potential subterfuge.

When he reached the pinecone, he placed a wary paw on it. When nothing bad happened, he gave it a tiny shove. The pinecone rolled over and landed with an awkward clunk due to its peculiar shape. The chipmunk skittered backward a few steps, but when the pinecone remained inert, he raced over and snatched it up, carrying it under the purple canopy of the nearest Russian sage.

The idea of the squirrel giving the chipmunk its hard-won prize tickled Quinn, and she let out a merry laugh. Or maybe that was the squirrel wife who, when learning her squirrel husband had swiped that pinecone from their chipmunk neighbor, returned it with her apologies. Or maybe she didn't appreciate her husband dragging a less-than-perfect pinecone into their well-ordered household.

Quinn wondered if squirrels could get OCD.

At any rate, she was relieved the drama had ended with a gift to the adorable chubby-cheeked chipmunk. Squirrel sightings were a dime a dozen in Chestnut Station, but chipmunks weren't as abundant for some reason. It felt to Quinn like a tiny gift the day had given her.

She wondered about all the unseen wildlife having adventures and achievements like this chipmunk. She shaded her eyes and glanced in the direction of the field where they'd found Donald Lee's bones, or at least where she thought the field was. It was hard to tell on this flat land. Nature always seemed harsh to Quinn, so she wondered about the rarity of this little exchange she'd witnessed.

Would the coyotes have purposely left the gift of some meat on the bones for the magpies to scavenge? Would the magpies use their sharp beaks to crack open the bones for the smaller birds or mice to reach the marrow? Would the foxes leave anything for the rabbits? It seemed unlikely, and yet it remained undisputable that everything survived just fine out here on the prairie.

Except Donald Lee, of course. Nobody left him a gift.

A wave of sadness washed over Quinn when she remembered Beany telling her that Donald Lee had a gift he wasn't able to give his daughter. With a start, she thought maybe it was the *Daruma* doll she'd found. Everything else they found in the vicinity of the bleached bones belonged to Donald Lee, so why would the doll be any different? Quinn squinched her eyes, trying to determine exactly where she'd found the faded toy. How many steps had she taken before reaching that skull?

She shook her head, memory failing her. If she'd found the bones first and then the doll, it would have made more of an impression, she presumed.

She pulled the *Daruma* from her bag, gently rubbing the smooth, worn wood, then setting it on the table behind her. She dialed Marion's number. Maybe Marion collected *Darumas* and this was another Donald Lee intended for her collection. That would at least solve one of these mysteries.

Marion's voice mailbox was full, so Quinn tried the home number Beany had given her. A deep male voice answered.

"I'm looking for Marion."

"She's at the shelter."

"She must volunteer there a lot," Quinn said.

The man laughed good-naturedly. "Marion is the founder of the shelter. Not only does she volunteer, she also fund-raises, staffs the place, cooks meals, and cleans the bathrooms on occasion." He sounded proud, Quinn thought, not like he was complaining. "Have you tried her cell?" he asked.

"Yes, the mailbox was full."

"Typical. I can take a message if you like."

"Thanks. Just tell her it's Quinn and I had a quick question for her. Make sure she knows it's not urgent. Not about her mother or anything. Maybe I'll try texting her later."

"Will do."

Quinn retrieved the *Daruma* doll as she tried to formulate how the curator—if they were even there today—could help her decipher it. Even if it was intended for Marion, Quinn still wanted to know who the artist was, and assumed Marion would too. Part of the problem was that it was so faint and faded. But now that the contours of the mouse logo were so obvious, maybe the rest would come easier.

Quinn pulled a mechanical pencil from her bag and clicked it. Holding the *Daruma* in the bright sunlight just at the edge of the picnic table, she leaned with her elbows on her knees and her face just an inch or two from it. She began gently and carefully dotting along the faint lines of the cartoon mouse taking clear shape with each poke of the pencil. When she'd made the outline of the mouse as clear as she could, she began the painstaking process of attempting the same with the Japanese characters. The problem with that, she realized, was her lack of any sort of knowledge about Japanese writing. She could only rely on her eyesight and the bright sunshine to help her. Since her eyesight was dubious, as was made very clear to her by Mary-Louise Lovely a couple of hours ago, she had no idea the outcome of her endeavors. It was a good thing she was enjoying the weather so much.

A flash of movement out of the corner of her eye made Quinn turn in time to see a pencil-sized garter snake flick out its tongue, getting a taste of its surroundings. It dove back into the weeds when a car drove up and expelled an Asian family of two women, a man, and three rowdy elementary school–age boys.

"Grandma, can you read this? Some of it is in Japanese!" One of the boys had raced over to the kiosk with the map of the museum grounds almost before the adults were out of the car. Without waiting for her to answer, he challenged his brothers to a footrace and they sped off, kicking up gravel.

"I'm so sorry," the younger woman said to Quinn. "We've been in the car for a while."

"No worries." Quinn straightened up, smiled at her, and stretched her back.

The woman turned to the man while she sauntered away. "Honey, we'd better let them blow off some steam out here for a while before we go in."

The man held the older woman by her elbow as they meandered around the outside exhibits.

Quinn snuck curious glances at the family while she worked, wondering if they had any historical ties to this place. She wanted to ask, but didn't want to seem rude. Just because they were Japanese didn't mean anything. After all, just because Quinn went to the Pro Rodeo museum didn't mean she barrel raced.

She was studying her handiwork, completely stuck as to where she should fill in next, when the older woman approached. "May I sit?" she asked.

"Of course." Quinn scooted down to make more room on the bench, now the only table with shade.

The elderly woman studied Quinn studying the bottom of the doll. "That's a very old *Daruma* you have there."

"It seems to be. I'm trying to decipher what it says here on the bottom." Quinn pointed to the writing, then handed the doll to the woman. Quinn thought about the boy's question earlier. "You wouldn't happen to read Japanese, would you?"

"I would. I was born in Osaka and lived there until I was a teenager." The woman squinted for a long time at the doll. Finally she said, "That's not Japanese. That's a picture of a mouse."

Quinn leaned over and pointed again. "I think these are Japanese characters."

The woman handed the *Daruma* back to Quinn. "These old eyes won't be any help to you." She called to the man. "Elliott, come here for a minute."

He hurried over. "Are you all right, Mom?"

"I'm fine. But this girl needs some translating help."

He laughed. "Forgot all your Japanese, Mom?"

"I just can't see it well enough, smartypants. Can you make it out?" She handed the doll to him.

"That's a cartoon mouse."

"Next to it," Quinn and the woman said simultaneously.

The three boys raced over, kicking up gravel, wanting to know what was going on. The man turned the doll every which way, finally handing it back to Quinn. "I think that might be an artist's mark and signature."

"Can you make out the signature?" Quinn asked hopefully.

He shrugged. "It might be Ichikawa, but I'm not sure. It's so faint."

Quinn pulled a small spiral notepad from her bag. She held out the pencil and pad to him. "Could you please draw the characters for Ichikawa, so I can try to compare it?"

"Sure." He made some beautiful marks on the page, then showed it to his mother, who nodded her approval.

He handed the notepad back to Quinn, and with her index finger she lightly traced what he'd drawn.

The boys began tugging on the adults' hands.

"Can't we go in?"

"I'm bored."

"Is there a gift shop in there?"

The mom rolled her eyes at Quinn, and the family disappeared into the museum, leaving Quinn alone again.

She compared the faint marks to the character drawn by the man. "Ichikawa," she said softly, tracing the image again. "Is that you? Did you make this?"

Quinn turned the *Daruma* over and stared at the faint outlines of the missing eyes. She knew this doll represented two tasks in front of her, one she wanted to do, and one she felt obligated to do. She wanted to find the artist or owner of the *Daruma*. But she needed to figure out about Donald Lee, making sure Bernard's name remained untarnished and determine one way or the other if Chief Chestnut was involved in his father's death.

Try as she might, however, she couldn't figure out a valid way to investigate Chief Chestnut. She couldn't let go of the idea of his involvement but had to acknowledge that if the CBI concluded there was no case, then maybe there really was no case.

It also weighed on her that she only had Wilbur's assurance that her grandfather wasn't involved, but she couldn't figure out how to determine once and for all that Bernard wasn't guilty. For all she knew, now that the entire town was talking about it, Abe the handyman's accusation was on the lips of everyone and Chief Chestnut was doing his own investigation into her grandfather. What better way to keep suspicion off himself?

She called Rico and asked him point-blank. "Is anyone at the Chestnut Station Police Department investigating Bernard Dudley for the murder of Donald Lee Chestnut?"

"Who is this?"

"Very funny. Just answer the question."

"No. Nobody at the Chestnut Station Police Department is investigating Bernard Dudley for the murder of Donald Lee Chestnut. Why do you ask?"

"What about the CBI?"

Rico's voice dropped to a quieter, more serious level. "Quinn, what's going on?"

"Nothing. Well, maybe a little something. Abe said he thought Grandpa could be a prime suspect and—"

"And your brain is going a mile a minute. Take a breath." After she blew a tornado into the phone, he said, "Do you think your grandpa is the prime suspect in Donald Lee's murder?"

Quinn thought about Odell Nilssen. "No. I'm just being silly."

"There's no murder investigation open on Donald Lee—"

"That you know of."

"That I know of. But I'd be the one to know, now, wouldn't I?"

"Yes," she said. "I guess you would."

"Okay. I'll see you at lunch."

"I'm not working today."

"And this is how you're spending your day off?"

"I'm actually out at the museum at Camp Chestnut. It's a beautiful day, and I'm working on the mystery of this *Daruma* doll." Quinn didn't tell him what she'd be doing after she left the museum.

* * * *

The sun had crept up past her ankles while she sat using her mechanical pencil to carefully place dots along what she hoped were the characters forming the name Ichikawa. As she studied her handiwork, a shadow fell across the doll, startling her.

A middle-aged woman in slacks and a blazer stood before her. "Oh! I'm so sorry! I didn't mean to startle you. I was just curious about what you were doing out here. Most visitors to the museum keep on the move out here, just glance at the exhibits on their way to climb the guard tower. Unless they've brought a picnic."

"No picnic for me, and I've been to the guard tower already. It's really cool up there." Quinn blanched. "I mean, it's terrible that it's a guard tower, but...the view," she ended weakly.

"I know. I still find it hard to wrap my mind around this place, and I've been the director out here for seven years." She held out her hand. "I'm Colleen Murray."

"Quinn Carr. I don't think I've ever seen you in town before. I work at the diner, and most people come through there at some point."

Colleen hitched a thumb over her shoulder. "I live the other direction, closer to Burlington." She pointed at Quinn's project. "Is that a *Daruma* doll?"

Quinn offered it to her. "Yes. Can you tell me anything about it? I found it in the field the other day." She waved vaguely across the road.

Colleen turned the *Daruma* over and over, finally squinting at the markings on the bottom. "I don't really know anything more about *Daruma*s than what's in the exhibit we have inside. Have you been in there yet?"

Quinn nodded. "Now that I know what it is, I'm trying to see if I can figure out if this is the artist's signature or maybe the owner to see if I can track them down. I was lucky enough that one of your visitors today might have cracked the code for me." Quinn displayed the notepad with the characters Elliott had drawn so they could compare them to the *Daruma*.

"Ooh, I love a good quest. Is there anything I can do to help?"

"Maybe." Quinn thought for a minute, thinking about how Donald Lee might have come in contact with this particular *Daruma* doll. "I saw from the exhibits inside that this camp was like a little town, and it even had an art studio." Colleen nodded. "Is it possible that whoever made this doll was locked up in here and, I don't know, sold them in town or something?"

"It's certainly possible the artist lived here, but I doubt he sold them outside the camp. Maybe he sold some inside the camp, to other inmates, but not a lot of money changed hands here."

Quinn did some quick math. Even if this artist had sold these to shopkeepers in Chestnut Station during the war years, how would Donald Lee have gotten his hands on it in the 1970s?

"If the artist lived here, how do you think this got out into that field?"

Colleen glanced across the road and shrugged. "Inmates left camp on occasion. Some held positions that required them to go to town every so often to do business for the camp. They'd have to be trusted inmates, of course. And there were townspeople coming and going all the time. Maybe one of them picked it up?"

"Maybe." Quinn's theory that Donald Lee had something to do with this doll was fading fast.

"Have you used the computers inside yet?"

Quinn nodded. "I listened to some of the first-person accounts of life here. Really fascinating. And sad."

"I agree. On both counts." They held a respectful silence.

"On those computers inside...is there a listing of all the internees?" Quinn asked.

"Oh, yes. That's one of the first things we did. We wanted people to be able to see if their people were sent here. Most families talked fairly openly about their time in the camps, but not all of them."

"So I can go in and search for any Ichikawas who were imprisoned here? Maybe find my artist?"

"Absolutely."

Quinn gathered up her things and followed Colleen into the museum. Colleen said, "Let me just put my things away, and I'll help you with the computers."

"No need. I know where they are."

"Well, give me a holler if I can help." She bustled away, greeting the family in the gift shop area, where the three boys were trying to decide on the best souvenirs to buy. Apparently they were using their own money because one was trying to get them to pool their money, much to the dubious reservations of the other two.

Quinn paid her admission and stuffed a ten-dollar bill into the donation box before signing in with a docent to use the computer.

An hour later, she left with a list of all the Ichikawas who had been incarcerated there. She'd have to research their specifics some other time, but she felt much closer to solving the mystery of the *Daruma* doll, and maybe how it came to be out in that field.

If only she felt like she was getting anywhere solving the mystery of how Donald Lee came to be out there as well.

Chapter 25

From the museum, Quinn headed to the county clerk's office to have another chat with Sandy. After some small talk about the weather, Quinn said, "Can you show me that map we were looking at again? I've been thinking about it and wanted to ask you something."

"Sure." Sandy dragged the big leather-bound book to the table near her desk and used her whole arm to flip the pages. "Here it is." She puffed from the exertion.

Quinn leaned over the book and pointed at some of the small properties that she saw up on the maps in the guard tower. "Out at the museum at Camp Chestnut, they have some maps of the area covered in Lucite or something—"

Sandy nodded. "Yeah, I've seen them."

"But they're not very clear. I was trying to figure out who all these small properties belong to." Quinn pointed to several of the finger-shaped farms and properties that seem to be poking into the big belly of all the Chestnut land.

"I think it's… Let me just check to be sure." Sandy plucked a magnifying glass off her desk and leaned close to the map. She wrote down a number, then waddled over to her computer. She plopped down into her chair, causing the pneumatic lift to hiss and drop her an extra inch. After consulting her sticky note with her password and typing it in, she next typed the number that she'd written down. "I thought so." She swiveled her chair toward Quinn. "Read me those other numbers."

Quinn picked up the magnifier and rattled off the lot numbers to Sandy.

"Yep. All those belong to a man named Odell Nilssen, Junior."

Quinn dropped the magnifier, and her face puckered like she sucked a lemon. "I met him today."

"I could have guessed by the look on your face. Still as smarmy as ever, I take it."

"Ugh. He's the worst. Worse than the worst."

"Always been that way. A while back, late sixties or early seventies, when all the farmers were struggling and the banks were foreclosing, Nilssen got it in his head to offer them pennies on the dollar and buy them out. But he didn't do his homework."

"What do you mean?"

Sandy struggled to her feet and joined Quinn in front of the map. "Look at the properties he bought." She pointed them out, tapping her finger on each one. "See how they're all spread out?"

Quinn nodded.

"He had grand plans to develop some big thing out there, can't remember what. Golf resort? Amusement park?"

"An amusement park next to an internment camp museum?" Quinn asked incredulously.

"Well, that wasn't there at the time, but it wouldn't have stopped him." Sandy snapped her fingers. "Outlet mall. That's what it was. So anyway, he started buying up all these tiny properties from those poor farmers who really had no other choice but to sell for what little they could get from him. It was either that or let the bank take it outright."

"How awful." Quinn didn't think it was possible for her to dislike Odell Nilssen even more. And yet now she did.

"Turns out the joke was on him anyway. It was like he never looked at a map. None of the properties he bought even touched one another. Not contiguous, they say in the property biz."

"So he couldn't develop any of it." Quinn smirked. "Should have done his homework."

"Best part of this whole story, though, is that he couldn't even sell the property back to the farmers because Daniel Chestnut found out about Odell's little scheme and sold all the farmers parcels from his own property. Gave them all better property at better terms, and Daniel carried the paper so the farmers didn't have to be beholden to the banks."

Quinn politely ignored Sandy's misidentification of Donald Lee's name.

"Poor ol' Odell has never been able to sell off any of the land he bought. Lost his shirt."

"Serves him right," Quinn said.

"Damn skippy."

Chapter 26

Quinn left the county clerk's office with a new number-one suspect. It was clear now why Odell Nilssen clammed up when she mentioned Donald Lee. If he was still miffed at Bernard for a little thing like not letting him be the Realtor on record when he sold his house to Georgeanne and Dan, imagine the pure hatred that must have coursed through Nilssen's veins every day knowing how he'd been bested by Donald Lee and would never see his outlet mall come to fruition.

Both Bernard's and Chief Chestnut's involvement seemed inconsequential now.

Even though Quinn knew that Chief Chestnut didn't want to pursue the circumstances of his father's death, she also knew he needed to arrest Odell Nilssen for the murder of Donald Lee Chestnut.

Marion hadn't returned her call yet. Quinn tried her cell, but got the full voice-mail message. She decided to shoot off an email to Marion, rather than texting, since this conversation was a bit more formal.

Even though they had become friendly, bonding over their love of the old *Cagney & Lacey* TV show, Quinn wanted to be very precise right now. It had been fun emailing and texting old clips and trivia back and forth, trying to see who was really the number-one fan. So far Quinn was well in the lead because Marion didn't have the benefit of an entire set of the seven seasons on videotape, no less, bequeathed to her by a neighbor. Quinn spent an entire summer as a child with every waking moment spent watching each episode repeatedly, then color-coding them with a complicated formula involving whether she had figured out the killer and the cuteness of any guest stars. Marion didn't stand a chance.

But this was different. Quinn composed her message to Marion carefully. "I know this might be a touchy subject with you and your brother, but there's gossip linking my grandpa to your father's death. It's absolutely false, though, and there's a guy by the name of Odell Nilssen, Junior, who might actually be responsible for Donald Lee's death. I hate the idea of my grandpa having his reputation tarnished"—she went back and added "elderly" before grandpa—"this late in his life, when it's hard for him to stick up for himself. Would it be possible for you to prod Myron to look into this Odell Nilssen? It might give some closure for you in your dad's death. I know your brother doesn't really care about that, but maybe you do? If you could convince him, it would also be a way to exonerate my grandfather"—she paused and then added—"before he dies." Bernard Dudley was healthier than most people his age and many who were much younger, but she hoped to appeal to Marion's emotions. "If you could talk to your brother, I'd really appreciate it." Quinn thought about attaching a YouTube clip of Cagney and/or Lacey fighting crime and/or sexism in the workplace, but decided against it. This was too serious.

After she pressed send, she set about making a crossword puzzle to plant that seed in another way in Chief Chestnut's mind. The theme would be real estate, but she already knew ODELL would be the answer to the clue, "Brewing company in Fort Collins," and NILSSON would be the answer to the clue, "Everybody's Talkin' singer." The spelling of Harry Nilsson's name was a little off, but she didn't think that would matter for her purposes.

With so many theme words as entries, it was very difficult to set up the grid and place the black squares properly. It was already late before she even started filling in the entries, but she finally finished placing all of them into the grid, and allowed herself a satisfied sigh.

Writing the clues was much easier and definitely more fun. She breezed through them until she came to a screeching halt when she went to write the clue for 58-down, almost the last one she needed to write. "Oh no!" she wailed, then clamped a hand over her mouth. Her voice was so much louder this early in the morning. She stared in dismay at her beautiful puzzle. She hadn't seen it earlier, but now the word she'd duplicated seemed like it flashed in neon from the screen. How had she not noticed using the same word? "It's like the number-one rule in making crosswords," she whispered to Fang.

Fang shook his head and blew a very judgmental bubble at her.

"I know! You don't have to rub it in." Quinn stared at the grid, trying to see a way to fix either of the quadrants and change one of the words.

Her brain was too frazzled. All the letters looked like hieroglyphics at this late hour. She used both hands to rub her face as she came to a decision.

She left them both in the puzzle, hoped her idol, Will Shortz, never saw, and wrote what she thought was a funny clue for 58-down.

Then she held her breath while she emailed it to Vera with a plea to publish it in the next edition.

ODELL NILSSEN PUZZLE

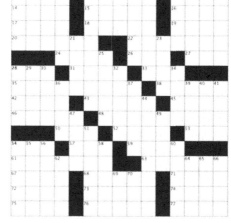

ACROSS

1. Slangy insult
5. Brewing company in Fort Collins
10. With 63-across, industry involved in buying and selling housing
14. Part of a foot
15. Slammer
16. British bum
17. Scientific agency dealing with major waterways, for short
18. Award given by the Mystery Writers of America
19. Juan's kitty
20. One of a reindeer's set
22. Everybody's Talkin' singer
24. Flair
26. H.S. curriculum subj.
27. Before, poetically
28. Palindromic women's name
31. Located on the peak
33. The Old Man and the ___
35. Someone who works to construct buildings on a piece of property
38. East coast, west coast, or on a playground
42. Spot to build a house
43. Taken back Outbacks
45. Word before hygiene, argument, or tradition
46. Seat for second-stringer
48. Buying property hoping to resell at a profit
50. "___ Just Not That Into You"
52. ___ Saint Laurent
53. Georgeanne Carr ___ Dudley
54. When doubled, a large biting fly
57. Tough ___ to follow
59. Rotten little twerp
61. Person with lots to show you?
63. See 10-across
67. Paintballs, snowballs, and cannonballs, for short
68. The lowest point
71. Milo's canine friend
72. Conked out
73. Teach
74. Dessert wine
75. Cicero's "to be"
76. Dr. who wrote "The Lorax"
77. Hook's sidekick in "Peter Pan"

DOWN

1. Delaney, Carvey, or Perino
2. Pump this to get strong
3. "Shoo, Garfield!"
4. Easily flaked sedimentary rock
5. Sade's "Smooth ___"
6. U.S. agency supervising nat'l security
7. Heart chart, for short
8. Emulates a Pisa tower
9. 5-down's include "Coast to coast, LA to Chicago"
10. ___ to riches
11. Rub to delete
12. Richest passenger on the Titanic when it sunk
13. Sierra ___
21. Israeli airline
23. "Big Little ___"
25. "Yup" opposites
28. Brylcreem amount?
29. Editor's removal instruction
30. Shakespeare's river
32. Energetic
34. Runaway soldier, (abbr.)
36. ___ A Sketch
37. With Wade, landmark Supreme Court ruling protecting womens' rights
39. You raced from a Middle Eastern country
40. Children's book series "___ the Great"
41. TV show set in a high school
44. "This tour's a great drive! The ___ gorgeous!"
47. Furnace output
49. GI hangouts
51. Treats often served with clotted cream
54. Swap
55. They're more important than quarters
56. Charles or Ray, famous for a modern lounge chair
58. If you swap this for 54-down, you get the same thing!
60. Sunroof choices (hyph)
62. Miner's bonanza
64. Eensy weensy thing
65. One of four on a car
66. Sunrise direction in Guadalajara
69. Fishing town in western India known for its fortress and old Portuguese cathedral
70. "No ___, ands, or buts!"

Chapter 27

Even though her eyes and brain were bleary from puzzle creation, Quinn still couldn't fall asleep. In an attempt to battle her OCD monster about that duplicate word, she used distraction, focusing instead on a deep dive into the internet searching the Ichikawa name. She traveled down so many wrong paths looking for the correct Ichikawa, she began to doubt she'd ever find him. Or her. What was worse, though, was the nagging feeling that even though she might find the *Daruma* artist, what did it have to do with anything? The odds were crazy that this was the gift Donald Lee was going to give Marion. And even if she could link the *Daruma* to Donald Lee, so what?

The only reason she kept investigating was, well, her OCD, but also if she could find a link, it would be a gift for Marion. Or would it? Quinn had no experience with bad fathers. She'd surely love a token from her own father if he had disappeared when she was a teenager, knowing he'd been thinking about her at the time of his death. But her father was fantastic and loving. How would she feel receiving something like that if she knew her father was about to desert the family for a job in Alaska?

Quinn wondered if she should even share what she found out about the *daruma* doll with Marion. "Ah well," she said quietly to Fang as she crawled out of bed. "That's a bridge to cross if I actually find out anything." She pressed her index finger on the side of the bowl, and he swam over to her. "I need a snack. How 'bout you?"

Fang blew a bubble that broke on the surface. Quinn used the tweezers to pluck one flake from the jar of food. He gobbled it up almost before it hit, then blew another bubble.

Quinn accepted it as a thank-you and not a fishy belch.

She turned on lights as she made her way to the kitchen, trying to be as quiet as possible so as not to wake her parents. She grabbed a box of graham crackers but tiptoed into the living room before opening its crinkly packaging.

Quinn hadn't finished cleaning out Grandpa's desk. She'd wanted to, every time she walked into the living room. She stared at all the drawers and cubbies she hadn't cleaned and organized yet. Maybe just that little one. Her hand reached out. She yanked it back.

No, she scolded herself. She didn't want to fail the test she'd set out for herself. Just as importantly—maybe more importantly—she didn't want to find any more surprises that might upset Georgeanne or cast Grandpa in a bad light.

Nobody else had touched the desk, either. The pile of books she'd set on it were still in the exact place she'd left them. She plucked off the top one, *Grimm's Fairy Tales*, and settled into the corner of the couch with it and a sleeve of graham crackers. A book and a snack would distract her.

She tucked her feet up under her and tugged on the noisy plastic wrapping. Pulling it apart in super slo-mo was the only way to keep her midnight snacking quiet. Not that her parents would care. They were much more concerned about her *not* eating because that was a sure sign her depression had roared back. Quinn had finally begun putting a bit of weight back on.

The package of graham crackers open beside her, Quinn thumbed through the fairy tales. She'd never actually opened this book, even though it had been in the same place on the living room shelves for as long as she could remember. It was a gorgeously illustrated edition. She flipped through the pages studying the artwork and seeing many of the well-known stories she was familiar with. Rapunzel. Little Red Riding Hood. Cinderella. The Bremen Town Musicians. There were more she'd never heard of, however, and she stopped to read one called "Mary's Child."

It was all about a girl who told lies who grew up to be a woman who told lies, even though it cost her the lives of her children and condemned her to death. At the last minute, the woman confessed and was spared, and her children were brought back to life and returned to her.

The entire premise was far-fetched and heavy-handed, Quinn thought, munching graham crackers, but it was probably written to teach kids not to tell lies. Weren't all fables and fairy tales used as teachable moments back in the day? But in this story, those poor kids were the pawns. They were taken away solely because of the sins of the mother.

Quinn nibbled one more graham cracker, surprised to see she'd plowed through almost the entire sleeve. "I wonder which fable is supposed to teach kids not to eat so many cookies?" she murmured before returning the book to the stack on Grandpa's desk. As quietly as she could, she closed up the crinkly paper in the box. Halfway to the kitchen, she noticed the crumbs she'd dropped in a trail across the floor. "Oh, yeah. Hansel and Gretel."

Chapter 28

Loma was waiting for Quinn outside the diner early the next morning before her breakfast shift. Jethro seemed miffed by the encroachment into his space. Loma held two coffees and handed one to Quinn.

Quinn stared at her outstretched hand. "You know I work in a place with coffee. In fact, I usually make it." She squatted to give Jethro a good-morning face rub.

"I know. This is a peace offering." Loma wiggled the cup at her. "The only other thing open so early in this town is the gas station out by the highway. Didn't think you'd want windshield wiper fluid."

Quinn stood, wiping Jethro's drool from her hand, and took the cup. "This probably tastes better." Taste didn't matter, though. She knew she'd never get enough coffee today.

"Don't count on it. It's from the gas station too."

Quinn couldn't help but smile as she unlocked the door. "Inside, you goof."

Loma wrapped her in a bear hug from behind. "I've missed you!"

"Fine. Whatever." Quinn tried to pretend she hadn't missed Loma, but her friend saw right through her ruse.

When they got inside, Loma did a bump-and-grind while singing, "Quinny-poo done missed me, Quinny-poo done missed me."

Jake came out of the kitchen wiping his hands on his apron. "Oh, should've known it was you caterwauling."

Loma danced up on him, grinding and twerking. He laughed and backed away, but she kept after him.

"You used to love dancing with me." Loma pouted melodramatically.

"I just pretended to, for the sake of a happy marriage."

"You're such a bad liar." Loma wiped a sheen of sweat from her brow while she retrieved her coffee. "Got any bear claws to get rid of the taste of this coffee?" she asked him.

"You mean diabetes claws? No, not for you, my love. I can rustle you up a bowl of berries, though." Jake was constantly on Loma to take better care of herself, now that she'd been diagnosed.

"Fine. If that's all you're offering." Loma waggled her eyebrows at him.

Quinn had never seen two divorced people flirt so much with each other. She found them a constant state of amusement. "Would you two like some privacy?"

Jake laughed again and headed back to the kitchen while Quinn put her things away. She didn't clock in yet because she assumed she'd be talking to Loma for a bit. She knew Jake let a lot slide—especially when it came to her friendship with his ex-wife—but she wanted an honest day's pay for an honest day's work.

They sat down in Jake's office with their bad gas station coffee.

"I'm so sorry about my big mouth. Really I am." She sipped from her cup and wrinkled her nose. "I can't believe you're actually letting me talk now."

"When the customers come in, I can slip your muzzle on."

"Harsh. But fair."

Quinn removed the lid from her cup, but when the aroma assaulted her, she put it back on. Okay, taste did matter. "Want real coffee? Jake's probably got some going already."

When Quinn came back with two steaming porcelain mugs, Loma said, "I was just so surprised when you told me you thought Chief Chestnut killed his own dad."

Quinn nodded. "I know."

"How could Myron—what was he, a thirteen-year-old boy—kill his dad?"

"Donald Lee was always pranking people. I was thinking maybe Myron tried to prank him back and it backfired. You know how boys are, never really thinking before they do something. And then he panicked." Quinn sipped her coffee.

"But how would he get Donald Lee's body to that field? He was too young to drive," Loma said.

"Maybe they were already in that field when the prank went wrong."

"Or they were hunting," Loma said. "Had an accident."

"But CBI didn't find a gunshot wound or any other suspicious injury. Besides, why would Myron keep that a secret? More importantly, how could he keep that a secret?" Quinn tapped a fingernail on her mug. "But now I don't really think Chief Chestnut—"

Loma interrupted. She had clearly been thinking this over since Quinn mentioned her theory about Chief Chestnut. Quinn let her go on, as if she could stop her anyway. "You said that Donald Lee was a drinker. Maybe he was driving drunk—wasn't this about the time they started doing those anti-drunk-driving assemblies in schools? Myron tried to take his keys, bonked his head or passed out, and he died from hypothermia or exposure or whatever." Loma warmed up to her scenario and talked faster and louder. "And maybe Myron *did* know how to drive—he was a country kid, right?—and drove home without Donald Lee."

"Settle down." Quinn glanced toward the restaurant, even though she knew the chime hadn't jingled and there were no customers out there. "You think Myron would leave him in that field to die?"

"Would a kid know he'd die out there?"

"Probably. He's not dumb."

"Well, then," Loma mused. "Maybe he didn't care. Maybe it was the last straw for him. You told me he didn't grow up with much money. Maybe Myron figured out they were poor because of Donald Lee's alcohol consumption."

Quinn shrugged. "I read an article from back then about Donald Lee smashing up the car when he hit somebody's mailbox. I'm sure even a kid as young as Myron would have realized the family would have more money if the car didn't always need repairs." She sipped her coffee. "Chief Chestnut told me and Jake a story about Donald Lee not getting him to a football game one time, which got him kicked off the team. He was an awful father."

"Maybe something similar happened, but this time Myron flew into a rage. Do they play football at that time of year?" Loma was working herself up again. "Maybe it wasn't football. But something could have set him off. You said his own mother told you he got into plenty of fights. And we know Donald Lee did too. That apple probably didn't fall too far from the parental tree. Then strutting around in that trophy parka? Shameful." Loma *tsk-tsk*ed.

They were quiet for a minute.

The more Loma reiterated the same thoughts Quinn had been having, the less sure she was about her new suspect, that smarmy Odell Nilssen. What was it Rico always told her? *You follow all facts to their logical conclusion. An investigation doesn't end until it ends.*

"But how would we prove any of that about Chief Chestnut?" Quinn said. "Talk to Beany again?"

"Maybe. But what do I say? Hey, did your son kill your husband in a fit of rage and you covered it up all these years? Okay, have a nice day."

"I probably wouldn't word it like that," Loma said dryly.

"Then how?"

Loma set her mug down with conviction and a tiny splash. "Lead her down a path until you get to a fork. One direction leads to guilt, the other to innocence."

"You make it sound easy." Quinn stood. "I've gotta clock in."

"I haven't had my berries yet!"

Quinn chuckled. "It's cute you really think Jake was making a bowl of berries for you to waste."

"I wasn't going to waste them." Loma pouted. When she saw the look on Quinn's face, she said, "Okay. I was probably going to waste them. But in my defense, when a big girl wants a bear claw, berries are a poor substitute."

Quinn moved down the hall to the time clock. Behind her she heard Loma bellow, "What kind of diner is this that doesn't have bear claws?" After a low rumble that Quinn knew was Jake's retort, she heard Loma again. "Berries or nothing? What kind of a terrible Sophie's Choice is that?"

Chapter 29

All through her shift, Quinn had to mediate between the town factions, half who only wanted to discuss theories with her about Chief Chestnut murdering Donald Lee, and the other half who wanted to debate with her why Chief Chestnut couldn't possibly have murdered Donald Lee. Unfortunately, everything anyone said made perfect sense and was something she'd already thought of herself. Nothing jumped out at her as a new avenue to investigate, but taken together, it all made her more determined to find out the truth. The theories and arguments, however, all got bottled up in her brain.

It was a small relief when only a couple of old-timers mentioned Bernard's name as a potential suspect in Donald Lee's death. Wilbur and Abe double-teamed the accusers and shut down any more discussion about him. Abe's guilt must have gotten the better of him.

Quinn quietly thanked them both, but she couldn't help wondering how much was being said about Bernard around town that Wilbur and Abe couldn't shut down.

She wanted to mention Odell Nilssen, Junior to all of them but held her tongue. She was already in enough trouble for slandering Chief Chestnut; she didn't need to heap on more.

The only respite she got was when her phone dinged to tell her Marion had replied to her email. "I'll talk to Myron. I'd hate if my Grandpa Dan had anything like that happen to him before he passed." It was a short message, but it made Quinn do a little dance in the diner. Now Chief Chestnut—or realistically, Rico—would start looking into Odell Nillsen, Junior for any involvement in Donald Lee's death. If she didn't fall asleep first, she'd call Rico to talk about it later and see what he'd found out.

Quinn thought about going to see Beany again. She still wanted to gift the *Daruma* doll to Marion if it was supposed to be hers. She could also try to find that fork in Beany's road that Loma mentioned. While she wasn't as convinced of Chief Chestnut's involvement in Donald Lee's death as she had been, she also hadn't learned anything to exonerate him. The arguing between town factions didn't clear up anything for her, rather it only served to muddy up her thinking.

The fact remained, Myron's own mother said he was a violent kid, and he himself talked about how bad a father Donald Lee was.

Yes, a visit with Beany might clear it up. She'd have time if she left right after her lunch shift.

In fact, she was so deep in thought about Beany that when Chief Chestnut came in, Quinn almost asked him if his mother liked all chocolates, or had specific favorites. She caught herself just in time, limiting her contact with him to pouring his coffee and nothing else, which, by his lack of eye contact with her, was perfectly fine with him.

One disturbing idea flickered through her mind, though. If Chief Chestnut actually did have something to do with his father's death, and his sister was pressuring him to look at Odell Nilssen, would it cause him to find some way to produce evidence against Nilssen? Had Chief Chestnut already noticed and acted on the scuttlebutt about Bernard to clear his own name? Quinn knew personally of several instances where Chief Chestnut had been involved in less-than-stellar policework, only serving his own need to railroad innocent suspects.

* * * *

Quinn made it to Beany's assisted living facility in Arvada just after three and found her knitting on the same bench in the same grotto. Only the color of her yarn was different today. Blue instead of yellow.

She handed Beany a box of chocolates as big as a board game. "Hi, Mrs. Chestnut. Do you remember me? I'm Quinn, I know your son."

Beany stared at her from behind her round, wire-framed granny glasses for so long that Quinn began to get anxious. Had Chief Chestnut warned her not to talk to Quinn?

Beany dug into the candy. "There was some girl named Quincy here the other day, but she's a nurse, I think."

"No, that was me. Just a visitor."

"Well, sit a spell and let's visit then." Beany transferred her knitting to the bag at her feet so Quinn had room on the bench.

"It's nice to see you again. You must like it out here." Quinn nodded at their surroundings.

"Best spot in the whole dang place. It used to be Velma would get out here first and stay all day. But I convinced her that everyone was inside watching *Jeopardy!* without her and getting every answer wrong." Beany leaned toward Quinn and looked over the rim of her glasses. "Velma has kind of an ego about her." She bit a chocolate in half and talked around it. "So now the grotto belongs to me. Everybody knows it too."

Quinn was a bit taken aback by Beany's forcefulness. It was only a bench, after all, and there seemed to be plenty of lovely places to enjoy the gardens. Perhaps it was just a control issue. The loss of autonomy in a facility like this—no matter how lovely—must be difficult to accept. She made a mental note to make it a point to allow her grandfather to make as many decisions as she could when they were together.

Beany held out the box of candy to Quinn.

"No thanks." Instead, Quinn pulled the *Daruma* doll from her bag and showed it to Beany. "Does this look familiar to you?"

Beany chewed another piece of candy while she looked it over. "Nope. Ugly little thing. Did you make it?"

Quinn snickered. Even when directed her way, it always struck her funny when elderly people lost their politeness filter. Or maybe they chose to unplug it. "No, it's not my handiwork. It's a Japanese doll. Did Marion ever have anything like this? Maybe Donald Lee would have given her something like this?"

Beany barked out a laugh, almost choking on her chocolate. "That's a laugh. Donald Lee never bought presents for anyone."

Quinn deposited it back in her bag, wondering if that was true or just another product of Beany's faulty memory. Hadn't she told Quinn in their first visit about the present Donald Lee had for Marion? And didn't she rattle off a long list of the presents they'd given their children—bikes and a dollhouse sprang to mind. But had Beany included Donald Lee in her statement, or just taken singular credit? Now that Quinn thought about it, maybe it was the latter.

Beany jabbed the box of candy at Quinn again, and she accepted one this time, hoping the sugar would help her stay awake. They munched on their assorted truffles in silence for a bit until Quinn said, "Can I ask you some more about Myron?"

Beany frowned. "We've been talking about Myron?"

"Not today," Quinn said quickly. "That was the other day when I was here."

Beany guffawed. "Just pulling your leg. I'm not that far around the bend." She pawed through the chocolates. "What do you want to know?"

"I'm curious about his relationship with Donald Lee. What was it like?"

"Didn't have much of one. Donald Lee was always out with that no-good Bernard what's-his-name. Came home drunk as a skunk, like as not. And he wasn't one of those fun drunks neither." Beany bit into a chocolate, then spit it out into her hand and tossed it toward a tree. "Coconut. Ew. Want it?" She held out the other half to Quinn, who shook her head vaguely, still trying to digest the description of her grandfather as a no-goodnik. Beany dropped the half-eaten offensive chocolate back into the box and chose another, which she bit into very tentatively. She smiled. "Cherry."

"Did Donald Lee ever hit Myron?"

"Nah. Ignored him, mostly."

Quinn watched Beany stuff the other half of the chocolate-covered cherry in her mouth and chew, making yummy noises. She wasn't sure of a good way to phrase this question, so she just blurted it out. "Beany, do you think it was possible that Myron killed Donald Lee?"

Another guffaw escaped Beany's mouth, sending a fine spray of chocolate down her chin. "Anything's possible."

"This?"

Beany wiped her chin with her hand, then turned and stared Quinn directly in the eyes. "No. Myron was a good boy. Didn't have it in him."

"You told me before that he got into a lot of fights."

"Well, yeah, but not so's bad as to kill somebody!"

"You're sure?"

"Sure as I am that water is wet."

They were quiet for a bit again, watching a couple of hummingbirds battle for space at the feeder.

If Myron and Donald Lee didn't have a relationship, and if Beany was positive that Myron couldn't have killed anyone, what was the deal with him wearing Donald Lee's parka all the time? If it wasn't an homage to his deep and abiding love for his father, and it wasn't a trophy ripped from his cold, dead body, then what was it? "Beany, why did Myron always wear Donald Lee's parka after he was gone?"

"Ever spend a winter in Colorado, child? It's cold. He was cold. All elbows and knees, Myron was. Still skinny to this day. Never grew any insulation." Beany stared at the hummingbird feeder even though the hummingbirds had disappeared. "Donald Lee left us high and dry. We only had a tiny emergency fund I'd been stashing, hiding it where Donald

Lee couldn't drink it away. Needed all that and more before I got hired on as a cashier at the feed store. Old Duane had all the employees he needed but hired me anyway. Whole town rallied 'round us. Everyone loves an underdog story. Folks brought us food and paid toward our bills, what little they could. Guess they felt responsible for us." Beany patted Quinn's knee. "Good folks in Chestnut Station. Don't let nobody tell you different. They did everything they could for us. But at least Donald Lee left behind that nice parka. Like—what do you call it?—his estate."

"I guess I still don't understand why Donald Lee wouldn't be wearing it out in a storm like that."

Beany actually shifted in her seat so she faced Quinn. "Anything I say about Donald Lee make you think he was smart?"

Quinn nibbled on a chocolate. Something didn't make sense. "You said the only thing Donald Lee left in his estate was that parka. What about all that land?"

"All what land?"

"Outside Chestnut Station."

"That land didn't belong to Donald Lee."

"It didn't? I thought it was all Chestnut land." Quinn frowned at Beany.

"It is all Chestnut land. Just not Donald Lee's. Never was. Dan—God rest his soul—knew what kind of man Donald Lee was. Even though Donald Lee was his only son—something he mourned every day—he didn't leave him a plug nickel."

"Then who owned the land?"

"Back then Dan put it in trust for Marion and Myron, upon his death. I was trustee, and it was iron-clad that Donald Lee couldn't get his grubby hands on a penny of it. Then when Marion turned eighteen, she became trustee." Beany rooted through the box of candy, searching for another favorite.

Quinn remembered Sandy at the county clerk's office mentioning the name Daniel, and she thought she'd just misspoken. And Marion talked about her grandpa Dan. Now it was clear that Donald Lee didn't have anything to do with thwarting Odell Nilssen's plans to develop an outlet mall. It was Daniel, Donald Lee's father, who did the thwarting.

"Beany, when did Daniel die?"

Without having to think about it, Beany said, "Summer of Woodstock. Nineteen sixty-nine."

If Daniel was the one who'd thwarted Odell Nilssen's plans and he died four years before Donald Lee did, then it made no sense that Nilssen would have killed Donald Lee. Even if Nilssen "hadn't done his homework" before buying up the properties, surely it didn't take long before he knew that Daniel Chestnut controlled that property and he'd never see his outlet mall because of him. Donald Lee had nothing to do with any of it.

Sure, people held grudges, but killing Donald Lee to get back at someone who had been dead for four years? Even for someone as odious as Odell Nilssen, that didn't make a whole lot of sense.

Quinn felt the chocolate churn in her stomach. Her main suspect didn't do it.

* * * *

On the drive back to Chestnut Station, fighting her exhaustion and her pinging brain, Quinn had to admit it also seemed very unlikely that thirteen-year-old Myron Chestnut could have had anything to do with Donald Lee's death, either.

That left Bernard Dudley.

She immediately put that thought out of her head and concocted a way for everything—every word, every accusation, every clue, everything—to fade away.

Even if Marion convinced Chief Chestnut to look at Odell Nilssen, he'd find the same information she had. And if Marion hadn't been able to convince him to look into it, then even better. Nobody would look into this any further, and all the gossip would die down. If Chief Chestnut hadn't heard any scuttlebutt about Bernard, he would have no reason to suspect her grandfather of any crime, either.

If Chief Chestnut and the CBI were still willing to keep this case closed, then now so was Quinn. She hoped she and her monster hadn't rung some bell that couldn't be unrung.

She needed to act like everything was normal and that she didn't suspect her grandfather of killing anyone.

By the time she got back to town, she knew what she needed to do, and it gave her the perfect opportunity to stop into the diner and meet Rachel, the new waitress.

She pulled open the door, and Jake looked up from the novel he was reading in the big corner booth in the back.

"What are you doing here?" he asked.

"Came to meet Rachel and talk to you about something."

"Dinner was as slow as lunch so I sent her home." Jake dog-eared the page of his paperback, a mystery by Charlemagne Russo.

Quinn looked heavenward. "Lord, help me. Does this girl even exist? Are you punking me?"

Jake called to a man at a four-top by the wall. "Jimmy, who refilled your coffee?"

Without looking up from his pie, Jimmy said, "You did."

"Oh."

"Then who brought out your pie?"

"You did."

"I did?" Jake raked his fingers through his thick hair.

"Jimmy," Quinn said. "Have you seen any waitress here tonight?"

He looked up. "Do you count?"

"I'd like to think so, but not in this particular scenario."

"Then no." Jimmy shoveled another bite of pie in his mouth.

Quinn pointed her finger at Jake.

He laughed. "I swear to God, Quinn. There is a waitress named Rachel who works the dinner shift."

"Is she imaginary?"

"No."

"A ghost?"

"Hm. Maybe, now that you mention it…" He started to slide out of the booth. "Is that what you wanted to talk about?"

"No." Quinn waved him back and slid into the booth opposite him. "I need your blessing for something I have to do."

Chapter 30

Quinn worked the next Wednesday dinner shift, giving the mythical Rachel a much-needed night off. They closed the diner at seven like normal, but didn't lock the door. People continued to stream into the jam-packed restaurant.

Wilbur shoved his way through the crowd, followed by the other Retireds. "This oughta be good," he growled in his raspy voice. He waved the ad clipped from the *Chestnut Station Chronicle* she'd placed earlier.

She could have simply written a letter to the editor, or written an article, or even agreed to be interviewed by Vera, but instead she placed a half-page display ad announcing her public apology to Chief Chestnut. Since the accusation was public, the apology should be too. "Chestnut Diner serving crow Wednesday at 7 p.m.....but only to Quinn Carr. Everyone else gets to enjoy a slice of free pie while listening to Quinn publicly apologize to Chief Chestnut for casting aspersions on his character and his past."

She'd found a cartoon crow to illustrate and draw attention to the ad.

Unconsciously doing her finger thing, Quinn stood in the hallway near the time clock with Loma. They peeked out into the restaurant. It seemed like most of the town was there, but Quinn knew that probably wasn't the case. For instance, Rachel wasn't there. That was to say, she wasn't aware of her presence, but if Rachel was Jake's imaginary friend, it was incumbent upon him to introduce them.

She saw Chief Chestnut enter the diner. Earlier, she'd seated Georgeanne and Dan on either side of a chair reserved for him, and they waved him over. Quinn was a bit relieved to see he looked as uncomfortable as she felt.

Loma grabbed her hand. "Quit it. You'll be fine. Are you sure you don't want me to do this? I mean, I was the one who actually said it."

Quinn shook off Loma's hand and clenched her fists, opening and closing them, trying to focus on them like Mary-Louise Lovely had taught her. "But everyone knows you were just repeating what I said. Thinking it and verbalizing it to you was way worse than you just spilling it."

"If you say so."

"Besides, it'll go a long way with my mom." Quinn glanced at Georgeanne, who patted Chief Chestnut's knee.

Dan looked in Quinn's direction and tipped his chin at her, shorthand for asking if she was okay. She gave a small nod and a thumbs-up.

Rico strode into the diner, stowing his duty cap between his elbow and ribs. "Am I too late for the ceremonial eating of the crow?"

"Nope. Still coming up on the agenda," Quinn said.

"Pie's still on the agenda too," Loma said, smacking her lips.

Rico glanced around the room and spoke quietly to Quinn. "You really think this is a good idea?"

"No, but I think I have to do it anyway. Besides, too late now for second thoughts." She swung a hand, Vanna White–style, indicating the packed house.

"You'll be fine!" Loma spoke too loud, and several people turned their way. She and Quinn exchanged a silent glance that spoke volumes.

"This reminds me of that time in eleventh grade when—"

Quinn interrupted Rico with a raised palm, effectively stopping his words. "I do not want to be reminded right now of some equally stupid thing I did in high school."

"It wasn't you, it was Wyatt McNulty."

"Who's Wyatt McNulty?" Loma asked.

"Some guy we knew who was constantly making bad decisions." Quinn turned to Rico. "Tell me later. But only if you think it'll make me feel better."

"Did Wyatt ever do anything that made you feel better?" Rico asked.

"Oooh-la-la." Loma did a sexy shimmy.

"Gross," Quinn said to her. "And no," she said to Rico.

Jake ambled over, after greeting his regulars as well as the customers he saw less frequently. "You ready?"

"As I'll ever be."

Jake dragged the chair they'd stashed away earlier, knowing there might not be an empty one when they needed it, and placed it in the doorway just in front of the hallway leading to the back. It was literally the only open space in the diner. He helped Quinn stand up on it, then he and Loma stepped out of the way.

An immediate hush fell over the diner. Expectant faces turned toward Quinn, but who knew what they expected? Crying? Defiance? A boxing match between her and Chief Chestnut? It suddenly dawned on her that it was entirely possible everyone would leave disappointed somehow. No fight, no crying, maybe not even their preferred flavor of pie.

Quinn took a deep breath and jammed her hands in the pockets of her favorite dress. It wasn't really a good dress to work in all day, but she'd specifically worn it today because she felt confident when she wore it. It fit perfectly, the jade color complemented her complexion, and, splendidly, it had pockets.

"Thank you all for coming tonight, especially you, Chief Chestnut." She turned toward him and earned a small nod of acknowledgment. She cleared her throat. "We're gathered here tonight"—her pause drew some laughs—"because I'm an idiot." More laughs. But not from Georgeanne, who pursed her lips. But was that almost a smile from Chief Chestnut? Quinn felt a surge of confidence that this might have actually been a good idea after all. "Let me rephrase before my mom blows a gasket."

"Because you're not an idiot, dear." Georgeanne's stern face softened at the good-natured laughs from the crowd. "Well, she isn't," she said to them.

"Preaching to the choir, Georgie," Wilbur shouted. "Let her get on with it. I want my pie!"

Laughs exploded in the diner. Quinn waited for them to quiet, then said, "We're gathered here tonight because I said something I had no business saying—"

"And I had no business repeating." Loma spoke loudly but continued leaning against the wall.

"—about Chief Myron Chestnut, a...diligent"—Quinn had to scrounge for the right word but didn't quite land on it. Nobody in their right mind thought Chief performed his duties diligently, and she hoped it wouldn't draw another laugh due to its irony—"public servant of this town named for his ancestor."

"Better look up the definition of 'diligent!'" Silas yelled across the room to laughter.

Quinn didn't pause. "The fact of the matter is that my thoughts and actions began a rumor I truly regret. I wanted to publicly say that I am absolutely convinced that Chief Chestnut did *not* kill his father, Donald Lee, nor did he have any hand in Donald Lee being out in that field. When I spoke with his mother—"

Chief Chestnut looked up from his hands folded in his lap and stared into Quinn's face. "You talked to my mother?" he asked incredulously.

"And I regret not doing that *before* I shoved my foot in my mouth." People began murmuring to each other, restless and getting bored since there was no crying or fighting. "So, to summarize, I was out of line and shouldn't have opened my big mouth. Enjoy your pie."

Jake helped her off the chair and stowed it back in his office. He, Loma, and Quinn had earlier arranged assorted slices of pie on plates and now began serving them.

Quinn carried a plate with cherry pie topped with a swirl of whipped cream over to Chief Chestnut. He glanced around the room. "I'm the only one who gets whipped cream? Is it poisoned?" He grudgingly accepted the pie from her.

"I'll take it, Myron." Dan reached for it, but Chief Chestnut held it out of his reach.

Georgeanne had taken it upon herself to deliver forks to everyone and held one out to Myron. He took one and jabbed it in his pie. Before taking a bite, he looked up at Quinn. "I can't believe you talked to my mother."

"She says you should visit more often, by the way."

He swirled his fork in the whipped cream. "I don't have time to get up there like I should."

"Take her some chocolates. She'll forgive you."

"How'd you find her, anyway?"

Quinn thought she heard the teensiest bit of admiration in his voice. She didn't want to drag Jake into anything, so she simply said, "I have my ways."

"That's what Rico keeps telling me." Chief scooped the triangle tip of his pie into his mouth.

Quinn took the opportunity to scoot away while he was being nice. It would be a shame to ruin the one and only nice moment they'd had when he hadn't scowled at her.

Loma, Jake, Georgeanne, and Quinn served pie until everyone had left the diner. It had turned out to be quite a nice little town party, although Quinn eyed the pies as they dwindled down. Running out of pie on Free Pie Night would have turned the happy, jovial crowd into an unruly mob. Luckily everyone left fully sated, with two pieces left.

Georgeanne asked if she could help clean up, but Jake shooed her and Dan out of the diner and on their way.

Loma took her chance to escape before cleanup began. She called loudly after Georgeanne and Dan, "You two need a ride, or do you have your car here?"

When the diner was quiet, Quinn handed Jake a piece of pie and a fork and took the other for herself. She collapsed into a chair. "So, what do I owe you for the pies?"

"The pie is on me." Jake grinned. "Totally worth it to see you publicly humiliate yourself like that."

Quinn's eyes widened. "Humiliate? Really?"

"Nah. You did a good thing here. The rumor is officially laid to rest. Chief's happy. Nobody's fighting or taking sides. Everyone was reminded what delicious pie we serve here at the Chestnut Diner." He raised his fork and clinked it against Quinn's. "Yep, we're all winners tonight."

"Except Donald Lee. We still don't know what happened to him," Quinn said.

"Maybe we never will."

Quinn chewed thoughtfully. "But that's not right. Not acceptable in any way."

Chapter 31

Quinn had a phone appointment with Mary-Louise Lovely before work. She hadn't received any texts from Quinn lately and decided she'd better check in.

"The spices remain alphabetized because I can't keep my hands out of there. Twice I've found myself just standing and staring at the pantry, and before I know it, everything is in order again. My mom has gotten tired of unarranging them, I think. And she never asks me to help in the kitchen anymore." Quinn paused and then spoke dramatically. "I think I've broken my mom."

Mary-Louise Lovely laughed brightly, and for a split second Quinn thought everything might be okay with her OCD. *Maybe, if Mary-Louise Lovely can laugh about my monster like that, someday I'll be able to also.*

"You haven't broken your mom, Quinn. But let's take a step back from the spice cabinet for a few days. Let's not even think about it. How's everything else going?"

"Oh, I used that FADE technique you showed me, and I think I'm becoming more aware of my finger thing. I had to give a…a speech last night, and I don't think I even did it once."

"That's great, Quinn! Remember what I said about *fall down seven times, get up eight*?"

Quinn nodded and then remembered she was on the phone. "Yes."

"That's what I'm hearing from you. You fell down with the spices, but you got up with the FADE technique and your finger thing. You're making progress."

"It doesn't feel that way."

"I know. But you are. Trust me." She paused. "What else is going on with you?"

"Nothing. Same old—oh! You know that Japanese *Daruma* doll I showed you? I think I found the artist."

"That's great!"

"Well, not the artist him- or herself, but at least the name has been deciphered."

"You know, Quinn, one of your great strengths is your perseverance. That's why I keep harping to you about not changing all of your behaviors in an effort to get rid of your OCD."

"I know, I know. I can't get rid of my OCD."

"It truly is a part of you, and it's not all bad. This perseverance—the way you glom on to a puzzle to solve—that's a good thing! It only turns bad when it overtakes your life. But what I'm hearing these days is that you are creating some balance for yourself. The old Quinn would have dived headfirst into the internet to find this artist—"

"Um…"

"But you've also"—Mary-Louise Lovely hit the word hard and drew it out a bit—"been dealing with the exercises I've given you, gone to work your shifts at the diner, and apparently delivered a speech."

Quinn thought for a moment about her trips to see Beany and her grandfather, and helping clean out his desk. "I guess you're right. Maybe I am figuring all this out."

* * * *

Quinn spent the morning joking with the Retireds and fielding their many and varied demands. It suddenly occurred to her that maybe running her ragged was a game they enjoyed. Perhaps they tried to top one another with their excessive and often ridiculous requests. Quinn always wanted to make the diner's customers happy, but maybe she was the butt of an extended practical joke by these guys. When she'd first started at the diner, she was grappling with so many personal issues, many days just trying to put one foot in front of another until she made it through her shift. Her default usually ran to pleasing others anyway, so perhaps she wasn't even aware she'd been falling for their shenanigans and soon enough it became just another part of her job, like filling the saltshakers.

When she delivered Silas's diagonally cut toast with a single, but different, berry in each quadrant, she asked them, "Are you guys pranking me with all your weirdo requests?"

"Weirdo? You calling me a weirdo?" Silas yanked his plate from her, but Quinn saw a smile forming in the corners of his mouth.

"I knew it!" she said.

"You didn't know it for a long time, though," Wilbur said with a chuckle.

Quinn stared at each of them in turn, trying to be angry. A halfhearted, "You guys," was all she could muster.

She refilled their cups while she was there. When she bent between Wilbur and Herman, Wilbur kissed her cheek. And when she came around to the front of the table, Hugh offered her a slice of his bacon. She accepted it just like Jethro accepted his bacon payment for patrolling the diner, but with less slobber. She and Hugh smacked their strips of bacon together as if they were crystal flutes of champagne. After they both crunched their bites, Hugh said, "You're one of us now!"

"Perish the thought!" she said to laughter as she hurried away to bus table four.

She carried the tub to the kitchen and spoke over the noise of Jake's griddle and the running water at her sink. "Did you know the Retireds were punking me?"

Jake barked out a laugh. "Took you long enough!"

"So they're not completely crazy, ordering their food the way they do?"

"Oh, they are completely crazy, but none of the other waitresses ever put up with them. That's why they like you so much."

"Is that why they're here all the time?"

"No, they'd be here anyway. Punking you just gives them something to do *while* they're here."

Quinn finished spraying the dishes and loading them into the dishwasher rack. "I don't know whether to be mad at them or not."

"What good would being mad do?"

Of course Quinn knew she wasn't mad at the old men. They had grown on her like barnacles. But they had run her ragged, and while they tipped, they didn't tip excessively like they should have, knowing what she knew now.

"I'll get them back," she vowed with a smile.

"Let me know how I can help." Jake handed her two plates. "Table six."

After Quinn finished with the breakfast rush, and the Retireds were the only ones still in the diner, she sat in the back corner booth. When Bob waved his cup at her, she waved him away. "Get it yourself," she called. The rest of the men laughed at Bob and cajoled him to get coffee for all of them.

"Put on one of those cute aprons!" Silas told him.

"Those aprons are only cute when Quinn wears them," Wilbur said.

Herman cocked his head, a puzzled look crossing his face. "I don't think that's how aprons work."

Quinn ducked her head so they wouldn't see her laugh. Then she ignored them while she did some more searching for the artist Ichikawa. Instead of searching by the name, she tried a different tactic and searched for anyone using the cartoon mouse as an artist's mark. She uploaded a photo of the mouse to Instagram with a note asking if anyone had ever seen it before, specifically attached to a Japanese artist. Then she found some Facebook pages devoted to *Daruma* dolls, so she posted it in there too.

Rico came into the diner for lunch, giving them a chance to catch up.

"Guess what I found out today?" Quinn said. Without waiting for an answer, she tipped her chin toward the Retireds' table. "They've been pranking me the whole time I've been working here. For months now, I've been pandering to their crazy demands thinking I was simply a marvel at excellent customer service."

Rico laughed. "Took you long enough!"

"That's what Jake said." Quinn sipped from her water glass. "Why didn't you tell me, Mr. Cannot-Tell-A-Lie?"

Rico's eyebrows knit together. "You never asked."

"Did everyone know?"

Rico glanced around the diner. "Guaranteed."

"Even my parents?"

Rico shrugged. "I think they were catching on."

"Honestly. Small towns." Quinn pretended to be annoyed, but secretly knew that now she fit in here in Chestnut Station. Not just because her parents lived here, but because people saw her, Quinn Carr, for herself. And they seemed to like her, despite everything. She changed the subject. "So what's new at the police station? Any more news about Donald Lee or Chief Chestnut?"

"Based on your public pie apology, I thought you'd given up on Chief Chestnut and Donald Lee." Rico took a bite of his BLT and wiped mayonnaise from his mouth.

"I don't think he killed his dad anymore, but that still leaves the fact that his father died in the middle of a piece of property that Myron may or may not have given my mother."

"May or may not?"

"I don't know exactly where Donald Lee was found in relation to the official property lines. And the deed is weird so it maybe didn't get filed properly. But whether it was on that property or not, Donald Lee still died out there."

"True." Rico bit a potato chip in half, and Quinn cringed.

"Geez, Rico. Can't you use your fingers to break an appropriate mouth-sized bite of chip? Are you a Neanderthal?" She picked an oversized chip from his plate, made a show in front of his face of breaking it in half, dropped one half back to the plate, then broke the remaining half in half. This she popped into her mouth, overdramatizing chewing with her mouth closed. After she swallowed, she primly took the corner of a paper napkin and delicately wiped the corners of her mouth.

Rico watched all this calmly, like he had the previous seven thousand times he'd seen it. "Now you need a finger bowl. Like at Buckingham Palace." Rico picked up the largest potato chip remaining on his plate and bit into it, making overzealously disgusting chewing noises and showering bits all over.

Quinn used his glass of water like a finger bowl. As she was drying them, her phone pinged. She picked it up while Rico started going on and on about how rude it was when people answered their phones while they were with friends, something Quinn had heard seven thousand times from him.

"Ohmygosh! Rico, I found him!" Quinn showed her screen to him.

He took it from her and squinted at it. "What am I looking at?"

"Remember that roundish doll I found out at the site? That faded wooden thing CBI didn't think was important?"

"Oh, yeah." He looked up at her and went into cop mode. "Is it important now?"

"Yes, but not like that. Beany said something that made me think that it had been a gift for Marion from Donald Lee."

Rico raised his eyebrows and handed the phone back to her.

"No, I don't have proof of anything like that, and I can't imagine it has anything to do with his death. But I thought if I could figure out the artist, I'd have some information about it and I could give it to Marion. Maybe she'd like to have something from her dad. I know I would."

"How do you know it belonged to Donald Lee?"

"I don't. But it was found right there with everything else, so maybe it does."

"CBI didn't think so."

Quinn scrutinized Rico's face to see if his nose twitched like a bunny smelling ammonia because he knew something more about it.

"Is there anything else you know about that doll or CBI's investigation of it?" she asked.

"Nope." Rico ate another chip, but not before he broke it into miniscule bits, which he then placed on his tongue.

"You're hopeless." Quinn brought her phone to life again. "Anyway…I've been trying to find this artist. If Marion doesn't want it, maybe I can get it back to the artist. If the artist was interned out there, maybe I can hear some stories about Camp Chestnut and try to figure out how it got out in that field."

Rico held the last bite of his sandwich in front of his mouth. "Interesting. So whatever that is on your phone leads you to the artist?"

"Yes. His daughter"—Quinn looked at her phone—"Keiko Kimura responded to something I put on Facebook. Listen to this. She said, 'That cartoon mouse accompanied everything my father Hiroshi Ichikawa signed, whether it was a toy or fine art. If you're ever near Denver, I'd love to see the *Daruma* in person.' Rico, she's here in Denver! I can meet up with her. Isn't that cool?"

"Very." He crunched the last few chips on his plate. "Just don't meet up anywhere that serves potato chips."

Chapter 32

On her next day off, Quinn made plans to meet Keiko Kimura for lunch at a ramen house in the Sakura Square area of Denver. They'd been chatting over Facebook messages and texts, so Quinn felt like she knew her even before she got to the restaurant.

The restaurant was clean and well lit, but Quinn still had to wait as her eyes adjusted from the bright sunshine outside. She blinked and looked around the restaurant, surprised to see an elderly woman with a gray pixie cut waving her over to a table. Her Facebook photo was a pink-and-white lotus flower. Her chatty correspondence belied her age. She half-stood as Quinn approached.

"Don't get up. I'm Quinn Carr." She held out her hand to the petite woman, then slid into a chair next to her.

"I'm so pleased to meet you. I'm Keiko Kimura." She spoke in a soft voice that Quinn strained to hear. "I could tell by your face that you weren't expecting to see a seventy-six-year-old woman."

Quinn blushed.

"I was born at the camp."

Keiko hadn't mentioned that during their exchanges but had explained that her father had a long career as an artist before he died. He and her mother had settled in Santa Fe in a thriving arts community, raising Keiko and her sister there.

Quinn pulled the *Daruma* doll from her bag. "Here it is."

Keiko caressed the doll on all sides, finally turning it over. Tears filled her eyes and threatened to spill over. "It's so faded, but my father's signature is so bold." She looked questioningly at Quinn.

"I used a pencil and a million little dots to try to decipher what he'd written on there." Quinn pointed at the mouse. "See that crack? I thought he was a spider for a while. And then someone out at the museum—have you been to the Camp Chestnut Museum?"

Keiko nodded.

"Someone at the museum helped me figure out those were the characters of the Ichikawa name. I used their genealogy computer, but there were so many Ichikawas interned there." In her excitement, Quinn realized she was babbling. "It wasn't until I talked to you that I used a fine-tipped black marker to finalize his signature."

Keiko had been staring at and stroking the doll the entire time Quinn had been speaking. "It's beautiful," she murmured, before handing it back to Quinn.

Quinn refused to take it from her. "I brought it for you to have."

Keiko continued to stroke the *Daruma*, but looked at Quinn. "While he was interned, my father made many of these traditional dolls. They are not toys, though. They serve a very distinct purpose. They're a reminder to whoever owns one to hammer away at whatever might challenge them. He gave them away to anyone who wanted one." Keiko lowered her eyes. "There were a lot of challenges in the camp."

"I can only imagine."

"My father was a generous man and a gifted artist. He would have been proud of how you persevered to figure out his signature and find me. You should keep this." She again held it out to Quinn. Keiko nodded encouragement and smiled. "I'm ancient and not in need of such things. I have already persevered for seventy-six years, after all. You have your entire life to chip away at."

Quinn slowly reached for the *Daruma*.

Keiko continued. "You never gave up finding me. Your research into the camp showed you all the instances of abuse and humiliation that happened there. Imprisoning all those people, stealing their property, never compensating them or the owners of the land they stole to build the camps. You could have looked away, but you didn't. And now you tell me a dead man was found right outside its gates, his family without him all those years, never knowing what happened to him." She shook her head sadly. "But I want you to understand there was beauty in the camp as well. Like my father carving and painting and distributing his art to anyone who desired it. Everyone shared what they had."

Quinn considered this and wondered how she and her family would have dealt with internment. "What was your mother like?"

Keiko's face lit up. "Her Japanese name was Mariko but everyone called her Mary. She was as generous as my father. I was very young, but I have a distinct memory of her giving her winter coat to another family who had recently arrived at Camp Chestnut in the middle of winter from Los Angeles. They were ill-prepared, but my mother said she and my father could share my father's coat, like it was no sacrifice at all."

"Literally, she gave them the coat off her back." Quinn marveled at the generous spirit of the Ichikawa family, all three of them. She cradled the *Daruma* in both hands. "Thank you for this. I will always treasure it."

They spent the next two hours eating spicy miso ramen and gyudon rice bowls and talking. Quinn wanted to hear more about Keiko's parents and what she remembered about living in the camp. Keiko wanted to hear about Quinn's life in Chestnut Station and about finding Donald Lee's bones.

When they parted company, they vowed to keep in touch and made tentative plans for Keiko to visit the diner and join Quinn for an excursion out to the museum together.

Driving home, Quinn's mind was on Keiko's mother, Mary, and how selfless and generous she was in giving her coat away. Her own family had practically nothing at the camp, but when she met someone who had even less, she didn't hesitate to share.

Quinn also thought of her own mother, who pitched in whenever and wherever she was needed, and always stuck up for her friend Myron Chestnut, even though he had more than his share of flaws.

Quinn thought about her visits with Beany, who defended, protected, and boasted about both Myron and Marion and shared the chocolates she so obviously loved.

"Do selfless, generous women become mothers?" Quinn mused. "Or does motherhood make you selfless and generous?"

Mariko/Mary, Georgeanne, and Beany notwithstanding, Quinn remembered the story she'd read in *Grimm's Fairy Tales* about a different kind of mother. The opposite of these real-life women. In that story, the woman consistently put herself and her desires over those of her children, and didn't repent until it was almost too late.

A sudden realization made Quinn swerve, earning her an angry blast from the horn of a nearby car. An exit was coming up. Quinn signaled to get across the interstate and nudged her way to the exit. She took it, then headed off in the direction of Arvada.

She had a question for Beany.

Chapter 33

"What? No candy?" Beany sighed.

"I'm sorry. This is kind of a spur-of-the-moment visit today."

"Then I'm going to keep on knitting, if you don't mind." She glanced up at Quinn, and a sly grin crossed her face. "Even if you do mind, actually."

"I understand completely. I don't want to interrupt. Can I sit?"

"Of course." Beany scooted over.

Quinn sat down but didn't speak for a long time. She was formulating her thoughts and becoming a bit hypnotized by the speed with which Beany's needles flashed through the yarn. Beany's words from the other day came back to her.

I always took care of things at home, but worried about the little ones, whole town did. Watched out for 'em.

A flea can bite a horse.

Sometimes you gotta take charge.

Finally, she spoke, gently and quietly. "Beany…did you kill Donald Lee?"

Beany didn't even flinch, just kept on with her knitting. "Darn tootin', I did. Couldn't let him hurt her, but nobody'd put him away when he hurt me."

"Nobody believed you?"

"Everyone believed me. That's why they all said he'd gone to Alaska. But nobody'd put him away. Times were different then. But when he told me he had a present for Marion, I knew I had to do something."

Quinn was confused. A present made her kill him? "Was it the *Daruma* doll?" That had been her working theory, but it really didn't make sense anymore.

Beany stopped her knitting and shook her head, eyes boring through Quinn's, willing her to understand the truth without forcing her to speak the unspeakable.

Quinn gasped when it dawned on her that it wasn't a present at all, and certainly nothing you'd want from your father. "Oh my gosh…" She thought about it but wondered if Beany was truly grounded in reality. Even if you suspected your husband of depravity like that, could someone as delicate and fragile as Beany take down a full-size man like Donald Lee, even if it was to protect her daughter? "How'd you do it?"

"Rat poison in his booze. Told him we were going to a party and drove him out to the property. Parked in a wide spot just before the old guard tower. Said we had to walk the last little bit, due south." Beany glanced up at Quinn and rolled her eyes. "Donald Lee was never all that bright." She took up her knitting again. "Walked him until he fell, took his coat and shoes to help nature take its course. Waited in the car to make sure he stayed put out in that field."

Quinn realized she and Loma had parked in that exact spot, also walked due south. She put herself in Beany's shoes and walked into that storm too.

"Came home, had a cup of tea, and the next day told everyone he went off to Alaska to work on that pipeline. Nobody was too upset he was gone."

When Quinn had detoured to come talk to Beany, she had a similar story to this in mind, although she'd thought the abused person was Beany herself and not Marion. But the calm, matter-of-fact way that Beany spoke continued to make Quinn wonder if this was another flight of fancy.

Was this another story like the grotto being the portal to the Rapture?

Chapter 34

Quinn returned to her car in the parking lot of Beany's assisted living facility, but instead of driving away, watched her as she continued to knit, sitting on the stone bench. Quinn realized she was doing her finger thing and clenched her fists in her lap.

Was Beany living in a fantasy world? One in which she'd killed her husband forty years earlier? Or was that real?

Quinn dialed her phone.

Marion answered with an apology. "I'm so sorry I never called you back. Is my mom okay?"

"She's fine. I think." Quinn wasn't sure how to say what she needed to say to Marion.

She was silent long enough for Marion to say, "Quinn...what's wrong?"

"Donald Lee didn't just wander out into that field, did he?"

Now it was Marion's turn for silence. Quinn held her tongue too.

After a lengthy delay, Marion said firmly, "No. I killed him."

"You were only fifteen."

"But I'm...strong." Marion's voice faltered.

Softly Quinn said, "Did your dad abuse you, Marion?" Quinn heard a throaty noise through the phone.

"He tried. Just the once, though." Marion cleared her throat once, twice, three times before she could speak. "The night he came for me, Mom told me to go hide. I went to a friend's house. When I got back the next morning, Mom said Dad left for Alaska and wouldn't be darkening our doorstep ever again. I never knew what had happened, but I could see a huge weight had been lifted from Mom's shoulders."

"Beany just told me she poisoned him and left him out in that storm."

Marion began crying. Quinn heard deep, gasping sobs. Marion sniffled and blew her nose. "I always suspected she did, but we never spoke of it. We were better off without him, and if Mom did kill him, it was after years of abuse against her, and she knew I was his next target."

"Did Myron know?"

"I doubt it. We've never talked about it, but he went around wrapped up in Dad's old coat like it was a talisman or something. Finally, Mom couldn't stand the sight of it anymore. Told him it had lice and she burned it. He should probably know the truth of who his father was."

They both sat with the weight of this knowledge for a minute.

"What are you going to do with this information?" Marion finally asked.

Without even needing to think about it, Quinn said, "Not one thing."

"Will you tell my brother?"

"Do you want me to?"

"I don't want to tell him, but I'm tired of carrying this burden alone."

"Then I'll tell him for you."

* * * *

When Quinn got back to Chestnut Station, she drove straight to the police department.

Rico stood up from his desk when she came in. He smiled at her until he noticed her pinched features and busy fingers. "What's up, Quinn?"

She walked up and hugged him tight, taking a few deep, cleansing breaths while pressed up against his broad, comforting chest. He knew her well enough to let it happen. When she pulled away, he looked questioningly at her.

"I'm okay. Everything's fine." She smiled what she hoped was her normal, carefree smile, and not some toothy, horror-movie grin. "Just need to talk to Chief Chestnut for a minute." She began her finger thing again, stopped briefly, then began again.

Rico didn't buy it for a second, resting against his desk and watching her as she knocked on Chief Chestnut's office door.

Chief Chestnut looked surprised to see her, but even more surprised when she closed the door behind her and sat down.

"If I found out something about your dad, would you want to know?"

Chief Chestnut scowled at her suspiciously. "I guess so," he said slowly.

Quinn proceeded to tell him about Donald Lee abusing Beany and his attempted abuse of Marion. She ended with Beany's confession.

Chief Chestnut never changed expression, nor did he twitch a single muscle. He still grasped the pen he was writing with when Quinn entered his office.

"Marion wanted me to tell you. She couldn't bring herself to."

Chief Chestnut peered down at the paper he'd been writing on and lowered the pen to continue his work. Without looking at her, he growled, "Get out of my office."

Rico still leaned against his desk with his arms crossed when she emerged.

At that moment Quinn knew three things with absolute certainty: Her face was blotchy and red. She couldn't tell Rico any of this. And if she didn't get out of there, she'd make a spectacle of herself by bawling. She waved off Rico's concern. "I'll call you later," she said.

Then she fled.

Chapter 35

Over the weekend, after the big piano recital went off without a hitch, Georgeanne threw a Japanese-themed potluck as an homage to the Camp Chestnut Museum, whose board of directors allowed them to take over the grounds for their event. They'd loaded a piano on the back of a flatbed truck, and all the piano students took their turn climbing up and playing their chosen piece. Because there were so many of them, some only played half of their memorized song, and some played duets. The beginner students played first, then the intermediate, then the advanced students. As the quality of the musicians increased, the anxiety level of the audience decreased.

Afterward everyone agreed it had been a delightful concert, and many of them—most of the town, it seemed to Quinn—headed back to the Carr house for the party.

Georgeanne made a new recipe, just for the occasion, Pineapple Potpie. The buffet table groaned with Japanese-inspired noodle dishes, stir fries, and tempura that people brought, as well as American potluck staples like cream cheese pinwheels, green salads, meatballs, and bags of every kind of chip invented. Quinn's contribution to the feast was fancy sushi from the Japanese restaurant in Sakura Square she'd visited with Keiko Kimura. Picking it up in Denver gave her another opportunity to have a meal there, this time with Loma and Rico.

As everyone was filling their plates, *ooh*ing and *aah*ing over the variety and quality of the selections, the doorbell rang.

When Quinn answered, she was surprised to see Chief Chestnut standing there in his street clothes.

"I came to apologize for telling you to get out of my office."

"It's okay."

"Not really. It was rude."

He looked over her shoulder into the party, but Quinn didn't think he actually focused on any of it.

"You were—"

He interrupted. "I didn't know you were having a party. I just wanted to say I'm grateful for knowing what really happened. Grateful for closure." He looked her in the eye. "I don't think Marion would have ever been able to tell me, and Mom…well, Mom…" He looked at the floor.

"I'm glad I could help. I know it must be hard."

Chief Chestnut looked up again. "It never really made sense. Why didn't he take his parka or anything else if he was on his way to Alaska? Even at the time, I think I knew something was off. But I also knew not to talk about it. Nobody told me to keep anything quiet, but I just knew. Maybe that's why I always wore that stupid coat. Hoping someone would notice it and wonder the same things I was wondering. All these years…" He was quiet for a moment. "I've been thinking a lot these last few days. Maybe it's why I became a police officer."

Quinn nodded, unsure of what to say. Were they having a moment here? And if so, how long would it last? She took a chance and asked him a question that had bothered her for more than twenty years. "Why do you hate me?"

Anyone else would have flinched or acted somewhat ashamed, but Chief Chestnut simply pressed his thin lips together. "When Georgeanne turned down my proposal and gift of land to build our house on, and then turned around and married Dan, well, it…it broke my heart. You look so much like him." He studied her face. "When you were a kid, I hardly ever had to see you, but then you moved back here, and I have to see you every damn day in the diner. I thought I'd gotten over it, but you reminded me I hadn't."

They stared at each other.

While Quinn was glad to finally know the truth, it disappointed her to know that there was not a thing she could do to help Chief Chestnut get over his unrequited love for her mother. Nor could she look less like her dad without major reconstructive surgery. The tense relationship between her and Chief Chestnut would probably never change. But at least she could quit obsessing over it and trying to figure out new and trickier ways to get Rico to find out for her. That was something positive, at least.

Remembering her gaffe of letting the town know she thought he had been somehow involved in the death of his father, and how the gossip had spread—in Mary-Louise Lovely's words, *like chlamydia in koalas*—she looked him in the eye. "Your secret is safe with me." She mimed zipping her lips and throwing away the key.

"Maybe you're not so bad after all," he said.

Chief Chestnut turned to leave, but Dan came to the door and invited him in. Georgeanne was right behind him, scolding Quinn for making Chief Chestnut stand on the threshold. Georgeanne looped her arm through his and pulled him into the living room. "Myron, I won't hear of you leaving. We have scads of food here, and we need to get some meat on your bones."

After most everyone had eaten their fill and the buffet had been ravaged, Quinn stood in the corner chatting with Loma, Jake, and Rico. Out of the corner of her eye, she saw Georgeanne crook a finger at Chief Chestnut, beckoning him to follow her into the hallway.

Quinn excused herself and crept through the kitchen, peeking around the corner to see what they were doing. She saw Georgeanne hand Chief Chestnut the property deed.

Georgeanne said something Quinn couldn't hear, but Chief responded. "I gave that to your dad to show him I was serious about marrying you and that I had something to offer. I hoped he'd convince you to change your mind."

Georgeanne smiled sadly. "I always thought he'd given it back to you. I'm so sorry this went on for so long, Myron."

They embraced, and Quinn ducked back into the kitchen thinking how bizarre and enigmatic small towns were. Georgeanne and Myron had lived in Chestnut Station their entire lives, constantly bumping elbows with each other, sixty-some years of history together. Myron, brokenhearted and reminded of it each day. Georgeanne, protecting him, as best she could.

Then there was the entire population of Chestnut Station, not holding Donald Lee accountable for his actions, but also not holding Beany accountable. They supported her—emotionally and financially—everyone in cahoots with whatever happened. Everyone in town seemed to know about Donald Lee's abuse, maybe not the particulars, but so many of them saying they knew "for a fact" that he was in Alaska was proof of their complicity. They closed ranks about Donald Lee's disappearance, rallying around Beany in an unspoken way, protecting one of their own. Exactly like the Japanese internees had protected each other in the camp.

People in small towns, Quinn concluded, seemed to cherish a level of autonomy and self-sufficiency, but they weren't opposed to seeing to the greater good, even if it meant looking the other way at a murder. Of course, they didn't see it as murder, did they? They knew Beany, Marion, and probably Myron were in danger from Donald Lee, and if the law was going to look the other way at Donald Lee's behavior, well, then they'd look the other way at Beany's.

Quinn returned to where she'd left Rico, Loma, and Jake. A girl had just walked away from them and left out the front door.

"Who was that?" Quinn asked.

"Rachel," Jake said.

"The new waitress?"

"In the flesh."

"Are you yanking me?"

"Why would I do that?" Jake grinned at her.

Quinn turned to Rico. "Did you just meet the new waitress at the diner? Don't lie to me."

"As if." Loma snorted.

"Yes, I did," Rico said.

"Her name's Rachel?"

"Yes, it is."

Quinn raced to the door, flung it open, and threw herself into the yard, searching.

When she came back in, Jake asked, "Did you catch her?"

"No," she said glumly. "I feel like I'm in a *Twilight Zone* episode."

The party crowd thinned out as everyone said their good-byes.

Quinn helped her mom clear the rest of the empty serving dishes from the buffet.

Georgeanne took the final platter from her but didn't carry it to the sink. Instead she said, "I know these last couple of weeks have been hard on you, and I wish I could have been more forthcoming. But I knew those bones were found on Myron's property, I knew even as a girl that Donald Lee's disappearance felt sudden and coincidental, and I knew Myron could be a hotheaded kid. I believed Myron might have had something to do with all this, and I was afraid for him. I didn't want you finding out something that would implicate him."

"I know, Mom."

"I never thought Beany..."

"I know."

"And when you found that property deed in my name, I was afraid it would dredge up all those old feelings. Myron and I...well, that was a long time ago. I know he wished for more, but then I met your father. I didn't want any gossip starting up or the whole town feeling sorry for Myron." Georgeanne smiled sadly at Quinn.

"That's what we get for loving small-town life, eh?"

"Yep." Georgeanne carried the platter to the sink and began rinsing it. "Go make sure your grandpa is okay. See if he needs anything."

Quinn found Bernard sitting on the couch. "Need anything, Grandpa?"

"Just the pleasure of your company." He patted the seat next to him.

She cuddled up next to him. After a bit, she said, "Can I ask you something?"

"Sure."

"You won't get mad?"

"At you? Never." He squeezed her knee.

"Did you know that Donald Lee abused Beany?"

The smile left Bernard's face, and he looked down at his lap. "Yes. I'm not proud of it now, but at the time, I thought it was none of my business what happened in another man's house." He looked up at Quinn. "But we all tried to take care of Beany and those kids. That's partly why I carried on so much with Donald Lee. I figured the longer I could keep him out of the house, the better."

Bernard's phrase from the other day made more sense now. An important friendship, he'd called it. It was important to Bernard that he and Donald Lee were friends so he could keep an eye on him.

"But he always seemed to go home drunk. That couldn't have helped the situation."

He shook his head. "You asked me before why Donald Lee and I fought so much. I'm not proud of this, either, but I picked most of those fights. I think it was my way of passive-aggressively punishing Donald Lee for his terrible behavior. If he was going to abuse Beany, then, by golly, I was going to abuse Donald Lee."

Quinn smiled sadly at her grandfather. "My therapist would have a field day with you."

"I'd do it completely differently today. I suspect we all would. I don't have many regrets in my life, but that's one of them."

"It was a different time back then." Quinn paused but quickly added, "Not that that's an excuse."

"Not a good one, that's for sure." Bernard patted her knee, then pointed up on the bookshelf. "What is that?"

Quinn followed his finger, then jumped up. "Oh, I almost forgot!" She reached for the diorama and carefully carried it over to him, setting it on the coffee table. "I made it with those army men I found in your desk. I glued them down so they wouldn't constantly fall over." Bernard admired the diorama, complete with a full-color photo wrap of a forest Quinn had downloaded.

"Just like you always described it."

"So you *do* pay attention when I talk," he said with a grin. "I'm never sure."

"I can bring it over to your place the next time I come, or we can help you take it back to your room tonight."

He stood and returned the diorama to its place on the shelf. "I want you to keep it here. With the desk." He looked over the contents on top of the desk and in the drawers and cubbies, now completely organized. He noticed Quinn's *Daruma* doll with both eyes completely painted in now, with the original red, black, and white colors spruced up. "What's this?"

"It's my reminder to keep getting up. No matter what."

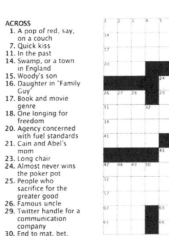
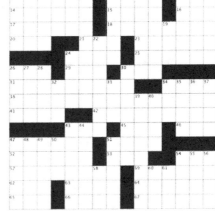

ACROSS

1. A pop of red, say, on a couch
7. Quick kiss
11. In the past
14. Swamp, or a town in England
15. Woody's son
16. Daughter in "Family Guy"
17. Book and movie genre
18. One longing for freedom
20. Agency concerned with fuel standards
21. Cain and Abel's mom
23. Long chair
24. Almost never wins the poker pot
25. People who sacrifice for the greater good
26. Famous uncle
29. Twitter handle for a communication company
30. End to mat, bet, and let
31. What do cows do to have a cow
34. HBCU in SE US
38. Egregious civil rights violations
41. Type of salmon
42. What's a cow who can't have a cow?
43. Opp. of ant.
45. "Would you like a hot dog ___ hamburger?"
46. Blog feed initials
47. Cat or fabric
51. Agency that protects rights of employees
52. Tolerated
53. Ugandan President, played by Forest
54. Body image, for short
57. People interned at Camp Chestnut
59. Rough fights, often drunken

62. Kidney or bladder malady, for short
63. What do u do when u ROTF?
64. Controversial novel by Nabokov
65. Homer's neighbor
66. Forensic examiners
67. Vera Greenberg is a great one

DOWN

1. First black player selected to the Davis Cup team
2. Comes after a clip
3. Countess of Grantham
4. One of the conts.
5. Nonprofit operating independently, for short
6. Shake a fist at
7. Beats rock but not scissors
8. Make an oopsie
9. Hackneyed phrase
10. Food satisfying Jewish dietary law
11. Procedure where fluid is removed from uterus, for short
12. Honkers
13. Fairy tale baddies
19. Crew need
22. C, D, or B12
24. Catherine, the last of Henry VIII's wives
26. Comes before span
27. River in Tuscany
28. Erratic flyer
30. Exponential increase
32. VIP at the Co
33. Number in commandments or countdowns
34. "Salt, ___, Acid, Heat"
35. Arison, Johnson, or Talai
36. Major city in Minn.
37. Employs
39. What some of these clues are
40. Fiddler or ghost
43. "Let's take the ___ route"
44. Songs that frequently change pitch
47. Like some gumbo and jambalaya
48. Subside or lessen
49. Type of fatty acid
50. Early leader in civil rights movement, ___ B. Wells
51. Physicist Bohr
54. Nincompoop
55. Choir voice
56. Russian ruler
58. "___ sez to my friend, I sez..."
60. Stewart who wants to know if you think he's sexy
61. Mahershala in Hollywood

ACROSS

1. Slangy insult
5. Brewing company in Fort Collins
10. With 63-across, industry involved in buying and selling housing
14. Part of a foot
15. Slammer
16. British bum
17. Scientific agency dealing with major waterways, for short
18. Award given by the Mystery Writers of America
19. Juan's kitty
20. One of a reindeer's set
22. Everybody's Talkin' singer
24. Flair
26. H.S. curriculum subj.
27. Before, poetically
28. Palindromic women's name
31. Located on the peak
33. The Old Man and the ___
35. Someone who works to construct buildings on a piece of property
38. East coast, west coast, or on a playground
42. Spot to build a house
43. Taken back Outbacks
45. Word before hygiene, argument, or tradition
46. Seat for second-stringer
48. Buying property hoping to resell at a profit
50. "___ Just Not That Into You"
52. ___ Saint Laurent
53. Georgeanne Carr ___ Dudley
54. When doubled, a large biting fly
57. Tough ___ to follow
59. Rotten little twerp
61. Person with lots to show you?
63. See 10-across
67. Paintballs, snowballs, and cannonballs, for short
68. The lowest point
71. Milo's canine friend
72. Conked out
73. Teach
74. Dessert wine
75. Cicero's "to be"
76. Dr. who wrote "The Lorax"
77. Hook's sidekick in "Peter Pan"

DOWN

1. Delaney, Carvey, or Perino
2. Pump this to get strong
3. "Shoo, Garfield!"
4. Easily flaked sedimentary rock
5. Sade's "Smooth ___"
6. U.S. agency supervising nat'l security
7. Heart chart, for short
8. Emulates a Pisa tower
9. 5-down's include "Coast to coast, LA to Chicago"
10. ___ to riches
11. Rub to delete
12. Richest passenger on the Titanic when it sunk
13. Sierra ___
21. Israeli airline
23. "Big Little ___"
25. "Yup" opposites
28. Brylcreem amount?
29. Editor's removal instruction
30. Shakespeare's river
32. Energetic
34. Runaway soldier, (abbr.)
36. ___ A Sketch
37. With Wade, landmark Supreme Court ruling protecting womens' rights
39. You raced from a Middle Eastern country
40. Children's book series "___ the Great"
41. TV show set in a high school
44. "This tour's a great drive! The ___ gorgeous!"
47. Furnace output
49. GI hangouts
51. Treats often served with clotted cream
54. Swap
55. They're more important than quarters
56. Charles or Ray, famous for a modern lounge chair
58. If you swap this for 54-down, you get the same thing!
60. Sunroof choices (hyph)
62. Miner's bonanza
64. Eensy weensy thing
65. One of four on a car
66. Sunrise direction in Guadalajara
69. Fishing town in western India known for its fortress and old Portuguese cathedral
70. "No ___, ands, or buts!"

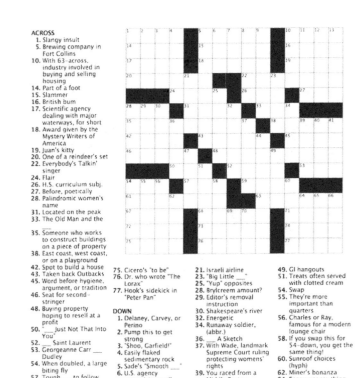

Weeknight Funfetti Casserole

Makes 12 servings

Note: Bacon is much easier to dice when it's a bit frozen.

16 oz. package bacon, diced
1 box (15 1/4 oz) Funfetti Cake Mix
4 eggs
1 C water
1/2 C oil OR 1/2 C unsweetened applesauce
8 oz (2 C) shredded cheddar cheese

Cook diced bacon until crisp. Set aside. No need to drain, just leave it in the pan. (Drain bacon on paper towels if you want. But everyone knows that the flavor comes from the fat. You can pretend to drain it on paper towels, but really let it soak in the bacon fat for a while. Your secret is safe with me.)

Spray 13x9 baking dish with nonstick spray.

Beat cake mix, eggs, water, and oil (or applesauce) until smooth. Stir in cheese by hand.

With slotted spoon, scoop cooked bacon into batter and stir.

Pour into baking dish.

Bake at 350° for 30 minutes or so. Use a toothpick to test. If it comes out clean, it's done. Cool a bit, then cut into 12 pieces.

Pineapple Potpie

Makes 8 servings

2 C diced, cooked ham
12-oz bags EACH frozen pearl onions, peas and carrots, and cut green beans
20-oz can crushed pineapple in juice—don't drain!
Whatever spices you like (Cinnamon? Chinese five-spice powder? Smoked paprika? You do you.)

Combine ham, veggies, pineapple with juice, and spices in large pot and bring to boil. Simmer until veggies are soft.

While filling is simmering, make your crust. In large mixing bowl, combine:
1 1/2 C white whole wheat flour
2 tsp. baking powder
1 1/2 tsp. salt

Make a well in the center and add:
1 1/4 C (10 oz) plain Greek yogurt

Pull flour into yogurt until dough forms. Turn it on to counter, kneading a few times to make sure it's mixed well. You and your dough can both rest for a bit.

Now taste your filling to make sure it's properly seasoned. When you're happy, it's time to thicken it. In small bowl, measure 1 T cornstarch. Add a little bit of cold water and mix to form a smooth paste. Add it to your simmering filling and stir. The cornstarch will thicken your filling fairly quickly, but this is where your artful cooking comes in. If you like more gravy in your potpie than what you're seeing in your pan, add a bit of water and stir. If you like your gravy thicker, you can do another round of 1T cornstarch paste.

Let's talk about cornstarch for a bit. It's a handy tool, as long as you remember the rules. First, never add it directly to whatever you want to thicken. Always make it into a paste and mix that in. Second, it only works to thicken hot foods.

Okay, back to the recipe. Dump your filling into a 9x13 baking dish. Using your hands, pat or roll the dough on your lightly floured countertop until it's large enough to crimp over the edge of your potpie. Make it pretty like Grandma would, or flop it on there like I do—strictly functional. Make 2 or 3 knife cuts in the dough to allow steam to escape.

Bake at 350° for 20–25 minutes or until the filling is bubbly and crust is lightly browned.

Acknowledgments

Camp Chestnut is fictional, but based on the Granada Relocation Center, also known as Camp Amache, which held Japanese American citizens as prisoners in southeastern Colorado, not far from the Kansas border. The history is as fascinating as it is heartbreaking. If you'd like to know about the real camp and its history, visit https://amache.org.

My crossword testers were once again invaluable to me. They catch all kinds of mistakes I make and offer excellent critiques and comments, so Amy Loyall, Kirsten Akens, Judy Rose, Dru Ann Love, Matt Sautter, Lori Howard, Rebecca Rowley, and Bob Clark, thank you for making me look smarter than I am.

I also owe a huge debt to Diane France for her expertise as the director of the Human Identification Laboratory of Colorado. In addition to doing her important and real job as a forensic anthropologist, she happily and thoroughly answered all my questions about fictional bones left out in a field for many years. If I had to live my life over, I'd want to have her job.

A mere "thank you" doesn't seem like nearly enough to offer my agent, Jill Marsal, or the team at Kensington, including my editor, Norma Perez-Hernandez. Everyone I've had the pleasure to work with over there does their job so well that it allows me to concentrate solely on mine. It's a marvelous blessing.

And you, dear reader. Where would I be without you? A million thanks for spending your time with my story. I hope you enjoyed it, and the others in the series.

Printed in the United States
by Baker & Taylor Publisher Services